'Josephine Tey enjoys a category to herself, as a virtuoso in the spurious . . . the nature of the deception on this occasion is too good to give away' *New Statesman*

'Tey's style and h characters are among *...orker*

JOSEPHINE TEY

The Man in the Queue

arrow books

Published by Arrow Books 2011

1 3 5 7 9 10 8 6 4 2

Copyright © The National Trust 1929

In accordance with the late Josephine Tey's wish, all author's profits from this book
will go to the National Trust for Places of Historic Interest or Natural Beauty

The right of Josephine Tey to be identified as the author of this work has been
asserted with the Copyright, Designs and Patents Act, 1988

First published in Great Britain in 1929 as by Gordon Daviot by
Peter Davies Ltd
Reissued as by Josephine Tey 1953 by Peter Davies Ltd

Arrow Books
Random House, 20 Vauxhall Bridge Road
London SW1V 2SA

www.randomhouse.co.uk

Addresses for companies within The Random House Group Limited can be found at:
www.randomhouse.co.uk/offices.htm

The Random House Group Limited Reg. No. 954009

A CIP catalogue record for this book
is available from the British Library

ISBN 9780099556725

The Random House Group Limited supports The Forest Stewardship
Council (FSC®), the leading international forest certification organisation.
Our books carrying the FSC label are printed on FSC® certified paper.
FSC is the only forest certification scheme endorsed by the leading
environmental organisations, including Greenpeace. Our
paper procurement policy can be found at
www.randomhouse.co.uk/environment

Printed and bound in Great Britain by Clays Ltd, St Ives PLC

To Brisena
who actually wrote it

CONTENTS

CHAPTER 1

MURDER

It was between seven and eight o'clock on a March evening, and all over London the bars were being drawn back from pit and gallery doors. Bang, thud, and clank. Grim sounds to preface an evening's amusement. But no last trump could have so galvanised the weary attendants on Thespis and Terpsichore standing in patient column of four before the gates of promise. Here and there, of course, there was no column. At the Irving, five people spread themselves over the two steps and sacrificed in warmth what they gained in comfort; Greek tragedy was not popular. At the Playbox there was no one; the Playbox was exclusive, and ignored the existence of pits. At the Arena, which had a three weeks' ballet season, there were ten persons for the gallery and a long queue for the pit. But at the Woffington both human strings tailed away apparently into infinity. Long ago a lordly official had come down the pit queue, and with a gesture of his outstretched arm that seemed to guillotine hope, had said, 'All after here standing room only.' Having thus, with a mere contraction of his deltoid muscle, separated the sheep from the goats, he retired in Olympian state to the front of the theatre, where beyond the glass doors there was warmth and shelter. But no one moved away from the long line. Those who were doomed to stand for three hours more seemed indifferent to their martyrdom. They laughed and chattered, and passed each other sustaining bits of chocolate in torn silver paper. Standing room only, was it? Well, who would not stand, and be pleased to, in the last week of *Didn't You Know?* Nearly two years it had run now, London's own musical comedy, and this was its swan song. The stalls and the circle had been booked up weeks ago, and many foolish virgins, not used to queues, had swelled the waiting throng at the barred doors because bribery and corruption had proved unsuccessful at the box office. Every soul in London, it seemed, was trying to crowd into the Woffington to cheer the show just once again. To see if Golly Gollan had put a new gag into his triumph of foolery – Gollan who had been rescued from a life on the road by a daring manager, and had been given his chance and had taken it. To sun themselves yet once more in the loveliness and sparkle of Ray Marcable, that comet that two years ago had blazed out of the void into the zenith and had dimmed the known and constant stars. Ray danced like a blown leaf, and her little aloof smile had killed the fashion for dentifrice advertisements in six months. 'Her indefinable charm,' the critics called it, but her followers called it many extravagant things, and defined it to each other with hand-wavings and facial contortions when words proved inadequate to convey the whole of her faery quality. Now she was going to America, like all the good things, and after the last two years London without Ray Marcable would be an unthinkable desert. Who would not stand for ever just to see her once more?

It had been drizzling since five o'clock, and every now and then a light chill air lifted the drizzle and half-playfully swept the queue from end to end with it in one long brush-stroke. That discouraged no one – even the weather could not take itself seriously tonight; it had merely sufficient tang to provide a suitable apéritif to the fare in front of them. The queue twiddled its toes, and Cockneywise made the most of whatever entertainment provided itself in the dark canyon of the lane. First there had come the newsboys, small things with thin, impassive faces and wary eyes. They had flickered down the queue like wildfire and disappeared, leaving behind a trail of chatter and fluttering papers.

Then a man with legs shorter than his body laid a ragged strip of carpet on the damp pavement and proceeded to tie himself into knots until he looked as a spider does when it is taken unawares, his mournful toad's eyes gleaming now and then from totally unexpected places, in the writhing mass, so that even the most indifferent spectator felt his spine trickle. He was succeeded by a man who played popular airs on the fiddle, happily oblivious of the fact that his E string was half-a-tone flat. Then, simultaneously, came a singer of sentimental ballads and a syncopated orchestra of three. After they had scowled at each other for a moment or two, the soloist tried to rush things on the possession-being-nine-points principle, by breaking into a wailing *Because you came to me*, but the leader of the orchestra, handing his guitar to a lieutenant, proceeded to interview the tenor, with his elbows out and his hands lifted. The tenor tried to ignore him by looking over his head, but found it difficult, because the musician was half a head taller than himself and appeared to be ubiquitous. He persevered for another two lines, and then the ballad wavered uncertainly into bitter expostulation in his natural voice, and two minutes later he faded up the dark alley, mumbling threats and complaints, and the orchestra broke into the latest dance tune. This being more to the taste of the moderns than inappropriate resurrection of decayed sentiment, they promptly forgot all about the poor victim of *force majeure*, and twiddled their toes in time to the lively measure. After the orchestra, and severally, came a conjurer, an evangelist, and a man who allowed himself to be tied up in a rope with imposing-looking knots, and as imposingly worked himself free.

All these did their little turn and moved on to another performance elsewhere, and each one before leaving made a tour of the line, thrusting limp but importunate head-gear into the meagre interstices of the queue, and saying, 'Thank you! Thank you!' as encouragement to the bountiful. By

way of punctuation to the programme, there had been
vendors of sweetmeats, vendors of matches, vendors of
toys, vendors even of picture postcards. And the crowd
had parted good-naturedly with their pence and found
amusement sufficient to their needs.

Now a shudder ran down the line – a shudder that
the experienced recognised as but one thing. Stools were
given up or folded into hand-bags, food disappeared, purses
appeared. The doors were open. The lovely exciting gamble
had begun. Was it to be win, place, or lose by the time
they came to the wicket? Up in the front of the queue
where the order was less mathematically two-and-two than
down in the open, the excitement of the door-opening had
for a moment or two overcome the habitual place-keeping
instincts of the Englishman – I say Englishman advisedly;
the Scot has none of it – and there had been a mild pushing
and readjustment before the queue had become immobile
in a wedged and short-breathing mass before the *guichet*
which was immediately inside the pit door. The clink and
rattle of coin on brass proclaimed the continual hurried
transactions which made the lucky ones free of paradise.
The very sound of it made those behind strain forward
unconsciously, until the crowd in front protested as audibly
as their crushed lungs permitted, and a policeman went
down the queue to remonstrate. 'Now then, now then,
stand back a bit. There's plenty of time. You won't get
in by pushing. All in good time.' Now and then the whole
line tottered forward a few inches as the emancipated ones
ran in twos and threes from the head of it, like beads
rolling from a broken string. Now a fat woman held them
up by fumbling in her bag for more money. Surely the fool
could have found out before now the exact amount required
instead of keeping them back like this. As if conscious of
their hostility she turned to the man behind her and said
angrily:

"Ere, I'll thank you to stop shoving. Can't a lady be

allowed to take out her purse without everyone losing their manners?'

But the man she addressed took no notice. His head was sunk on his chest. Only the top of his soft hat met her beady indignant gaze. She snorted, and moving away from him to face the box office squarely laid down the money she had been searching for. And as she did so the man sank slowly to his knees, so that those behind almost fell over him, stayed like that for a moment, and then keeled still more slowly over on his face.

'Chap fainted,' said someone. No one moved for a moment or two. Minding one's own business in a crowd today is as much an instinct of self-preservation as a chameleon's versatility. Perhaps someone would claim the chap. But no one did; and so a man with more social instinct or more self-importance than the rest moved forward to help the collapsed one. He was about to bend over the limp heap when he stopped as if stung and recoiled hastily. A woman shrieked three times, horribly; and the pushing, heaving queue froze suddenly to immobility.

In the white clear light of the naked electric in the roof, the man's body, left alone by the instinctive withdrawal of the others, lay revealed in every detail. And rising slantwise from the grey tweed of his coat was a little silver thing that winked wickedly in the baleful light.

It was the handle of a dagger.

Almost before the cry of 'Police!' had gone up, the constable had come from his job of pacification at the other end of the queue. At the first of the woman's shrieks he had turned. No one shrieked like that except when faced by sudden death. Now he stood looking for a moment at the picture, bent over the man, turned his head gently to the light, released it, and said to the man at the *guichet*:

'Phone for the ambulance and the police.'

He turned his rather shocked gaze on the queue.

'Anyone here know the gentleman?'

But no one claimed acquaintance with the still thing on the floor.

Behind the man there had been a prosperous suburban couple. The woman was moaning continuously and without expression, 'Oh, let's go home, Jimmy! Oh, let's go home!' On the opposite side of the *guichet* stood the fat woman, arrested by this sudden horror, grasping her ticket in her black cotton gloves but making no effort to secure a seat now that the way lay open to her. Down the waiting line behind, the news went like fire in stubble – a man had been murdered! – and the crowd in the sloping vestibule began to mill suddenly in hopeless confusion as some tried to get away from the thing that had spoiled all thought of entertainment, and some tried to push forward to see, and some indignant ones fought to keep the place they had stood so many hours for.

'Oh, let's go home, Jimmy! Oh, let's go home!'

Jimmy spoke for the first time. 'I don't think we can, old girl, until the police decide whether they want us or not.'

The constable heard him and said, 'You're quite right there. You can't go. You first six will stay where you are – *and* you, missus,' he added to the fat woman. 'The rest come on.' And he waved them on as he would wave the traffic past a broken-down car.

Jimmy's wife broke into hysterical sobbing, and the fat woman expostulated. She had come to see the show and didn't know anything about the man. The four people behind the suburban couple were equally reluctant to be mixed up in the thing they knew nothing about, with results that no one could foresee. They too protested their ignorance.

'Maybe,' said the policeman, 'but you'll have to explain all that at the station. There's nothing to be scared of,' he added for their comfort, and rather unconvincingly in the circumstances.

So the queue came on. The doorkeeper brought a green

curtain from somewhere and covered up the body. The automatic clink and rattle of coin began again and went on, indifferent as rain. The doorkeeper, moved from his habitual Jovian abstraction by their plight or by the hope of reward, offered to keep their rightful seats for the seven derelicts. Presently came the ambulance and the police from Gowbridge Police Station. An inspector had a short interview with each of the detained seven, took names and addresses, and dismissed them with a warning to be ready to come up if called upon. Jimmy took his sobbing wife away to a taxi, and the other five straggled soberly in to the seats over which the doorkeeper was brooding, just as the curtain rose on the evening performance of *Didn't You Know?*

CHAPTER 2

INSPECTOR GRANT

Superintendent Barker applied a carefully manicured fore-finger to the ivory bell-push on the under side of his table, and kept it there until a minion appeared.

'Tell Inspector Grant that I want to see him,' he said to the minion, who was doing his best to look obsequious in the great man's presence, but was frustrated in his good intention by an incipient embonpoint which compelled him to lean back a little in order to preserve his balance, and by the angle of his nose which was the apotheosis of impudence. Bitterly conscious of failure, the minion withdrew to deliver the message and to bury the memory of his confusion among the unsympathetic perfection of files and foolscap from which he had been summoned, and presently Inspector Grant came into the room and greeted his chief cheerily as one man to another. And his chief's face brightened unconsciously in his presence.

If Grant had an asset beyond the usual ones of devotion to duty and a good supply of brains and courage, it was that the last thing he looked like was a police officer. He was of medium height and slight in build, and he was — now, if I say dapper, of course you will immediately think of something like a tailor's dummy, something perfected out of all individuality, and Grant is most certainly not that. But if you can visualise a dapperness that is not of the tailor's dummy type, then that is Grant. Barker had for years striven unsuccessfully to emulate his subordinate's chic; he succeeded merely in looking too carefully dressed. He lacked the flair for things sartorial as he lacked flair in most things. He was a plodder. But that was the worst that could be said about him. And when he started plodding after someone, that someone usually wished he had never been born.

He regarded his subordinate now with an admiration untinged with any resentment, appreciated his son-of-the-morning atmosphere – he himself had been awake most of the night with sciatica – and came to business.

'Gowbridge are very sick,' he said. 'In fact, Gow Street went so far as to insinuate that it was a conspiracy.'

'Oh? Someone been pulling their legs?'

'No, but last night's affair is the fifth big thing in their district in the last three days, and they're fed up. They want us to take this last affair over.'

'What is that? The theatre-queue business, is it?'

'Yes, and you are O.C. investigations. So get busy. You can have Williams. I want Barber to go down to Berkshire about that Newbury burglary. The locals down there will want a lot of soft soap because we have been called in, and Barber is better at that than Williams. I think that is all. Better get down to Gow Street right away. Good luck.'

Half an hour later Grant was interviewing the Gowbridge police surgeon. Yes, the surgeon said, the man had been dead when he was brought into hospital. The weapon was a thin, exceedingly sharp stiletto. It had been driven into the man's back on the left side of the backbone with such force that the hilt had pressed his garments to a wad which had kept any blood from flowing. What had escaped had oozed out round the wound without coming to the outer surface at all. In his opinion the man had been stabbed a considerable time – perhaps ten minutes or more – before he had collapsed as the people in front moved away. In a squash like that he would be held up and moved along by the crowd. In fact, it would have been a sheer impossibility to fall if one had wanted to in such a closely packed mob. He thought it highly unlikely that the man was even aware that he had been struck. So much pressing and squeezing and involuntary hurting went on on these occasions that a sudden and not too painful blow would not be noticed.

'And about the person who stabbed him. Anything peculiar about the stabbing?'

'No, except that the man was strong and left-handed.'

'Not a woman?'

'No, it would need more strength than a woman has to drive the blade in as it has been driven. You see, there was no room for a back-sweep of the arm. The blow had to be delivered from a position of rest. Oh no, it was a man's work. And a determined man's, too.'

'Can you tell me anything about the dead man himself?' asked Grant, who liked to hear a scientific opinion on any subject.

'Not much. Well nourished – prosperous, I should say.'

'Intelligent?'

'Yes, very, I should think.'

'What type?'

'What type of occupation, do you mean?'

'No, I can deduce that for myself. What type of – temperament, I suppose you'd call it?'

'Oh, I see.' The surgeon thought for a moment. He looked doubtfully at his interlocutor. 'Well, no one can say that for a certainty – you understand that?' and when Grant had acknowledged the qualification, 'but I should call him one of the "lost cause" type.' He raised his eyebrows interrogatively at the inspector and, assured of his understanding, added, 'He had practical enough qualities in his face, but his hands were a dreamer's. You'll see for yourself.'

Together they viewed the body. It was that of a young man of twenty-nine or thirty, fair-haired, hazel-eyed, slim, and of medium height. The hands, as the doctor had pointed out, were long and slim and not used to manual work. 'Probably stood a lot,' said the surgeon with a glance at the man's feet. 'And walked with his left toe turned in.'

'Do you think his assailant had any knowledge of anatomy?' asked Grant. It was almost incredible that so small a hole had let a man's life out.

'It wasn't done with the precision of a surgeon, if that's what you mean. As for a knowledge of anatomy, practically everyone who is old enough to have lived through the war has a working knowledge of anatomy. It may have been just a lucky shot – and I rather think it was.'

Grant thanked him and came to business with the Gow Street officials. On a table were laid out the scanty contents of the man's pockets. Grant was conscious of a faint dismay when he saw their fewness. A white cotton handkerchief, a small pile of loose change (two half-crowns, two sixpences, a shilling, four pennies, and a halfpenny), and – unexpected – a service revolver. The handkerchief was well worn but had no laundry mark or initial. The revolver was fully loaded.

Grant examined them in a disgusted silence. 'Laundry marks on his clothes?' he asked.

No, there were no marks of any kind.

And no one had come to claim him? Nor even anyone to make inquiries?

No, no one but that old madwoman who laid claim to everyone the police found.

Well, he would see the clothes for himself. Painstakingly he examined each article of clothing. Both hat and shoes were well worn, the shoes so much so that the maker's name which should have been on the lining, had been obliterated. The hat when new had been bought from a firm who owned shops all over London and the provinces. Both were good of their kind, and though well worn neither was shabby. The blue suit was fashionable if rather too pronounced in cut, and the same might be said of the grey overcoat. The man's linen was good if not expensively so, and the shirt was of a popular shade. All the clothes, in fact, had belonged to a man who either took an interest in clothes or was accustomed to the society of those who did. A salesman in a men's outfitter's, perhaps. As the Gowbridge people had said, there were no laundry marks. That meant either that the man had wanted to hide his identity or that his linen was washed habitually at home. Since there was no sign of any obliteration of marks it followed that the latter was the reasonable explanation. On the other hand, the tailor's name had been deliberately removed from the suit. That and the scantiness of the man's belongings pointed certainly to a desire on his part to conceal his identity.

Lastly – the dagger. It was a wicked little weapon in its viperish slenderness. The handle was of silver, about three inches long, and represented the figure of some saint, bearded and robed. Here and there it was touched with enamel in bright primitive colours such as adorn sacred images in Catholic countries. In general it was of a type fairly common in Italy and along the south coast of Spain. Grant handled it gingerly.

'How many people have had their hands on it?' he asked.

The police had commandeered it as soon as the man had arrived in hospital and it could be removed. No one had touched it since. But the expression of satisfaction was wiped from Grant's face when the information was added that it had been tested for fingerprints and had been found blank. Not even a blurred one spoiled the shining surface of the smug saint.

'Well,' said Grant, 'I'll take these and get on.' He left instructions with Williams to take the dead man's fingerprints and to have the revolver examined for peculiarities. To his own sight it seemed to be an exceedingly ordinary service revolver of a type which since the war has been as common in Britain as grandfather clocks. But, as has been said, Grant liked to hear authorities on their own subject. He himself took a taxi and spent the rest of the day interviewing the seven persons who had been nearest the unknown when he collapsed the previous night.

As the taxi bore him hither and thither he let his thought play round and over the situation. He had not the faintest hope that these people he interviewed would be of use to him. They had one and all denied any knowledge of the man when first questioned, and they were not likely to alter their minds as to that now. Also, if any of them had seen a companion with the dead man previously, or had noticed anything suspicious, they would have been only too ready to say so. It was Grant's experience that ninety-nine people proffered useless information where one was silent. Again, the surgeon had said that the man had been stabbed some time before it had been noticed, and no assassin was going to stay in the immediate neighbourhood of his victim until the deed was discovered. Even if the possibility of a bluff had occurred to the murderer, the chances of a connection between himself and his victim being established were too good to allow a sensible man – and a man bent on self-preservation is usually shrewd enough – to indulge in it. No, the man who did it had left the queue some time before. He must find someone who had noticed the murdered man before his death and had seen him in converse with someone. There was, of course, the possibility to be faced that there had been no converse, that the murderer had merely taken up a place behind his victim and slipped away when the thing was done. In that case he had to find someone who had seen a man leave the queue. That should not be difficult. The Press could be called to help.

Idly he considered the type of man it would be. No thorough Englishman used such a weapon. If he used steel at all he took a razor and cut a person's throat. But his habitual weapon was a bludgeon, and, failing that, a gun. This was a crime that had been planned with an ingenuity and executed with a subtlety that was foreign to an Englishman's habit of thought. The very femininity of it proclaimed the dago, or at the very least one used to dago habits of life. A sailor perhaps. An English sailor used to the Mediterranean ports might have done it. But then, would a sailor have been likely to think of anything so subtle as the queue? He would have been more likely to wait for a dark night and a lonely street. The picturesqueness of the thing was Latin. An Englishman was obsessed with the desire to hit. The manner of the hitting did not habitually concern him.

That made him think of motive, and he considered the more obvious ones: theft, revenge, jealousy, fear. The first was ruled out; the man's pockets could have been picked half a dozen times by an expert practitioner in such a crowd, without any more violence than a fly bestows in alighting. Revenge or jealousy? Most probably – dagoes were notoriously vulnerable in their feelings; an insult rankled for a lifetime, a straying smile on the part of their adored, and they ran amok. Had the man with the hazel eyes – he had, undoubtedly, been attractive – come between a dago and his girl?

For no reason whatever Grant did not think so. He did not for a moment lose sight of the possibility, but – he did not think so. There remained fear. Was the fully loaded revolver prepared for the man who slid that sliver of steel into the owner's back? Had the dead man intended to shoot the dago on sight, and had the assassin known it and lived in terror? Or was it the other way about? Was it the dead man who had carried a weapon of defence which had not availed him? But then there was the unknown man's desire to slough his identity. A loaded revolver in these circumstances pointed to suicide. But if he contemplated suicide, why postpone it while he went to the play? What other motive induced a man to make himself anonymous? A brush with the police – arrest? Had he intended to shoot someone and, afraid of not getting away, made himself nameless? That was possible.

It was fairly safe, at least, to suppose that the dead man and the man whom Grant had mentally christened the Dago had known each other sufficiently well to knock sparks from each other. Grant had very little belief in secret societies as the origins of picturesque murders. Secret societies delighted in robbery and blackmail and all the more squalid methods of getting something for nothing, and there was seldom anything picturesque about them, as he knew from bitter experience. Moreover, there were no impressive secret societies in London at present, and he hoped they would not start. Murder to order bored him stiff. What interested him was the possible play of mind on mind, of emotion on emotion. Like the Dago and the Unknown. Well he must do his best to find out who the Unknown was – that would give him a line on the Dago. Why had no one claimed him? It was early yet, of course. He might be recognised by someone at any minute. After all, he had only been 'missing' to his people for the space of a night, and not many people rush to see a murdered man because their son or brother has stayed out for the night.

With patience and consideration and an alert mind, Grant interviewed the seven people he had set out to see – quite literally to see. He had not anticipated receiving information from them directly, but he wanted to see them for himself and to sum them up. He found them all going about their various business, with the exception of Mrs James Ratcliffe, who was prostrate in bed and being attended by the doctor, who deplored the nervous shock she had received. Her sister – a charming girl with hair the colour of honey – talked to Grant. She had come into the drawing-room quite obviously hostile to the thought of any police officer being admitted to her sister in her present state. The sight of the police officer in reality was so astonishing that she looked again at his card quite involuntarily, and Grant smiled inwardly a little more broadly than he permitted himself to outwardly.

'I know you hate the sight of me,' he said apologetically and the tone was not wholly acting – 'but I wish you would let me talk to your sister for just two minutes. You can stand outside the door with a stop-watch. Or come in, if you like, of course, There is nothing at all private in what I want to say to her. It's only that I am in charge of investigations in this case, and it is my duty to see the seven people who were nearest the man last night. It will help me enormously if I can write them all off the slate tonight and start on fresh lines tomorrow. Don't you see? It's mere form but very helpful.'

As he had hoped, this line of argument was a success. After a little hesitation the girl said, 'Let me go and see if I can persuade her.' Her report of the inspector's charms must have been a rose-coloured one, for she came back in less time than he had dared to hope and took him up to her sister's room, where he had an interview with a tearful woman who protested that she had not even noticed the man until he had fallen, and whose wet eyes regarded him continually with a dreadful curiosity. Her mouth was hidden behind a barricade of handkerchief which she kept pressed to it. Grant wished that she would take it down for a moment. He had a theory that mouths gave away more than eyes – certainly where women were concerned.

'Were you standing behind him when he fell?'

'Yes.'

'And who was alongside him?'

She could not remember. No one was paying attention to anything but getting into the theatre, and in any case she never noticed people on the street.

'I'm sorry,' she said shakily, when he was taking his departure. 'I'd like to be of use if I could. I keep seeing that knife, and I'd do anything to have the man that did it arrested.' And as Grant went out he dismissed her from his mind.

Her husband, whom he had to travel into the City to see – he could have had them all to the Yard, but he wanted to see how they were occupying their time on this the first day after the murder – was more helpful. There had been a fair amount of churning in the queue, he said, as the doors were opened, so that their relations with their neighbours had altered a bit. As far as he could remember, the person who had stood beside the dead man and in front of himself was a man who had belonged to a party of four in front of that again, and had gone in with them. He, like his wife, said that he had not consciously seen the man until he had fallen.

The other five Grant found equally innocent and equally unhelpful. None had noticed the man. That amazed Grant just a little. How had *no one* seen him? He must have been there all the time. One doesn't shove in at the head of a queue without attracting a most uncomfortable amount of attention. And even the most unobservant of people will recall what their eyes have seen even if they were unconscious of taking notice at the time. Grant was still puzzling when he got back to the Yard.

There he sent a notice to the Press which asked anyone who had seen a man leave the queue, to communicate with Scotland Yard. Also a full description of the dead man, and as much of the progress of the investigations as was to be given to the public. Then he summoned Williams and demanded an account of his stewardship. Williams reported that the dead man's finger-prints had been photographed according to instructions and sent up for investigation, but he was unknown to the police. No corresponding finger-prints were to be found among those betraying dockets. The revolver expert could find nothing individual about the revolver. It was probably second-hand, had been used quite a lot, and was of course a very powerful weapon.

'Huh!' said Grant disgustedly. 'Some expert!' and Williams smiled.

'Well, he did say there was nothing distinctive about it,' he reminded.

And then he explained that before sending the revolver to the experts he had tested it for finger-prints, and finding quite a lot had had them photographed. He was now waiting for the prints.

'Good man,' said Grant, and went in to see the superintendent, carrying the print of the dead man's finger-tips with him. He gave Barker a *précis* of the day's events without adducing any theories about dagoes beyond remarking that it was a very un-English crime.

'Precious unproductive kind of clues we've got,' said Barker. 'All except the dagger, and that's more like something out of a book than part of an honest-to-goodness crime.'

'My sentiments exactly,' said Grant. 'I wonder how many people will be in the Woffington queue tonight,' he added irrelevantly.

The knowledge of how Barker would have speculated on this fascinating question was lost for ever to mankind by the entrance of Williams.

'The revolver prints, sir,' he said succinctly, and laid them on the table. Grant picked them up with no great enthusiasm and compared them with the prints he had absent-mindedly been carrying about. After a short time he stiffened to sudden interest as a pointer stiffens. There were five distinct prints and many incomplete ones, but neither the good prints nor the broken ones had been made by the dead man. Attached to the prints was a report from the finger-print department. There was no trace of these prints in their records.

Back in his room Grant sat and thought. What did it mean, and of what value was the knowledge? Did the revolver not belong to the dead man? Borrowed, perhaps? But even if it had been borrowed there would surely have been some indication that the dead man had had it in his possession. Or had the dead man not had it in his possession? Had it been slipped into his pocket by someone else? But one could not slip anything of the weight and bulk of a service revolver into a man's pocket unknown to him. No, not a living man, but – it could have been done after the knife-thrust. But why? Why? No solution, however far-fetched, presented itself to him. He took the dagger out of its wrappings, and considered it through the microscope, but could mesmerise himself into no hopeful state over it. He was stale. He would go out and walk a bit. It was just after five. He would go down to the Woffington and see the man who had been doorkeeper at the pit last night.

It was a fine still evening with a primrose sky, and London was painted against it, in flat washes of a misty lavender. Grant sniffed the air appreciatively. Spring was coming. When he had run the Dago to earth, he would wangle some leave – sick leave, if he couldn't get it any other way – and go fishing somewhere. Where should he go? You got the best fishing in the Highlands, but the company was apt to be darned dull. He would go fishing in the Test – at Stockbridge, perhaps. Trout were poor sport, but there was a snug little pub there, and the best of company. And he would get a horse to ride there, and turf to ride it on. And Hampshire in spring—!

So he speculated, walking briskly along the Embankment, on things far removed from the business on hand. For that was Grant's way. Barker's motto was: 'Chew it over! Chew it over continually, sleeping and waking, and you'll find the kernel that matters.' That was true for Barker but not for Grant. Grant had once retorted that when he had chewed to that extent he couldn't think of anything but the ache in his jaws, and he had meant it. When something baffled him he found that if he kept on worrying it, he got no further, and lost his sense of proportion in the process. So when he came to a dead stop he indulged in what he called 'shutting his eyes' for a little, and when he 'opened' them again he habitually found a new light on things that revealed unexpected angles and made the old problem a totally new proposition.

There had been a matinée that afternoon at the Woffington, but he found the theatre in its usual state of shrouded desolation in front and untidy dreariness behind. The doorkeeper was on the premises, but no one was very sure where he was to be found. In the early evening his duties were many and various, it seemed. After several panting messengers had returned from the bowels of the building with reports that, 'No, sir, there wasn't a sign of him,' Grant himself joined in the exploration and eventually ran the man to earth in a dim passage behind the stage. When Grant had explained who he was and what he wanted the man became voluble in his pride and eagerness. He was used to being within hailing distance of the aristocracy of the stage, but it was not every day that he had the chance of conversing on friendly terms with that much more august being, an inspector from the C.I.D. He beamed, he continually altered the angle of his cap, he fingered his medal ribbons, he dried his palms on the seat of his trousers, and he quite obviously would have said that he had seen a monkey in the queue if it would have pleased the inspector. Grant groaned inwardly, but the part of himself that always stood aloof whatever he did – the looker-on part of him which he had in such abundance – thought appreciatively what a character the old boy was. With that providing for a hypothetical future which is second-nature in a professional detective, he was taking a friendly farewell of so much devoted uselessness, when a charming voice said, 'Why, it's Inspector Grant!' and he turned to see Ray Marcable in her outdoor things, and evidently on the way to her dressing-room.

'Are you looking for a job? I'm afraid you can't have even a walking-on part at this late hour.' Her still small smile teased him and her grey eyes looked at him friendlily from under the slight droop of her lids. They had met a year previously over the theft of a fabulously expensive dressing-case which had been one of her richest admirers' gifts to her, and though they had not met again since she had evidently not forgotten him. In spite of himself he was flattered – even while the looker-on bit of him was aware of it and laughed. He explained his business in the theatre, and the smile faded from her face instantly.

'Ah, that poor man!' she said. 'But here is another,' she added immediately, laying a hand on his arm. 'Have you been asking questions all the afternoon? Your throat must be very dry. Come and have a cup of tea in my room with me. My maid is there and she will make us some. We are packing up, you know. It is very sad after such a long time.'

She led the way to her dressing-room, a place that was walled half with mirrors and half with wardrobes, and which looked more like a florist's shop than any apartment designed for human habitation. She indicated the flowers with a wave of her hand.

'My flat won't hold any more, so these have to stay here. The hospitals were very polite, but they said quite firmly that they had had as much as they could do with. And I can't very well say, "No flowers," as they do at funerals, without hurting people.'

'It's the only thing most people can do,' Grant said.

'Oh yes, I know,' she said. 'I'm not ungrateful. Only overwhelmed.'

When tea was ready she poured out for him, and the maid produced shortbread from a tin. As he was stirring his tea and she was pouring out her own his mind brought him up with a sudden jerk, as an inexperienced rider jabs at his horse's mouth when startled. *She was left-handed!*

'Great heavens!' he said to himself disgustedly, 'it isn't that you deserve a holiday, it's that you need it. What did you want to italicise a statement like that for? How many

left-handed people do you think there are in London? You're
developing the queerest kind of nerves.'

To break the silence and because it was the first thing
that came into his head, he said, 'You're left-handed.'

'Yes,' she said indifferently, as the subject deserved, and
went on to ask him about his investigations. He told her as
much as would appear in the morrow's press and described
the knife, as being the most interesting feature of the case.

'The handle is a little silver saint with blue-and-red
enamel decoration.'

Something leaped suddenly in Ray Marcable's calm
eyes.

'What?' she said involuntarily.

He was about to say, 'You've seen one like it?' but changed
his mind. He knew on the instant that she would say no,
and that he would have given away the fact that he was
aware that there was anything to be aware of. He repeated
the description and she said:

'A saint! How quaint! And how inappropriate! – And
yet, in a big undertaking like a crime, I suppose you'd want
someone's blessing on it.'

Cool and sweet she put out her left hand for his cup,
and as she replenished it he watched her steady wrist
and impassive manner and wondered if this too could be
unreasonableness on his part.

'Certainly not,' said his other self. 'You may be suffering
from attacks of flair in queer places, but you haven't got to
the stage of imagining things yet.'

They discussed America, which Grant knew well and to
which she was about to make her first visit, and when he
took his leave he was honestly grateful to her for the tea.
He had forgotten all about tea. Now it wouldn't matter
how late he had dinner. But as he went out he sought
a light for his cigarette from the doorkeeper, and in the
course of another ebullition of chatter and goodwill learned
that Miss Marcable had been in her dressing-room from six

o'clock the previous evening until the call-boy went for her before her first cue. Lord Lacing was there, he said, with an eloquent lift of his eyebrow.

Grant smiled and nodded and went away, but as he was making his way back to the Yard, he was not smiling. What was it that had leapt in Ray Marcable's eyes? Not fear. No. Recognition? Yes, that was it. Most certainly recognition.

CHAPTER 3

DANNY MILLER

Grant opened his eyes and regarded the ceiling of his bedroom speculatively. For the last few minutes he had been technically awake, but his brain, wrapped in the woolliness of sleep and conscious of the ungrateful chilliness of the morning, had denied him thought. But though the reasoning part of him had not wakened, he had become more and more conscious of mental discomfort. Something unpleasant waited him. Something exceedingly unpleasant. The growing conviction had dispelled his drowsiness, and his eyes opened on the ceiling laced across with the early sunlight and the shadows of a plane tree; and on recognition of the unpleasantness. It was the morning of the third day of his investigations, the day of the inquest, and he had nothing to put before the coroner. Had not even a scent to follow.

His thoughts went back over yesterday. In the morning, the dead man being still unidentified, he had given Williams the man's tie, that being the newest and most individual thing about him, and had sent him out to scour London. The tie, like the rest of the man's clothes, had been obtained from a branch of a multiple business, and it was a small hope that any shop assistant would remember the individual to whom he sold the tie. Even if he did, there was no guarantee that the man remembered was their man. Faith Brothers must have sold several dozens of ties of the same pattern in London alone. But there was always that last odd chance, and Grant had seen too much of the queer unexpectedness of chance to neglect any avenue of

24

exploration. As Williams was leaving the room an idea had occurred to him. There was that first idea of his that the man had been a salesman in some clothing business. Perhaps he did not buy his things over the counter. He might have been in the employ of Faith Brothers. 'Find out,' he had said to Williams, 'if anyone answering the dead man's description has been employed by any one of the branches lately. If you see or hear anything interesting at all – whether you think it is important or not – let me know.'

Left alone, he had examined the morning's Press. He had not bothered with the various accounts of the queue murder, but the rest of the news he scrutinized with some care, beginning with the personal column. Nothing, however, sounded an answering chord in his brain. A photograph of himself with the caption, 'Inspector Grant, who is in charge of the Queue Murder investigations,' caused him to frown. 'Fools!' he said aloud. He had then collected and studied a list of missing persons sent in from all the police stations in Britain. Five young men were missing from various places, and the description of one, who was missing from a small Durham town, might have been that of the dead man. After a long delay, Grant had succeeded in talking on the telephone to the Durham police, only to learn that the missing man had originally been a miner and was, in the opinion of the Durham inspector, a tough. And neither 'miner' nor 'tough' could be applied to the dead man.

The rest of the morning had been occupied with routine work – settling about the inquest and such necessary formalities. About lunch-time Williams had rung him up from the biggest branch of Faith Brothers, in the Strand. He had had a busy but unproductive morning. Not only did no one recall such a purchaser, but no one remembered even selling such a tie. It was not one of a range that they had stocked lately. That had made him want further information about the tie itself, and he had come to the headquarters and asked to see the manager, to whom he explained the situation. The manager now suggested that if the inspector would surrender the tie for a little it should be sent to their factory at Northwood, where a list could be furnished of the destination of all consignments of such ties within, say, the last year. Williams now sought permission to hand over the tie to the manager.

Grant had approved his action, and while mentally commending Williams' common sense – lots of sergeants would have gone on plodding round London because they were told to and it was their duty – thought not too hopefully of the hundred or so branches of Faith Brothers all over Scotland and England. The chances narrowed slightly, however, when Williams appeared with a fuller explanation. Ties like that, it appeared, were made up in boxes of six, each tie in the box being of a different shade though usually in the same colour-scheme. It was unlikely that more than one, or at the most two, ties of the exact shade of their specimen had been sent to any one branch. There was therefore more hope of a salesman remembering the customer who had bought it than there would have been if the tie had been merely one of a box all the same shade. The detective part of Grant listened appreciatively while the looker-on part of him smiled over the sergeant's fluency in the jargon of the trade. Half an hour with the manager of Faith Brothers had had the effect of studding the sergeant's habitual simplicity of word and phrase with amazing jewels of technicality. He talked glibly of 'lines' and 'repeats' and similar profundities, so that Grant had, through his bulk, in a queer television a vivid picture of the manager himself. But he was grateful to Williams and said so. That was part of Grant's charm; he never forgot to say when he was pleased.

In the afternoon, having given up hope of learning anything more by it, he had sent the dagger to the laboratory for analysis. 'Tell me anything you can about it,' he had said; and last night when he left he was still waiting for the answer. Now he stretched out an arm into the chilly air and grabbed at the telephone. When he got the number he had asked for, he said:

'Inspector Grant speaking. Any developments?'

No, there were no developments. Two people had viewed the body last night – two separate people – but neither had recognised it. Yes, their names and addresses had been taken and were lying on his desk now. There was also a report from the laboratory.

'Good!' said Grant, jammed the earpiece on the hook and sprang out of bed, his sense of foreboding dispelled by the clear light of reason. Over his cold bath he whistled, and all the time he was dressing he whistled, so that his landlady said to her husband, who was departing to catch an eight o'clock bus, 'I'm thinking it won't be very long now before that horrible anarchist is caught.' Anarchist and assassin were synonymous terms to Mrs Field. Grant himself would not have put it so optimistically perhaps, but the thought of that sealed package waiting on his desk was to him what a lucky packet is to a small boy. It might be something of no importance and it might be a diamond. He caught Mrs Field's benevolent glance on him as she set down his breakfast, and it was like a small boy that he said to her, 'This my lucky day, do you think?'

'I don't know about luck, Mr Grant. I don't know as I believes in it. But I do believe in Providence. And I don't think Providence'll let a nice young man like that be stabbed to death and not bring the guilty to justice. Trust in the Lord, Mr Grant.'

'And if the clues are *very* thin, the Lord and the C.I.D.,' Grant misquoted at her and attacked his bacon and eggs. She lingered a moment watching him, shook her head in a gently misgiving way at him, and left him scanning the newspapers while he chewed.

On the way up to town he occupied himself by considering the problem of the man's non-identification, which

became momentarily more surprising. True, a few persons
every year are thrown up by London to lie unclaimed for a
day or two and then vanish into paupers' graves. But they
are all either old or penniless or both – the dregs of a city's
being, cast off long before their deaths by their relations
and friends, and so, when the end came, beyond the ken
of anyone who might have told their story. In all Grant's
experience no one of the type of the dead man – a man
who must have had the normal circle of acquaintances if
not more – had remained unidentified. Even if he had been
a provincial or a foreigner – and Grant did not think he was;
the man's whole appearance had proclaimed the Londoner
– he must have had a dwelling in London or near it; hotel,
lodgings, or club, from which he must now be known to be
missing. And the appeals from the Press that the fact of a
missing person should be communicated to Scotland Yard
without delay would most certainly have brought someone
hurrying to report it.

Then, granted that the man was a Londoner – as Grant
most heartily believed – why did his people or his landlord
not come forward? Obviously, either because they had
reason to think the dead man a bad lot, or because
they themselves had no wish to attract the attention of
the police. A gang? A gang getting rid of an unwanted
member? But gangs didn't wait until they got their victim
into a queue before dispensing with his services. They chose
safer methods. Unless – yes, it might have been at once a
retribution and a warning. It had had all the elements of a
gesture – the weapon, the striking down of the victim while
in a place of supposed safety, the whole bravado of the thing.
It eliminated the backslider and intimidated the survivors at
one and the same time. The more he considered it the more
it seemed the reasonable explanation of a mystery. He had
scouted the thought of a secret society and he still scouted
it. The vengeance of a secret society would not prevent the
man's friends from reporting his loss and claiming him. But

the defaulting member of a gang – that was a different thing. In that case all his friends would either know or guess the manner and reason of his death, and none would be fool enough to come forward.

As Grant turned into the Yard he was revising in his mind the various London gangs that flourished at the moment. Danny Miller's was cock of the walk, undoubtedly, and had been so for some time. It was three years since Danny had 'seen the inside', and unless he made a grievous error, it would be still longer before he did. Danny had come from America after serving his second sentence for burglary, and had brought with him a clever brain, a belief in organisation that was typically American – the British practitioner is by nature an individualist – and a wholesome respect for British police methods. The result was that, though his minions slipped occasionally and served short sentences for their carelessness, Danny went free and successful – much too successful for the liking of the C.I.D. Now, Danny had all the American crook's ruthlessness in dealing with an enemy. His habit was a gun, but he would think no more of sticking a knife into a man than he would of swatting the fly that annoyed him. Grant thought that he would invite Danny to come and see him. Meanwhile there was the packet on his table.

Eagerly he opened it and eagerly skipped the slightly prosy unimportances with which it opened – Bretherton of the scientific side was inclined to be a pompous dogmatist; if you sent him a Persian cat to report on, he would spend the first sheet of foolscap in deciding that its coat was grey and not fawn – and picked out the salient thing. Just above the junction of the handle with the blade, Bretherton said, was a stain of blood which was not the blood on the blade. The base on which the saint stood was hollow and had been broken at one side. The break was merely a cut which did not gape and was almost invisible owing to the bloodstain. But when the surface was pressed, one edge of the rough

cut was raised very slightly above the other. In gripping
the tool the murderer had made the fracture in the metal
gape sufficiently to injure his own hand. He would now
be suffering from a jagged cut somewhere on the thumb
side of the first finger of the left hand, or finger side of
the thumb.

Good so far, thought Grant, but one can't sift London for
a left-handed man with a cut hand and arrest him for that.
He sent for Williams.

'Do you know where Danny Miller is living now?'
he asked.

'No, sir,' said Williams; 'but Barber will know. He came
up from Newbury last night, and he knows all about
Danny.'

'All right, go and find out. No, better send Barber to
me.'

When Barber came – a tall, slow man with a sleepy and
misleading smile – he repeated his question.

'Danny Miller?' Barber said. 'Yes, he has rooms in a house
in Amber Street, Pimlico.'

'Oh? Been very quiet lately, hasn't he?'

'So we thought, but I think that jewel robbery that the
Gowbridge people are busy with now is Danny.'

'I thought banks were his line.'

'Yes, but he has a new "jane". He probably wants
money.'

'I see. Do you know his number?'

Barber did.

An hour later, Danny, who was performing a leisurely
and painstaking toilet in the room in Amber Street, was
informed that Inspector Grant would be very much obliged
if he would have a short talk with him at the Yard.

Danny's pale grey, wary eyes surveyed the plain-clothes
man who had brought the message. 'If he thinks he
has anything on me,' he said, 'he has another guess
coming.'

The plain-clothes man did not think that the inspector wanted anything but some information from him.

'Oh? And what is the inspector inspecting at the moment?'

But that the plain-clothes man either did not know or would not tell.

'All right,' said Danny. 'I'll be along right now.'

When a portly constable led him into Grant's presence Danny, who was small and slim, indicated the departing one with a backward jerk of the head and a humorous lift of an eyebrow. 'It isn't often anyone troubles to announce me,' he said.

'No,' said Grant, smiling, 'your presence is usually announced after your departure, isn't it?'

'You're a wit, Inspector. I shouldn't have thought you'd need anyone to jog your brains along. You don't think you've got anything on me, do you?'

'Not at all. I thought you might be of some use to me.'

'You're certainly flattering.' It was impossible to tell when Miller was serious or otherwise.

'Did you ever know by sight a man like this?' While he described in detail the murdered man, Grant's eyes were examining Danny and his brain was busy with what his eyes saw. Gloves. How could he get the glove off Danny's left hand without deliberately asking for its removal?

When he came to the end of his description, particularised even to the turned-in-toe, Danny said politely, 'That's the deader from the queue. No, I'm very sorry to disappoint you, Inspector, but I never saw the man in my life.'

'Well, I suppose you have no objections to coming with me and having a look at him?'

'Not if it'll set your mind at rest, Inspector. I'll do anything to oblige.'

The inspector put his hand into his pocket and brought it out full of coins, as if to make sure of his loose change before setting out. A sixpenny piece slid through his fingers and rolled swiftly across the smooth surface of the table towards

Miller, and Miller's hand shot out in an abrupt preventive movement as it was about to drop off the table's edge to the floor. He fumbled for a moment with his gloved hand and then laid the coin down on the table.

'Trifling things, these,' he remarked in his flat amiable voice.. But it was his right hand that he had used to stop it.

As they were driving down to the mortuary in a car he turned to the inspector with the almost noiseless expulsion of breath that in him did duty for a laugh. 'Say,' he said, 'if any of my pals see me now, they'll all be boarding a dangler for Southampton inside five minutes and not waiting to pack.'

'Well, we'd do the packing – back,' said Grant.

'Got us all taped like that, have you? Would you bet on it? I'll lay you five to one in dollars – no, pounds – five to one in pounds that you don't have one of us settled inside two years. You won't take it? Well, I think you're wise.'

When Miller was brought face to face with the body of the murdered man, Grant's eager eyes could trace no shadow of expression on that poker face. Danny's cool grey glance wandered over the dead man's features in a half-interested indifference. And Grant knew certainly that, even had Miller known the man, his hope of a betraying gesture or expression had been a vain one.

'No,' Danny was saying, 'I never saw the man in my—' He stopped. There was a long pause. 'Say, but I did!' he said. 'Oh, gosh, let me think! Where was it? Where was it? Wait a minute and it'll come.' He beat a hectic tattoo on his forehead with his gloved palm. Was this acting, thought Grant? Good acting, if so. But then Miller would never make the mistake of acting badly. 'Oh, gosh, I can't get it! I talked to him, too. Don't think I ever knew his name, but I'm sure I talked to him.'

In the end Grant gave it up – he had the inquest in front of him – but it was more than Danny Miller did. The fact that his brain had gone back on him was an outrage in his eyes and quite insupportable. 'I never forget a man,' he kept saying, 'any more than a "bull" does.'

'Well, you can think it over and telephone to me,' said Grant. 'Meanwhile, will you do one thing more for me? . . . Will you take your gloves off?'

Danny's eyes shut suddenly to bright slits. 'What's the big idea?' he said.

'Well, there isn't any reason that you shouldn't take them off, is there?'

'How do I know that?' snapped Danny.

'Look here,' said Grant good-naturedly, 'a minute ago you wanted a gamble. Well, here's one. If you take your gloves off, I'll tell you whether you've won or not.'

'And if I lose?'

'Well, I have no warrant, you know.' And Grant smiled easily into the gimlet eyes boring into his own.

Danny's eyelids lifted. His old nonchalance came back. He drew his right glove off and held out his hand. Grant glanced at it and nodded. Then he slipped off his left glove and extended his hand, and as he did so the right hand went back into his coat pocket.

The left hand that lay open to Grant's gaze was clean and unscarred.

'You win, Miller,' said Grant. 'You're a sportsman.' And the slight bulge in Danny's right-hand coat pocket disappeared.

'You'll let me know the minute you have a brain-wave, won't you?' Grant said as they parted, and Miller promised.

'Don't you worry,' he said. 'I don't let my brain go back on me and get away with it.'

And Grant made his way to lunch and the inquest.

The jury, having swallowed at one nauseating gulp the business of viewing the body, had settled into their places with that air of conscious importance and simulated modesty which belongs to those initiated into a mystery. Their verdict was already certain, therefore they had no need to worry themselves over the rights or wrongs of the case. They could give themselves up wholly to the delightful occupation of hearing all about the most popular murder of the day from lips of eye-witnesses. Grant surveyed them sardonically, and thanked the gods that neither his case nor his life depended on their intelligences. Then he forgot them and gave himself up to the rich comedy of the witnesses. It was strange to compare the grim things that fell from their lips with the pretty comedy they themselves presented. He knew them so well by now, and they all ran so amusingly true to form. There was the constable who had been on duty at the Woffington pit queue, brushed and shining, his dampish forehead shining most of all; precise in his report and tremendously gratified by his own preciseness. There was James Ratcliffe, the complete householder, hating his unexpected publicity, rebelling against his connection with such an unsavoury affair, but determined to do his duty as a citizen. He was the type that is the law's most useful ally, and the inspector recognised the fact and mentally saluted him in spite of the fact that he had been unhelpful. Waiting in queues bored him, he said, and as long as the light was good enough he had read, until the doors opened and the pressure became too great to do anything but stand.

There was his wife, whom the inspector had last seen sobbing in her bedroom. She still clutched a handkerchief, and obviously expected to be encouraged and soothed after every second question. And she was subjected to a longer examination than anyone else. She was the one who had stood directly behind the dead man.

'Are we to understand, madam,' said the coroner, 'that you stood for nearly two hours in close proximity to this man and yet have no recollection of him or of his companions, if any?'

'But I wasn't next to him all that time! I tell you I didn't see him until he fell over at my feet.'

'Then who was next in front of you most of the time?'

'I don't remember. I think it was a boy – a young man.'

'And what became of the young man?'

'I don't know.'

'Did you see him leave the queue?'

'No.'

'Can you describe him?'

'Yes; he was dark and foreign-looking, rather.'

'Was he alone?'

'I don't know. I don't think so, somehow. I think he was talking to someone.'

'How is it that you do not remember more distinctly what occurred when it is only three nights ago?'

The shock had put everything out of her head, she said. 'Besides,' she added, her gelatinous backbone ossified suddenly by the coroner's ill-hidden scorn, 'in a queue one doesn't notice the people next one. Both I and my husband were reading most of the time.' And she dissolved into hysterical weeping.

Then there was the fat woman, shiny with satin and soap-and-water, recovered now from the shock and reluctance she had displayed at the crowded moment of the murder, and more than willing to tell her tale. Her plump red face and boot-button brown eyes radiated a grim satisfaction with her rôle. She seemed disappointed when the coroner thanked her and dismissed her in the middle of a sentence.

There was a meek little man, as precise in manner as the constable had been, but evidently convinced that the coroner was a man of little intelligence. When that long-suffering official said, 'Yes, I was aware that queues usually go two by two,' the jury allowed themselves to snigger and the meek little man looked pained. As neither he nor the other three witnesses from the queue could recall the murdered man, nor throw any light on any departure from the queue, they were dismissed with scant attention.

The doorkeeper, incoherent with pleasure at being so helpful, informed the coroner that he had seen the dead man before – several times. He had come quite often to the Woffington. But he knew nothing about him. He had always been well dressed. No, the doorkeeper could not recall any companion, though he was sure that the man had not habitually been alone.

The atmosphere of futility that characterised the inquest discouraged Grant. A man whom no one professed to know, stuck in the back by someone whom no one had seen. It was a sweet prospect. No clue to the murderer except the dagger, and that told nothing except that the man was scarred on a finger or thumb. No clue to the murdered man except the hope that a Faith Brothers employee might have known the person to whom he sold a fawn patterned tie with faint pink splashes. When the inevitable verdict of murder against some person or persons unknown had been given, Grant went to a telephone revolving in his mind the Ratcliffe woman's tale of a young foreigner. Was that impression a mere figment of her imagination, brought into being by the suggestion of the dagger? Or was it a genuine corroboration of his Dago theory? Mrs Ratcliffe's young foreigner had not been there when the murder was discovered. He was the one who had disappeared from the queue, and the one who had disappeared from the queue had most certainly murdered the dead man.

Well, he would find out from the Yard if there was anything new, and if not, he would fortify himself with tea. He needed it. And the slow sipping of tea conduced to thought. Not the painful tabulations of Barker, that prince of superintendents, but the speculative revolving of things which he, Grant, found more productive. He numbered among his acquaintances a poet and essayist, who sipped tea in a steady monotonous rhythm, the while he brought to birth his masterpieces. His digestive system was in a shocking condition, but he had a very fine reputation among the more precious of the modern littérateurs.

CHAPTER 4

RAOUL LEGARDE

But over the telephone Grant heard something which put all thoughts of tea out of his head. There was waiting for him a letter addressed in capitals. Grant knew very well what that meant. Scotland Yard has a wide experience of letters addressed in capitals. He smiled to himself as he hailed a taxi. If people only realised that writing in capitals didn't disguise a hand at all! But he sincerely hoped they never would.

Before he opened the letter that awaited him he dusted it with powder and found it covered with finger-prints. He slit the top delicately, holding the letter, which was fat and softish, in a pair of forceps, and drew out a wad of Bank of England five-pound notes and a half-sheet of notepaper. On the notepaper was printed: 'To bury the man who was found in the queue.'

There were five notes. Twenty-five pounds.

Grant sat down and stared. In all his time in the C.I.D. a more unexpected thing had not happened. Somewhere in London tonight was someone who cared sufficiently for the dead man to spend twenty-five pounds to keep him from a pauper's grave, but who would not claim him. Was this corroboration of his intimidation theory? Or was it conscience money? Had the murderer a superstitious desire to do the right thing by his victim's body? Grant thought not. The man who stuck another in the back didn't care a hoot what became of the body. The man had a pal – man or woman – in London tonight, a pal who cared to the tune of twenty-five pounds.

38

Grant called in Williams, and together they considered the plain, cheap white envelope and the strong, plain capitals.

'Well,' said Grant, 'what do you know?'

'A man,' said Williams. 'Not well off. Not used to writing much. Clean. Smokes. Depressed.'

'Excellent!' said Grant. 'You're no good as a Watson, Williams. You get away with all the kudos.'

Williams, who knew all about Watson – at the age of eleven he had spent hunted moments in a hay-loft in Worcestershire trying to read *The Speckled Band* without being discovered by Authority, who had banned it – smiled and said, 'I expect you have got far more out of it, sir.'

But Grant had not. 'Except that he's a poor hand at the business. Fancy sending anything as easily traced as English five-pound notes!' He blew the light soft powder over the half-sheet of notepaper, but found no finger-prints. He summoned a constable and sent the precious envelope and the bundle of notes to have all finger-prints photographed. The sheet of notepaper bearing the printed message he sent to the handwriting expert.

'Well, the banks are shut now, worse luck. Are you in a hurry to get back to the missus, Williams?'

No, Williams was in no hurry. His missus and the baby were in Southend with his mother-in-law for a week.

'In that case,' Grant said, 'we'll dine together and you can give me the benefit of your ideas on the subject of murders in queues.'

Some years before, Grant had inherited a considerable legacy – a legacy sufficient to have permitted him to retire into idle nonentity if such had been his desire. But Grant loved his work even when he swore and called it a dog's life, and the legacy had been used only to smooth and embroider life until what would have been the bleak places were eliminated, and to make some bleak places in other lives less impossible. There was a little grocer's shop in a southern suburb, bright as a jewel with its motley goods, which owed its existence to the legacy and to Grant's chance meeting with a ticket-of-leave man on his first morning out. It was Grant who had been the means of 'putting him away,' and it was Grant who provided the means of his rehabilitation. It was owing entirely to the legacy, therefore, that Grant was an habitué of so exclusive an eating-place as Laurent's, and – a much more astonishing and impressive fact – a pet of the head waiter's. Only five persons in Europe are pets of Laurent's head waiter, and Grant was thoroughly conscious of the honour, and thoroughly sensible of the reason.

Marcel met them half-way down the green-and-gold room, with his face screwed to an expression of the most excruciating sorrow. He was desolated, but there was not a table worthy of monsieur left. There were no tables at all except that much-to-be-condemned one in that corner. Monsieur had not let him know that he was to be expected. He was desolated, desolated simply.

Grant took the table without a murmur. He was hungry, and he did not care where he ate so that the food was good, and except for the fact that the table was directly outside the service door there was no fault to be found with it. A couple of green draught-screens camouflaged the door, and the door, being a swing one, kept the rattle of crockery to a faint castanet music that blossomed every now and then in a sudden fortissimo as the door swung wide and closed again. Over their dinner Grant decided that in the morning Williams should visit the banks in the area indicated by the letter's postmark, and with that as a basis, track down the history of the bank-notes. It shouldn't be difficult; banks were always accommodating. From that they turned to the discussion of the crime itself. It was Williams' opinion that it was a gang affair; that the dead man had fallen foul of his gang, had known his danger, had borrowed the gun from the only friendly member of the crowd, and had never had a chance to use it. The money that had arrived tonight had come from the secretly friendly one. It was a good enough theory, but it left out things.

'Why had he no identification marks on him, then?'

'Perhaps,' said Williams with electrifying logic, 'it's a gang habit. No identification if they're caught.'

That was a possible theory, and Grant was silent for a little, thinking it over. It was with the entrée that he became conscious, with that sixth sense which four years on the Western Front and many more in the C.I.D. had developed to an abnormal acuteness, that he was being watched. Restraining the impulse to turn round – he was sitting with his back to the room, almost facing the service door – he glanced casually into the mirror. But no one seemed to be taking the slightest interest in him. Grant continued to eat, and in a moment or two tried again. The room had emptied considerably since their arrival, and it was easy to examine the various people in the vicinity. But the mirror showed only a collection of self-absorbed people, eating, drinking, and smoking. And still Grant had that sense of being subjected to a long scrutiny. It made his flesh creep, that steady, unseen examination. He lifted his eyes above Williams' head to the screen that hid the door. And there, in the chink between the screens, were the eyes that watched him. As if conscious of his discovery, the eyes wavered and disappeared, and Grant went serenely on with his meal. A too curious waiter, he thought. Probably knows who I am, and just wanted to gape at anyone connected with a murder. Grant had suffered much from the gapers. But presently, looking up in the middle of a sentence, he found the eyes back at their examination of him. This was too much. He stared stolidly in return. But the owner of the eyes was evidently unaware that he was visible at all to Grant, and continued his watching uninterrupted. Now and then as a waiter came or went behind the screen the eyes disappeared, but always they returned to their furtive gazing. Grant was seized with a desire to see this man whose

interest in himself was of so absorbing a character. He said
to Williams, who was seated not more than a yard in front
of the screen, 'There is someone at the back of the screen
behind you who is taking a most abnormal interest in us.
When I click my fingers fling back your right hand and
knock the screen sideways. Make it look as much like an
accident as you can.'

Grant waited until the waiter traffic had lulled for a
little and the eyes were steady at gaze, and then gently
snapped his middle finger and thumb. Williams' brawny
arm shot out, the screen quivered for a moment and
collapsed sideways. But there was no one there. Only the
agitated swinging of the door showed where someone had
made his hasty exit.

Well, that's that, thought Grant, as Williams was apolo-
gising for the accident with the screen. You can't identify
a pair of eyes. He finished his dinner without further
annoyance and strolled back to the Yard with Williams,
hoping that the photographs of the prints on the envelope
would be ready for his examination.

No photographs had come, but there was a report on
the tie which had been sent to Faith Brothers' factory at
Northwood. The only consignment of that pattern of tie
sent out in the last year was a box of six in various shades
which had been sent as a repeat order at the request of
their Nottingham branch. They returned the tie and hoped
that if they could be of any further use the inspector would
command them.

'If nothing important turns up between now and tomorrow,' said Grant, 'I shall go down to Nottingham while you
are doing the banks.'

And then a man came in with photographs of the envelope prints, and Grant took from his desk the photographs
of the other prints in the case – the prints of the dead man's
finger-tips and the prints found on the revolver. Nothing
but smudges, the report said, had been found on any

of the bank-notes, so Grant and the sergeant applied themselves to the examination of the envelope prints. A variety of impressions were apparent since several people had handled the envelope since the writer had posted the letter. But clear and perfect and without possibility of doubt was the print of a forefinger to the right of the flap, and the forefinger was the same forefinger that had left its mark on the revolver found in the dead man's pocket.

'Well, that fits your theory about the friend who supplied the gun, doesn't it?' said Grant.

But the sergeant made a queer choked noise and continued to look at the print.

'What's the matter? It's as clear as a kid's alphabet.'

The sergeant straightened himself and looked queerly at his superior. 'I'll swear I hadn't a glass too much, sir. But it's either that or the whole finger-print system is balmy. Look at that!' He pointed with a not too steady forefinger at a print in the extreme lower right-hand corner, and as he did so he shoved the dead man's finger-prints, which had lain slightly apart, under Grant's nose. For a little there was silence while the inspector compared the prints and the sergeant, over his shoulder, half-fearfully corroborated his previous view. But there was no getting away from the fact that faced them in irrefutable whorls and ridges. The finger-print was that of the dead man.

It was only a moment or two before Grant realised the simple significance of that apparently staggering fact.

'Communal notepaper, of course,' he said offhandedly, while his looker-on half mocked at him for having allowed himself to be victimised even for a moment by the childish amazement that had overcome him. 'Your theory blossoms, Williams. The man who lent the gun and provided the money lived with the dead man. That being so, of course he can spin any kind of yarn he likes to his landlady or his wife or whoever would be interested about the disappearance of his chum.' He took up the telephone on his desk. 'We'll see what the handwriting people have to say about the piece of notepaper.'

But the handwriting experts had nothing to add to what Grant already knew or guessed. The paper was of a common type that could be bought at any stationer's or bookstall. The printing was that of a man. Given a specimen of a suspect's handwriting they would probably be able to say whether or not the printing had been done by him, but so far they could be of no more help than already indicated.

Williams departed to his temporarily bereaved home to comfort his uxorious mind by reminding himself how short a week was, and how pretty Mrs Williams would be when she came back from Southend; and Grant remained where he was, trying to mesmerise the dagger into giving up its tale. It lay on the dark green leather surface of his desk, a graceful, wicked toy-like thing, its business end in its slender viciousness making a queer contrast to the bluff saint on the handle with his silly, expressionless face. Grant considered the saintly features sardonically. What was it Ray Marcable had said? You'd want a blessing on an undertaking as big as that. Well, Grant thought, he would choose a more potent saint as O.C. affairs than the ineffectual holy one on the handle. His thoughts went to Ray Marcable. This morning's Press had been full of her projected departure for America, the popular papers expressing themselves in lamentation and the more high-brow in bitterness and indignation that British managers should allow the best musical comedy star of a generation to leave the country. Should he go to her, Grant wondered, before she left and ask her bluntly why she had looked surprised at the description of the dagger? There had been nothing to connect her even remotely with the crime. He knew her history – the little semi-detached villa in a dreary suburb that she had called home, the council school she had attended, her real name, which was Rosie Markham. He had even met Mr and Mrs Markham over the affair of the suitcase. It was exceedingly unlikely that she could throw any light on the Queue Murder. And it was still more unlikely that she would if she could. She had had her chance to be frank with him over that tea in her dressing-room, and she had quite deliberately kept him outside any knowledge she might have had. That knowledge, of course, might be entirely innocent. Her surprise might have been due to recognition of the dagger's description, and yet have nothing to do with the murder. The dagger was far from unique, and many people must have seen and handled similar weapons. No, either way he was not likely to get much satisfaction from another interview with Miss Marcable. She would have to depart for the United States uninterrogated.

With a sigh for its unproductiveness he locked the dagger away in its drawer again and set off for home. He came out on to the Embankment, to find that it was a fine night with a light, frosty mist in the air, and he decided that he would walk home. The midnight streets of London – always so much more beautiful than the choppy crowded ones of the daytime – fascinated him. At noon London made you a present of an entertainment, rich and varied and amusing. But at midnight she made you a present of herself; at midnight you could hear her breathe.

When at length he turned into the road where he lived he had come to the stage of walking automatically, and a starry mist possessed his brain. For a little while Grant had 'shut his eyes.' But he was not asleep, actually or metaphorically, and the eyes of his brain opened with a start at the dim figure that was waiting on the opposite corner just outside the lamplight. Who was hanging about at this hour?

He debated rapidly whether or not to cross and walk down the other side of the street, and so come within criticising distance of the figure. But it was rather late to change his direction. He held on, ignoring the loiterer. Only when he was turning in at his own gate he looked back. The figure was still there, almost indistinguishable in the gloom.

It was after twelve when he let himself in with his latchkey, but Mrs Field was waiting up for him. 'I thought you'd like to know that there has been a gentleman here asking for you. He wouldn't wait and he wouldn't leave a message.'

'How long ago was that?'

More than an hour, Mrs Field said. She didn't see him rightly. He had stood well out beyond the step. But he was young.

'No name?'

No, he had refused to give a name.

'All right,' said Grant. 'You go to bed. If he comes back, I'll let him in.'

She hesitated in the doorway. 'You won't do anything rash, will you?' she said solicitously. 'I don't like the thought of you bin here all alone with someone who might be an anarchist for all we know.'

'Don't you worry, Mrs Field. You won't be blown up tonight.'

'It isn't blowing up I'm afraid of,' she said. 'It's the thought of you lyin' here perhaps bleeding to death and no one knowing. Think how I'd feel when I came in in the morning and found you like that.'

Grant laughed. 'Well, you can comfort yourself. There isn't the slightest chance of anything so thrilling happening. No one has ever spilt my blood except a Jerry at Contalmaison, and that was more by luck than good management.'

She conceded the point. 'See and have a bite before you go to bed,' she said, indicating the food on the sideboard. 'I got you some English tomatoes, and the beef is Tomkins' best pickled.' She said good-night and went, but she could not have reached her kitchen before a knock sounded on the door. Grant heard her go to the door, and even while his brain was speculating about his visitor, the looker-on in him was wondering whether it was spunk or curiosity that had sent Mrs Field so willingly to answer the knock. A moment later she threw open the sitting-room door and said, 'A young gentleman to see you, sir,' and into Grant's eager presence came a youth of nineteen or twenty, fairly tall, dark, broad-shouldered, but slight, and poised on his feet like a boxer. As he came forward he shot a furtive glance from his brilliant dark eyes into the corner behind the door, and he came to a halt some yards from the inspector in the middle of the room, turning a soft felt hat in his slim gloved hands.

'You are Inspector Grant?' he asked.

Grant motioned him to a chair, and the youth, with a completely un-English grace, subsided sideways on to it, still clutching his hat, and began to talk.

'I saw you tonight at Laurent's. I am in the pantry there. I clean the silver and things like that. They told me who you were, and after I think for a while, I decided to tell you all about it.'

'A very good idea,' said Grant. 'Carry on. Are you Italian?'

'No; I am French. My name is Raoul Legarde.'

'All right; carry on.'

'I was in the queue the night the man was killed. It was my night off. For a long time I was standing next the man. He trod on my foot in accident, and after that we talked a little – about the play. I was on the outside and he was next the wall. Then a man came to talk to him and came in in front of me. The man who was new wanted something from the other man. He stayed until the door opened and the people moved. He was angry about something. They were not quarrelling – not as we quarrel – but I think they were angry. When the murder happened I ran away. I did not want to be mixed up with the police. But tonight I saw you, and you looked *gentil*, and so I made up my mind to tell you all about it.'

'Why didn't you come to Scotland Yard and tell me?'

'I do not trust the Sûreté. They make very much out of nothing. And I have no friends in London.'

'When the man came to talk to the man who was murdered, and pushed you back a place, who was between you and the theatre wall?'

'A woman in black.'

Mrs Ratcliffe. So far the boy was telling the truth.

'Can you describe the man who came and went away again?'

'He was not very tall. Not as tall as me. He had a hat like mine, only more brown, and a coat like mine' – he indicated his tight-fitting, waisted navy-blue coat – 'only brown too. He was very dark, without moustache, and these stuck out.' He touched his own beautifully modelled cheek and chin bones.

'Would you know him again if you saw him?'

'Oh yes.'

'Well enough to swear to?'

'What is that?'

'To take your oath on.'

'Oh yes.'

'What did the two men quarrel about?'

'I don't know. I didn't hear. I was not deliberately listening, you understand, and though I speak English, I do not understand if people talk very quickly. I think the man who came wanted something that the man who was killed would not give him.'

'When the man went away from the queue, how is it that no one saw him go?'

'Because just then the policeman was walking down saying "Stand back" to the people.'

That was too glib. The inspector took out his note-book and pencil and, laying the pencil on the open page, held it out to his visitor. 'Can you show me how you stood in the queue? Put marks for the people, and label them.'

The boy stretched out his left hand for the book, took the

pencil in his right, and made a very intelligent diagram, unaware that he had at that moment defeated the distrusted Sûreté's attempt to make something out of nothing.

Grant watched his serious, absorbed face and thought rapidly. He was telling the truth, then. He had been there until the man collapsed, had backed with the others away from the horror, and had continued backing until he could walk away from the danger of being at the mercy of foreign police. And he had actually seen the murderer and would recognise him again. Things were beginning to move.

He took back the book and pencil that the boy extended to him, and as he raised his eyes from the consideration of the diagram, he caught the dark eyes resting rather wistfully on the food on the sideboard. It occurred to him that Legarde had probably come straight from his work to see him.

'Well, I'm very grateful to you,' he said. 'Have some supper with me now, before you go.'

The boy refused shyly, but allowed himself to be persuaded, and together they had a substantial meal of Mr Tomkins' best pickled. Legarde talked freely of his people in Dijon – the sister who sent him French papers, the father who disapproved of beer since one ate grapes but not hops; of his life at Laurent's and his impression of London and the English. And when Grant eventually let him out into the black stillness of the early morning, he turned on the doorstep and said apologetically and naïvely, 'I am sorry now that I did not tell before, but you understand how it was? To have run away at first made it difficult. And I did not know that the police were so *gentil*.'

Grant dismissed him with a friendly pat on the shoulder, locked up, and picked up the telephone receiver. When he was through, he said:

'Inspector Grant speaking. This to be sent to all stations: "Wanted, in connection with the London Queue Murder, a left-handed man, about thirty years of age, slightly below middle height, very dark in complexion and hair, prominent cheek and chin bones, clean-shaven. When last seen was wearing a soft brown hat and tight-fitting brown coat. Has a recent scar on the left forefinger or thumb.'"

And then he went to bed.

CHAPTER 5

DANNY AGAIN

Running out of Marylebone into the sunlight of the morning, Grant looked out of his carriage window and felt more optimistic than he had since he had first interviewed the officials at Gow Street Police Station. The murderer had ceased to be a mythical being. They had a full description of him now, and it could only be a matter of time before they ran him down. And perhaps by tonight he would have settled the identity of the murdered man. He stretched his legs in the empty compartment and let the sun slide slowly back and fore over them as the train wheeled in its progress. A pleasant country, England, at ten of a bright morning. Even the awful little suburban villas had lost that air of aggressiveness born of their inferiority complex, and were shining self-forgetful and demure in the clear light. Their narrow, inhospitable doors were no longer ugly in the atrociousness of cheap paint and appliqué mouldings; they were entrances of jade and carnelian and lapis lazuli and onyx into particular separate heavens. Their gardens, with their pert, ill-dressed rows of tulips and meagre seedsown grass, were lovely as ever the Hanging Gardens of Babylon had been. Here and there a line of gay motley child's clothes danced and ballooned with the breeze in a necklace of coloured laughter. And farther on, when the last vestiges of the town fell away, the wide acres of the grass country smiled broadly in the sunlight like an old hunting print. All England was lovely this morning, and Grant knew it. Even Nottingham canals had a Venetian touch of blue today and their grimy, imprisoning walls were rosy as Petra.

Grant came out of the station into the drone and clamour
of trams. If he had been asked what represented the Midlands in his mind, he would unhesitatingly have said trams.
Trams in London always seemed to him alien incongruities,
poor provincials who had been inveigled to the Metropolis,
and drudged out a misanthropic and despised existence,
because they had never made enough money to get out
of it. Grant never heard the far-away peculiar sing of an
approaching tramcar without finding himself back in the
dead, airless atmosphere of the Midland town where he had
been born. The Midlanders did not hide away their trams
in back streets; they trailed them proudly through their
chiefest thoroughfares, partly from braggadocio, partly
from a misplaced idea of utility. A long yellow string
of them stood in Nottingham market-place, blocking the
view of the wide, almost continental square, and making
the passage from the pavement on one side to the stalls
of the market on the other a most exhilarating game of
hide-and-seek. But the natives, with that adaptability to
circumstances which is nature's greatest marvel, seemed
to enjoy the hop-skip-and-jump business, and to find it not
too dangerous to be indulged in. No one was killed during
the time that Grant walked down the street, at any rate.

At Faith Brothers' he produced the tie which had belonged
to the dead man, and explained that he wanted to know
whether anyone remembered selling it. The man at the
counter had no recollection of the transaction, but summoned a colleague, who was flipping a white and too
flexible forefinger up and down the wall of cardboard
boxes in an endeavour to find an article that would meet
with his customer's approval. Something told Grant that
in matters sartorial this youth would have the memory of
an oldest inhabitant, and he was right. After one glance at
the tie, he said that he had taken it out of the window –
or one exactly like it – for a gentleman about a month ago.
The gentleman had seen it in the window and, because it

matched the suit he was wearing, had come in and bought it. No, he did not think that he was a Nottingham man. Why? Well, he didn't *talk* Nottingham for one thing, and he didn't *dress* Nottingham for another.

Could he describe the man?

He could, and did, with minuteness and accuracy. 'I can tell you the date, if you like,' said this surprising youth. 'I remember because' – he hesitated, and finished with a refreshing lapse from his worldly-wise air to a pink *naïveté* – 'because of something that happened that day. It was the second of February.'

Grant noted the date and asked what his impression of the stranger had been. Was he a commercial traveller?

The youth thought not. He didn't talk business and he didn't seem interested in the growth of Nottingham or anything.

Grant asked if there was anything on in the town on that date that would bring a stranger to Nottingham, and the youth said yes, most emphatically. There had been a huge musical festival – a festival for all the Midlands; and there had been a good few people from London too. He knew, because he himself had taken part in it. He sang in a church choir and knew all about festivals. The stranger had looked much more like someone interested in the festival than a commercial traveller. He had thought at the time that that was probably what the man was in Nottingham for.

Grant thought it was quite likely. He remembered the man's sensitive hands. And he had been an habitué of the Woffington – which, if not high-brow, is at least invariably musical. It didn't march with the gang theory, but he could not afford to ignore it because of that. The gang theory had no support in fact. It was a theory and nothing else – pure speculation. He thanked the youth and asked for the name of someone in Nottingham who would know all about the festival and the people who came to it. The youth said that he had better go and see Yeudall, the solicitor. Yeudall wasn't the secretary, but he was a sort of chairman, and it was his hobby. He sat there from morning to night, all the three days of the festival, and he would be certain to know anyone who was interested enough to come from London for it.

Grant wrote down Yeudall's address, conscious that the youth's inquisitive mind was docketing him as it had docketed the dead man, and that years hence, if someone asked him to describe the man who took Yeudall's address, he would do it faithfully. He was wasted in a hatter's-and-hosier's.

'Are you looking for the man who bought the tie?' the youth asked. He said 'looking' in inverted commas, giving it its police sense.

'Not exactly,' said Grant, 'but I want to trace him if I can.' And he departed to interview Mr Yeudall.

In a little side street, near the castle – the kind of street that has never seen a tramcar and where one's footsteps echo until one involuntarily looks behind – were situated the small and gloomy offices of Yeudall, Lister & Yeudall. Three hundred years old they were, and the waiting-room was panelled in oak that extinguished the last valiant ray of light as it fought its way past the old greenish glass of the window-pane. The light died on the window-sill as the last survivor of a charge dies on the enemy parapet, murdered but glorious. But Mr Yeudall, of Yeudall, Lister & Yeudall, would have considered it heresy if it had been suggested that things might be otherwise. Otherwise! That meant a building like a meat-safe, fretted with windows until the walls were practically non-existent. A collection of plate-glass bound together by pilasters of an incredible ignobility! That was modern architecture! But, as if to make up for the dim dustiness of his surroundings, Mr Yeudall himself beamed and shone and welcomed all humanity with that sublime lack of suspicion which makes friends, and 'confidence' men, but never lawyers. Being the only

Yeudall of the third generation, he had been given in his youth a cupboard-like corner in the warren of small rooms that were the Yeudall offices, and, since he loved oak panelling and beams and greenish glass second only to symphonies and sonatas, he had stayed there. And now he was Yeudall, Lister & Yeudall – though a competent clerk kept anything too awful from happening.

To say that Mr Yeudall welcomed the inspector is an inadequate statement. Grant felt that he must have met the man before and have forgotten it. He betrayed none of the curiosity that was usually rampant on a man's face when the inspector followed his card into a room. Grant was to him merely another charming fellow-being, and almost before he had made his business clear Grant found himself being led away to lunch. It was so much nicer to talk over a meal, and it was long after one, and if the inspector hadn't eaten since breakfast, he must be famishing. Grant followed his unexpected host meekly enough; he had not yet got his information, and this seemed to be the only way of getting it. Moreover, a detective officer never throws away the chance of making an acquaintance. If Scotland Yard has a motto, it is You Never Know.

Over lunch he learned that Mr Yeudall had never to his knowledge seen the man he was looking for. He knew by sight or personally all the performers at the festival as well as a great number of those merely interested in it. But none tallied exactly with the description Grant furnished.

'If you think he was musical, try Lyons' orchestra or the picture-houses. Their orchestra performers are mostly Londoners.'

Grant did not bother to explain that the supposition that the man was musical had arisen only through his supposed connexion with the festival. It was easier and pleasanter to let Mr Yeudall talk. In the afternoon, however, after he had taken farewell of his cheerful host, he did sift the various orchestra in the town, with the lack of success that he had foreseen. He then telephoned to the Yard to find out how Williams had fared in his hunt after the history of the banknotes, and spoke to Williams himself, who had just come back after a long morning's work. The notes were with the bank just now. Nothing had transpired so far, but they were on a scent, and the bank were working it.

Well, thought Grant, as he hung up the receiver, one end of the tangle seemed to be working out slowly but surely. Nothing left so clear and incontrovertible a history behind it as a Bank of England note. And if he had failed at Nottingham to trace the dead man himself, their discovery of the friend's identity would inevitably lead them to the knowledge of who the dead man was. And from the dead man to the Dago would be only a step. Still, he was slightly depressed. He had had such a hunch this morning that before night an unexpected piece of information would have set him on the right track, that he surveyed his wasted day with something like disgust, and not even the after-effects of the good lunch Mr Yeudall had given him, nor the rosy afterglow of that gentleman's goodwill to men, was sufficient to comfort him. At the station he found that he had half an hour to wait for his train, and he betook himself to the lounge of the nearest hotel in the vague hope of picking up unconsidered trifles of information in that most gossipy of all public places. He surveyed the two waiters with a jaundiced eye. One was supercilious and like an overfed pug, and the other was absent-minded and like a dachshund. Grant felt instinctively that help was not in them. But the person who brought him his coffee was a charming middle-aged waitress. Grant's weary soul brightened at the sight of her. In a few minutes he was indulging in a friendly, if disjointed, exchange of generalities, and when she went away temporarily to attend to the wants of someone else, she always came back and hovered within speaking distance until the conversation was resumed. Realising that a verbal description of a man

who was not a hunchback or blind or otherwise abnormal
would convey nothing to this woman, who saw in one day at
least half a dozen men who might have fitted a description
of the dead man, Grant contented himself with giving leads
which might provoke useful information of a relative sort.

'You're quiet here just now,' he said.

Yes, she admitted; this was their quiet time. They had
slack times and busy ones. It just happened like that.

Did it depend on the number of people staying in
the hotel?

No, not always. But usually it did. The hotel was the
same; they had slack times and busy ones.

Was the hotel ever full up?

Yes; it had been full to bursting when the Co-operative
came. The whole two hundred rooms. It was the only time
she remembered such a crowd in Nottingham.

'When was that?' asked Grant.

'At the beginning of February,' she said. 'They come twice
a year, though.'

At the beginning of February!

Where did the Co-operative people come from?

From all over the Midlands.

Not from London?

No, she thought not; but some of them might have.

Grant went to catch his train, revolving the new possibility and not finding it acceptable, though he was not
quite sure why. The dead man had not looked that type.
If he had been a shop-assistant, it had been in a business
requiring considerable chic on the part of its employees.

The journey back to town was not a slow and pleasant
revolving of sunlit thoughts. The sun had gone, and a grey
mist blotted out the lines of the country. It looked flat,
dreary, and unwholesome in the wan evening. Here and
there a sheet of water gleamed balefully from among the
poplars with the flat, unreflecting surface of pewter. Grant
devoted himself to the papers, and when he had exhausted

them, watched the grey, formless evening flying past, and let
his mind play with the problem of the dead man's occupation. There were three other men in the compartment, and
their voluble and occasionally vociferous pronouncements
on the subject of casings, whatever they might be, distracted
and annoyed him unreasonably. A tangle of signal lights,
hung isolated and unrelated in their ruby and emerald
across the fading daylight, restored his good humour a
little. They were a wonder and a revelation, these lights.
It was incredible that anything so faery had its invisible
support in stout standards and cross bars, and its being in
a dynamo. But he was glad when the long roar and rattle
over the points proclaimed the end of the journey, and the
more robust lights of London hung above him.

As he turned into the Yard he had a queer feeling that
the thing he had set out to find was waiting for him
here. His hunch had not played him false. That scrap of
information that would be the key to the whole of the dead
man's story was about to be put into his hand. His steps
quickened unconsciously. He could hardly wait. Never had
lifts seemed so slow or passages so long.

And after all there was nothing – nothing but the written
report which Williams, who had gone to tea, had left for him
when he should come in – a more detailed recapitulation of
what he had already heard over the telephone.

But at the exact moment that Inspector Grant had turned
into the Yard a queer thing had happened to Danny Miller.
He had been seated sideways in an easy chair in an
upper room of the house in Pimlico, his neat feet in
their exquisite shoes dangling idly from the upholstered
arm, and a cigarette in a six-inch holder projecting at
an aggressive angle from his thin mouth. Standing in the
middle of the floor was his 'jane'. She was engaged in trying
on a series of evening frocks, which she wrested from their
cardboard shells as one thumbs peas from a pod. Slowly
she turned her beautiful body so that the light caught the

beaded surface of the fragile stuff and accentuated the long
lines of her figure.

'That's a nice one, isn't it?' she said, her eyes seeking
Danny's in the mirror. But even as she looked she saw the
eyes, focused on the middle of her back, widen to a wild
stare. She swung round. 'What's the matter?' she asked.
But Danny apparently did not hear her; the focus of his
eyes did not alter. Suddenly he snatched the cigarette holder
from his mouth, pitched the cigarette into the fireplace, and
sprang to his feet with wild gropings about him.

'My hat!' he said. 'Where's my hat? Where the hell's
my hat!'

'It's on the chair behind you,' she said, amazed. 'What's
biting you?'

Danny snatched the hat and fled out of the room as if all
the fiends in the lower regions were on his heels. She heard
him pitch himself down the stairs, and then the front door
closed with a bang. She was still standing with startled eyes
on the door when she heard him coming back. Up the stairs
he came, three at a time, as lightly as a cat, and burst into
her presence.

'Gimme tuppence,' he said. 'I haven't got tuppence.'

Mechanically she reached out for the very expensive
and rather beautiful handbag that had been one of his
presents to her, and produced two pennies. 'I didn't know
you were that broke,' she said in an effort to goad him into
explanation. 'What do you want them for?'

'You go to blazes!' he snapped, and disappeared again.

He arrived at the nearest call-box slightly breathless
but exceedingly pleased with himself, and without conde-
scending to anything so mundane as a consultation with
the Telephone Directory, demanded to be connected with
Scotland Yard. During the subsequent delay he executed
a neat shufle on the floor of the call-box as a means of
expressing at once his impatience and his triumph. At last
– there was Grant's voice at the end of the wire.

'I say, Inspector, this is Miller speaking. I've just remembered where I saw that guy you were talking about. 'Member? . . . Well, I travelled in a race train to Leicester with him, end of January, I think it was . . . Sure? I remember as if it was yesterday. We talked racing, and he seemed to know quite a lot about it. But I never saw him before or since . . . eh? . . . No, I didn't see any bookmaking things . . . Don't mention it. I'm pleased to death to be able to help. I told you my brain didn't go back on me for long!'

Danny quitted the box and set out, a little more soberly this time, to smooth down an outraged and abandoned female in a beaded evening frock, and Grant hung up his receiver and expelled a long breath. A race train! The thing had all the fittingness of truth. What a fool he had been! What a double-dyed infernal fool! Not to have thought of that. Not to have remembered that though Nottingham to two-thirds of Britain may mean lace, to the other third it means racing. And of course racing explained the man – his clothes, his visit to Nottingham, his predilection for musical comedy, even – perhaps – the gang.

He sent out for a *Racing Up-to-Date*. Yes, there had been a jumping meeting at Colwick Park on the second of February. And one in Leicester at the end of January. That checked Danny's statement. Danny had provided the key.

Information like that, Grant thought bitterly, *would* come on a Saturday evening when bookmakers were as if they had not been, as far as their offices were concerned. And as for tomorrow – no bookmaker was at home on a Sunday. The very thought of a whole day without travelling scattered them over the length and breadth of England in their cars as quicksilver scatters when spilt. Both bank and bookmaking investigations would be hindered by the intervention of the week-end.

Grant left word of his whereabouts and repaired to Laurent's. On Monday there would be more hack work

– a round of the offices with the tie and revolver – the revolver that no one so far had claimed to have seen. But perhaps before then the bank-notes would have provided a clue that would speed things up and obviate the laborious method of elimination. Meantime he would have an early dinner and think things over.

CHAPTER 6

THE DAGO

The green-and-gold room was half empty as he made his way to a corner, and Marcel lingered to talk. Things marched with the inspector, it seemed? Ah, but Inspector Grant was a marvel. To have built a whole man out of a little dagger! (The Press, with the exception of the early-morning editions, had blazoned the wanted man's description all over Britain.) It was a thing *à faire peur*. If he, Marcel, was to bring him a fish fork with the entrée, it might be made to prove that he had a corn on the left little toe.

Grant disclaimed any such Holmesian qualities. 'The usual explanation advanced for such little mistakes is that the guilty one is in love.'

'*Ah, non alors!*' laughed Marcel. 'I defy even Inspector Grant to find me guilty of that.'

'Oh? Are you a misanthrope?' asked Grant.

No; Marcel loved his kind, but his wife was an exacting woman, Grant should know.

'I think I made the acquaintance of a pantry boy of yours the other day,' Grant said. 'Legarde, was it?'

Ah, Raoul. A good boy, very. And beautiful too, *hein?* Such a profile and such eyes! They had wanted him for the cinema, but Raoul would have none of it. He was going to be *maître d'hôtel*, Raoul. And if Marcel was any judge, he would be.

A new arrival took the table opposite, and Marcel, the geniality gone from his face like snowflakes on a wet pavement, went to listen to his needs with that mixture of tolerant superciliousness and godlike abstraction which he used to all but his five favourites. Grant made a leisurely meal, but even after lingering over coffee it was still early when he found himself in the street. The Strand was brilliant as day and crowded, the ebb of the late home-goers meeting the current of the early pleasure-seekers and causing a fret that filled both footpath and roadway. Slowly he walked up the gaudy pavement towards Charing Cross, in and out of the changing light from the shop windows: rose light, gold light, diamond light; shoe shop, clothes' shop, jewellers. Presently, in the wider pavement before the old 'bottleneck,' the crowd thinned out and men and women became individual beings instead of the corpuscles of a mob. A man who had been walking several yards in front of Grant turned round as if to see the number of an oncoming bus. His glance fell on Grant, and in the bright diamond light from the window his placid face became suddenly a mask of horror. Without a second's hesitation or a look to right or left he plunged headlong into the traffic in front of the charging bus. Grant was held up by the bus as it thundered past, but before the end of it had swung by he was off the pavement and into the maelstrom after the man. In that crowded moment, when his eyes were more for a figure in flight than for the dangers that threatened himself, he thought distinctly, 'Won't it be awful to die under a bus in the Strand after dodging the bosche for four years!' A yell in his ear, and he hovered in flight sufficiently to let a taxi scrape past him by inches with a blasphemous driver howling vituperation at him. He dodged a yellow sports car, saw a whirring black thing at his left elbow which he recognised as the front wheel of a bus, leaped back, was charged on his right by another taxi, and sprang behind the bus as it passed, and a yard in front of the following one to safety on the far pavement. A quick glance to right and left. There was his man walking composedly towards Bedford Street. He had evidently not expected such a quick decision on the

inspector's part. Grant metaphorically vowed a candle to
the saint that had taken him safely across the street, and
fell to the casual stroll that kept him at the right distance
from his quarry. 'Now, if he looks round before Bedford
Street,' he thought, 'I'll know I wasn't mistaken – that it
really was the sight of me and not a sudden thought that
scared him.' But he did not need another glance at the man
to verify his impression of high cheek-bones, thin dark face,
and jutting chin. And he knew as surely as if he saw it that
on the man's left forefinger or thumb was a recent scar.

A second later the man looked back – not with that
momentary, absent-minded glance that one gives, not
knowing why, but with that two-second turn of the head
which means a deliberate scrutiny. And a second after he
had vanished up Bedford Street. And then Grant sprinted.
Vividly he could see in his mind that thin figure flying up
the dark and deserted street with none to say him nay.
As he turned the corner and pulled up he could see no
sign of his quarry. Now, not even a Burleigh could have
been out of sight in the time if he had taken a straight
course, so Grant, expecting a bluff, walked briskly up the
right-hand side of the street, his eye wary at each recess.
As nothing materialised he grew anxious; a consciousness
of being fooled grew within him. He stopped and looked
back, and as he did so, down at the Strand end a figure
moved from a doorway on the other side of the street and
fled back to the crowded thoroughfare it had left. In thirty
seconds Grant had gained the Strand again, but the man
was gone. Buses came and went, taxis floated by, shops were
open all up and down the street. The choice of a means of
escape was not wanting.

Grant cursed, and even as he cursed he thought, 'Well,
he fooled me very neatly, but I expect he's cursing harder
than I am for being such a fool as to show that he knew
me. That was a very bad break.' And for the first time he
felt pleased with the Press who had made so free with his

features in their desire to educate the public. He patrolled the street for a while, casting exploratory but unoptimistic glances into the shops as he passed. Then he withdrew into the shadow of a doorway, where he remained for some time, hoping against hope that the man had gone to ground instead of making a break for it, and would reappear when he thought the coast was clear. The only result of that was that an inquisitive policeman who had watched him for some time from across the street wanted to know what he was waiting for. Grant came out into the light and explained the circumstances to the apologetic officer, and, deciding that his man had bolted, went to telephone to the Yard. His first impulse when the man had tricked him and run for it had been to throw a squad into the Strand, but the sight of the swift traffic and the knowledge that by the time anyone arrived from the Embankment, even in a fast car, the wanted man might be well on the way to Golders Green or Camberwell or Elstree, had deterred him. It was hardly an occasion for turning out the force.

As he went slowly up to Trafalgar Square after the business of telephoning, his spirits lightened. For the last hour he had been disgusted with himself to an extent that beggared his vocabulary. He had had the Dago within six yards of him, and he had let him slip through his fingers. Now the lighter side of the situation was becoming apparent. He had made a backward slip certainly, but even at the end of the slip he was further on – much further on – than when he had started. He knew for a certainty that the Dago was in London. That was a tremendous advance. Until his description had been furnished to the police the previous night there had been nothing to prevent the murderer from leaving London at any moment. They would have had to consider reports from all over Britain – and Grant had bitter experience of such reports of wanted men – and perhaps the Continent, if it had not been for that chance meeting in the Strand, and the man's lack of

self-control in a delirious moment. Now they knew he was
in London, and could concentrate their forces. He might
leave it by road, but he could not by any other method,
and Grant had seen to it that he would have difficulty in
hiring a car from any recognised garage. That merely made
things difficult for him – it did not prevent him from going
if he wanted to, but it made his exit considerably slower. It
was strange in the circumstances that he had stayed at all
when the way was clear. But Grant knew the Londoner's
mulish habit of clinging to the town he knows, and the
dago's ratlike preference for the sewers rather than the
open. Both would be more likely to hide than to run. And
of course the wanted man, though his description had not
been broadcast, had no guarantee that the police were not
in possession of it. It would have required more courage or
more foolhardihood than most men possess to face a ticket
collector or a boat official in these circumstances. So the
man had stuck to the town. From now on he would be at
the mercy of a continual patrol of the flying squad, and his
chances of slipping through their fingers again were very
small. Moreover, Grant had seen him. That was another
enormous advance. They could never meet again, even in
the distance, without Grant recognising him.

The Dago in London, the dead man's friend in London
presumably, the Dago recognisable, the friend about to be
traced by his bank-notes – things, as Marcel had remarked
were marching. At the bottom of St Martin's Lane Grant
remembered that this was the last night of *Didn't You Know?*
He would drop in there for a little and then go back to the
Yard. His thoughts worked much better without goading,
and the quiet of the room at the Yard was a silent goad that
maddened him. His thoughts would never work to order.
There was more likelihood of a revelation being vouchsafed
him in the middle of the teeming streets, in the seething
mob that somewhere held the Dago, than in the imposing
isolation of his room.

The play had been in progress for about twenty minutes
when Grant, after a chat with the manager, found six square
inches of standing-room at the back of the dress circle. It
was a magnificent sight, looked at from the darkness of so
remote a vantage. The theatre, never a very accommodating
one, was packed from floor to ceiling, its rosy dimness filled
with the electric quality that is only found when every man
of an audience is an enthusiast. And they were all enthusiasts, that last-night crowd, devotees saying farewell to
the object of their adoration. Adulation, camaraderie, and
regret filled the house and made the gathering completely
un-British in its abandon to the emotion of the moment.
Now and then, when Gollan left out an old gag, someone
would call a correction. 'Give us all of it, Golly!' they cried.
'Give us all of it!' And Golly gave them all he had. Ray
Marcable trailed her loveliness over a nearly empty stage
with that half-reluctant lightness of a leaf in the wind. She
was always, when she danced, a mere fraction of a beat
behind the music, so that it seemed as if, instead of being
an accompaniment, the music was the motive power, as if it
was the music that lifted and spun and whirled her, floated
her sideways, and relinquished her gently as it died. Again
and again at their vociferous demands the music lifted her
into motion, held her laughing and sparkling and quivering,
like a crystal ball held poised on a jet of water, and dropped
her in a quick descending run to a fast-breathing stillness
broken by the crash of the applause. They would not let her
go, and when at last someone held her forcibly in the wings,
and an effort was made to get on with the story, there was
unconcealed impatience. No one wanted a plot tonight. No
one had ever wanted one. Quite a large number of the most
enthusiastic habitués were unaware that there was such a
thing, and few, if any, would have been able to give a lucid
account of it. And tonight to insist on wasting time with
such irrelevance was folly.

The entrance of the most perfect chorus in Britain

soothed them slightly. The fourteen Woffington girls were famous in two continents, and their studies in synchronised motion gave one the same feeling of complete satisfaction – the satisfaction that never becomes satiety – that one has on beholding the Guards in motion. Not a head turned too much, not a toe was out of alignment. No kick was higher than its neighbour, no flop was quicker than another. When the last of the fourteen flicked her black-and-orange columbine skirt in a little defiant motion as she disappeared behind the flats the audience had almost forgotten Ray. Almost, but not quite. Ray and Gollan possessed the house – it was their night, theirs and the public's. And presently the impatience with anything that was not Ray or Gollan became too marked to be ignored. The evening was one long crescendo of excitement that was rapidly reaching hysteria-point. Grant watched half pityingly the wry smile with which the leading man acknowledged the conventional plaudits accorded to his sentimental solo. That solo was sung by languishing tenors all over Britain, whistled by every errand boy, played, with lowered lights, by every dance orchestra. He had obviously expected it to be encored at least three times, but beyond humming the last chorus with him they had shown no marked appreciation of it. Something had gone wrong. They couldn't even see him. With as good a grace as he could muster he took his place as background to Ray Marcable, danced with her, sang with her, acted with her – and Grant suddenly caught himself wondering if his eclipse were merely the accident of Ray Marcable's vivid personality, or if she had used that personality deliberately to keep the limelight where she happened to be. Grant had no illusions about the theatre or about the professional generosity of leading ladies. Theatrical stars were easily moved to tears and a lavish expenditure over a hard-luck story, but their good nature withered at the fount when confronted with a successful rival. Ray Marcable had a reputation for all-round generosity and sweet reasonableness. But then, her press agent was wily beyond the average of that wily race. Grant himself had read 'pars' about her which he had not recognised as an agent's work until his eye had gone on to the next item of interest. He had that supreme quality, her press agent, of making the advertised one's presence in the story entirely and convincingly incidental to the main theme.

And then there was the suspicious fact that she had had three leading men in the two years, whereas the rest of the cast had stayed the same. Could her friendly air, her modesty, her – there was no other word for it – her ladylikeness be camouflage? Was London's fragile darling hard as nails underneath? He visualised her as he had met her 'off', unassuming, intelligent, eminently reasonable. No parade of temperament or idiosyncracy. A charming girl with her head screwed on the right way. It was hardly credible. He had known among crooks many women of the fluffy type who had no softer feelings whatever in their make-up. But Ray Marcable's was a sweetness that had no fluff about it, a sweetness that he could have sworn was genuine. He watched her closely now, trying to disprove for his own satisfaction – he had liked her enormously – that suggestion which his mind had thrown up involuntarily. But to his dismay he found his suspicions, now that they were acknowledged and made the subject of investigation, being slowly confirmed. She *was* keeping the man out of it. When he looked for indications they were all there, but they were done with a subtlety such as Grant had never witnessed before. There was nothing so crude as trying to share or divert his applause, or even cutting his applause short by an intrusion of her own. All these would have been recognisable for what they were, and therefore, from her point of view, not permissible. It occurred to him that she was not only too subtle to use such a method but too potent to need to. She had only to use her glowing personality with unscrupulousness, and rivals faded out as stars before the sun. Only with Gollan she was powerless – he was a sun as potent if not more so than herself – and so she suffered him. But with her leading man – good-looking, amiable, and a very fine singer – she had no difficulty. They had said, he remembered now, that it was impossible to find a leading man good enough for her. That was why. He did not doubt it now.

There was something uncanny about the clearness with which he suddenly read her mind, untouched by the glamour that surrounded him. Only he and she in all that intoxicated crowd were aloof, were poised above emotion and looking on. He watched her play with that unhappy wretch as coldly and deliberately as he would have played a trout in the Test. Smiling and sweet, she took what would have been a triumph from his hands, and tacked it on to her own dazzling outfit. And no one noticed that the triumph had gone astray. If they thought at all, they thought that the leading man was not up to the mark tonight – but, of course, it was difficult to get one good enough for her. And after having absorbed his worth she would, at the end of a turn, with a Machiavellian acuteness drag him forward by the hand to share the applause, so that everyone in the building thought, 'Well, *he* didn't deserve much of it!' and his inferiority was accentuated and remembered. Oh yes, it was subtle. This play within a play became for Grant the absorbing entertainment of the evening. He was seeing the real Ray Marcable, and the sight was incredibly strange.

So rapt was he that the final curtain found him still at the back of the circle, deafened by the cheers and feeling strangely cold. Again and again, and yet again, the curtain rose on the glittering stage, and the stream of presents and flowers began to flow over the footlights. Then the speeches came; first Gollan, clutching a large square bottle of whisky and trying to be funny, but not succeeding because his voice would not stay steady. Grant guessed that in his mind was

a picture of the heart-breaking years of squalid rooms in
squalid towns, twice-nightly performances, and the awful
ever-present fear of 'the bird.' Gollan had sung long for his
supper; it was no wonder that the feast choked him. Then
the producer. Then Ray Marcable.

'Ladies and gentlemen,' she said in her clear, slow voice,
'two years ago, when none of you knew me, you were
kind to me. You overwhelmed me then. Tonight you have
overwhelmed me again. I can only say thank you.'

'Very neat,' thought Grant, as they cheered her to the
echo. 'Quite in the part.' And he turned away. He knew
what was coming – speeches by everyone down to the
callboy, and he had heard enough. He went down through
the crimson and buff vestibule and out into the night with a
queer constriction in his chest. If he had not in his thirty-five
years cast overboard all such impedimenta as illusion, one
would have said that he was disillusioned. He had quite
liked Ray Marcable.

CHAPTER 7

THINGS MOVE

'It's not a Christian life at all,' said Mrs Field as she put the inevitable bacon and eggs in front of him. Mrs Field had tried to cure Grant of the bacon-and-eggs habit by providing wonderful breakfasts with recipes culled from her daily paper, and kidneys and other 'favours' wrested from Mr Tomkins at the threat of withdrawing her custom, but Grant had defeated her – as he defeated most people in time. He still had bacon and eggs, Saturday, Sunday, Monday. It was now eight o'clock on Sunday morning, which was the fact that had called forth Mrs Field's remark. 'Unchristian' in Mrs Field's vocabulary meant not any lack of conformity but an absence of comfort and respectability. The fact that he was having breakfast before eight on a Sunday morning shocked her infinitely more than the fact that his day was to be spent in the most mundane of work. She grieved over him.

'It's a wonder to me that the King doesn't give you inspectors decorations oftener than he does. What other man in London is having breakfast at this hour when he needn't!'

'In that case I think inspectors' landladies should be included in the decoration. Mrs Field, O.B.E. – for being an inspector's landlady.'

'Oh, the honour's enough for me without the decoration,' she said.

'I'd like to think of a good rejoinder to that, but I never could say graceful things at breakfast. It takes a woman to be witty at eight in the morning.'

'You'd be surprised really at the standing it gives me, you being an inspector at Scotland Yard.'

'Does it really?'

'It does, but don't you be afraid. I keep my mouth shut. Nothing ever comes out through me. There's lots would like to know what the inspector thought, or who came to see the inspector, but I just sit and let them hint. You don't have to see a hint unless you like.'

'It is very noble of you, Mrs Field, to achieve a reputation for obtuseness for my sake.'

Mrs Field blinked and recovered herself. 'It's my duty, if it wasn't my pleasure,' she said, and made a graceful exit.

As he was going away after breakfast she surveyed the untouched toast sorrowfully. 'Well, see that you have a good meal in the middle of the day. You can't think to any advantage on an empty stomach.'

'But you can't run to any advantage on a full one!'

'You'll never have to run very far after anyone in London. There's always someone to head them off.'

Grant was smiling to himself as he went down the sunny road to the bus-stop at this simplification of the work of the C.I.D. But there was no heading-off the people who claimed to have seen the wanted man. Nearly half London appeared to have set eyes on him – his back as often as not. And the number of cut hands that required investigation would have been incredible to anyone who has not witnessed a man-hunt from the inside. Patiently Grant sifted the reports through the long, bright morning, sitting at his desk and sending his lieutenants out here and there as a general arranges his forces on a battlefield. The provincial clues he ignored, with the exception of two, which were too good to be passed over – there was always the odd chance that the man in the Strand had *not* been the Dago. Two men were sent to investigate these – one to Cornwall and one to York. All day long the telephone at his elbow buzzed, and all day long messages of failure came over it.

Some of the men they had been sent out to observe had not, in the detective's opinion, the remotest resemblance to the wanted man. This valuable information was obtained often enough at the cost of a long afternoon's vigil behind the Nottingham lace curtains of a suburban villa waiting for 'the man three houses down' to pass within examining distance. One suspect proved to be a nobleman well known to the public as a polo player. The officer who tracked him down saw that he had aroused the earl's curiosity – the noble lord had been run to earth in a garage where he was collecting his car preparatory to having a little flip of three or four hundred miles as a slight Sunday diversion – and confessed what his business was.

'I *thought* you were tailing me,' said the peer of the realm, 'and as my conscience is particularly good at the moment I wondered what you were up to. I have been accused of taking many things in my short time, but never of looking like a murderer before. Good luck to you, by all means.'

'Thank you, sir, same to you. I hope your conscience will be as clear when you come back.' And the earl, who had more convictions for exceeding the speed limit than anyone else in England, had grinned appreciatively.

Truly it was the men who went out who found work light that Sunday, and it was Grant, sitting pulling strings with mechanical competence, who found it tedious. Barker came in in the afternoon, but had no suggestion to make which might expedite matters. They could afford to ignore nothing; the least helpful of the clues had to be investigated in the relentless process of elimination. It was spade-work, and most un-Christian, in the Field sense. Grant looked enviously from his window, through the bright mist that hung over the river, at the Surrey side, lit now by the westering sun. How good it would be to be in Hampshire today! He could see the woods on Danebury in their first green. And a little later in the evening, when the sun went, the Test would be just right for fly.

It was late when Grant got home, but he had not left an avenue of exploration untrodden. With the coming of evening the spate of reported appearances had gradually diminished and died away. But as he ate his supper – to Mrs Field a meal was a necessary concomitant to a home-coming – he was wearily conscious of the telephone by the fireplace. He went to bed and dreamed that Ray Marcable called him by telephone and said, 'You'll never find him, never, never!' She kept repeating the phrase, unheeding of his pleas for information and help, and he wished that the exchange girl would say 'Time up' and release him. But before that relief had come the telephone had turned into a fishing-rod without exciting any surprise on his part, and he was using it, not as a fishing-rod but as a whip to encourage the four-in-hand which he was driving down a street in Nottingham. At the end of the street was a marsh, and in front of the marsh, and exactly in the middle of the street, stood the waitress from the hotel. He tried to call out to her as the horses advanced, but his voice died in his throat. Instead, the waitress grew bigger and bigger, until she filled the whole street. As the horses were about to charge into her she had grown so that she towered over Grant and overwhelmed him, the horses, the street, and everything. He had that sense of inevitability which attends the moment of a catastrophe. 'It's come,' he thought, and woke to thankful consciousness of a safe pillow and a reasonable world where there was motive before action. 'Damn that cheese soufflé!' he thought, and, turning on his back, surveyed the dark ceiling and let his now wide-awake brain go its own way.

Why had the man hidden his identity? Was it perhaps mere accident? Nothing but the tailor's name had been obliterated from his clothes, and the makers' name had been left on the tie – surely a most obvious place if one had been deliberately eliminating identification marks. But if it were a mere accident that eliminated the tailor's name, how account for the scantiness of the man's belongings? Small change, a handkerchief, and a revolver. Not even a watch. It spoke loudly of intended suicide. Perhaps the man was broke. He didn't look it, but that was no criterion. Grant had known many paupers who looked like millionaires, and beggars with large bank balances. Had the man, at the end of his resources, decided to end it rather than sink slowly into the gutter? Had the visit to the theatre with his last few shillings been merely a snapping of fingers in the face of the gods who had defeated him? Was it merely the final irony that the dagger had anticipated his own revolver by an hour or two? But if he were broke, why had he not gone to the friend for money – the friend who was so free with his bank-notes? Or had he? and the friend had refused it? Was it conscience, after all, that had prompted that anonymous twenty-five pounds? If he decided to accept the presence of the revolver and the absence of clues as evidence of intended suicide, then the murder resolved itself into the outcome of a quarrel – probably between two members of a race gang. Perhaps the Dago had shared in the dead man's downfall and had held the dead man responsible. That was the most reasonable explanation. And it fitted all the circumstances. The man was interested in racing – probably a bookmaker – he was found without watch or money and evidently prepared for suicide; the Dago was heard to demand something which the dead man either could not or would not give, and the Dago had stabbed him. The friend who had refused him help in life – probably tired of pulling him out of tight places – had been seized with such a fit of remorse on learning of the man's end that he had provided lavishly, if anonymously, for his burial. Pure theory, but it fitted – almost! There was one corner where no amount of insinuation would make it fit. It did not explain why no one had come forward to claim the dead man. If the affair was merely a quarrel between two men, intimidation was washed out as a theory for the silence of

his friends. It was not credible that the Dago had them all
in such a state of subjection that not one of them risked even
that usual method of the craven and the circumspect, the
anonymous communication. It was a curious and almost
unique situation. Never in all Grant's experience had a
murderer been on the point of being captured before the
identity of his victim had been established.

A light rain fell across the window-pane with stealthy
fingers. The end of the good weather, thought Grant. A
silence followed, dark and absolute. It was as if an advance
guard, a scout, had spied out the land and gone away to
report. There was the long, far-away sigh of the wind that
had been asleep for days. Then the first blast of the fighting
battalions of the rain struck the window in a wild rattle.
The wind tore and raved behind them, hounding them
to suicidal deeds of valour. And presently the drip, drip
from the roof began a constant gentle monotone beneath
the wild symphony, intimate and soothing as the tick of a
clock. Grant's eyes closed to it, and before the squall had
retreated, muttering into the distance, he was asleep.

But in the morning, a grey morning veiled in dispirited
drizzle, the theory still looked watertight – with judicious
plugging at the weak spot, and it was not until, hard on
the track of the dead man's friend, he was interviewing the
manager of the Adelphi branch of the Westminster Bank
that he found his nicely-made house of cards pattering
round his ears.

The manager was a quiet, grey man whose unluminous
skin had somehow taken on the appearance of a banknote.
His manner, however, was more like that of a general
practitioner than a financial adviser. Grant found himself
momentarily expecting to feel Mr Dawson's dry finger-tips
on his wrist. But Mr Dawson this morning was a mixture
of Mercury and Juggernaut. This was his report.

The five notes in which the inspector was interested had
all of them been paid over the counter on the third of

the month as part of a payment of two hundred and
twenty-three pounds ten shillings. The money had been
drawn by a client of theirs who had a running account
in the bank. His name was Albert Sorrell, and he ran
a small bookmaker's business in Minley Street. The sum
drawn represented the whole of the money deposited with
them except a pound, which had been left presumably with
the intention of keeping the account open.

'Good!' thought Grant; 'the friend is a bookmaker too.'

Had Mr Dawson known Mr Sorrell by sight? he asked.

No, not very well, but his cashier would be able to tell the
inspector all about him; and he summoned the cashier.

'This is Inspector Grant from Scotland Yard. He wants
a description of Mr Albert Sorrell, and I have told him that
you will provide him with one.'

The cashier provided a very telling one. With a minuteness that defeated any hope of a mistake, he described
the dead man.

When he had finished, Grant sat thinking at top speed.
What did it mean? Had the dead man owed the money to
the friend, and had the friend taken all he possessed and
afterwards been seized with a too tardy charity? Was that
how the notes had come into the friend's possession? On
the third, too. That was ten days before the murder.

Did Sorrell draw the money himself? he asked.

No, the cashier said; the cheque had been presented by a
stranger. Yes, he remembered him. He was very dark, thin,
medium height or a little under, with high cheek-bones.
Foreign looking, a little.

The Dago!

Grant was seized with a mixture of exhilaration and
breathlessness – rather as Alice must have felt during her
express journey with the Red Queen. Things marched, but
at what a bat!

He asked to see the cheque, and it was produced. 'You
don't think that this is a forgery?' Such a thought had not

occurred to them. Both the amount and the signature had been made out in Mr Sorrell's handwriting, and that was unusual in an attempt at forgery. They brought out other cheques of the dead man's and exhibited them. They refused to entertain the thought that the cheque was not genuine. 'If it is a forgery,' Mr Dawson said, 'it is incredibly good. Even if it were *proved* a forgery, I should have difficulty in believing it. I think you may take it that it is a genuine cheque.'

And the Dago had drawn it. The Dago had had all Sorrell's deposit with the exception of twenty shillings. And ten days later he had stuck Sorrell in the back. Well, if it proved nothing else, it proved the existence of a relationship between the two men which would be useful when it came to evidence in a court of law.

'Have you the numbers of the rest of the notes handed over in the money to Sorrell?' They had, and Grant took a list of them. Then he inquired what Sorrell's address was, and was told that they had no home address, but that his office was at 32 Minley Street, off the Charing Cross Road.

As Grant walked up to Minley Street from the Strand he began to digest the news. The Dago had drawn the money with a cheque made payable to Sorrell and endorsed by Sorrell. Theft seemed to be ruled out by the fact that Sorrell had made no fuss in the ten days intervening between the paying out of the money and his death. Therefore the cheque had been given to the Dago by Sorrell himself. Why had it not been made payable to the Dago? Because it had been a transaction in which the Dago had no intention of letting his name appear. Had he been 'bleeding' Sorrell? Had his 'asking for something,' which Raoul Legarde had reported as being the tenor of their conversation on the night of the murder, been but a further demand for money? Had the Dago been not an unlucky companion in Sorrell's ruin but the means of it? At least that transaction over the counter of the

Westminster Bank explained Sorrell's pennilessness and
intended suicide.

Then who had sent the twenty-five pounds? Grant refused
to believe that the man who had had all Sorrell had, and
who had stuck him in the back at not getting more, would
have disbursed such a sum for so slight a reason. There
was someone else. And the someone else knew the Dago
well enough to be in receipt of at least twenty-five pounds
of the amount that the Dago had received from Sorrell.
Moreover, the someone else and the dead man had lived
together, as witnessed by the dead man's finger-print on
the envelope which had contained the twenty-five pounds.
The sentimentality of the action and the lavishness of the
amount spoke of a woman, but the handwriting people had
been very sure that the printing was a man's work. And
of course that someone else had also owned the gun with
which Sorrell had contemplated putting an end to himself.
It was a pretty tangle, but at least it *was* a tangle – closely
related and growing closer, so that at any moment he might
pick up a lucky thread which, when pulled, would unravel
the whole thing. It seemed to him that he had only to find
out about the dead man's habits and life generally and he
would have the Dago.

Minley Street has, in common with the lesser turnings
off Charing Cross Road, that half-secretive, half-disgruntled
air that makes it forbidding. A stranger turning into it has
an uncomfortable feeling of being unwelcome, as if he had
blundered unwittingly into private property; he feels as a
newcomer feels in a small café under the half-surprised,
half-resentful scrutiny of the habitués. But Grant, if he was
not an habitué of Minley Street, was at least no stranger
to it. He knew it as most of the Yard know the purlieus of
Charing Cross Road and Leicester Square. If the outwardly
respectable but sly faces of the houses said anything to him,
it was 'Oh, here again, are you?' At thirty-two a painted
wooden notice announced that on the first floor were the

offices of Albert Sorrell, Turf Accountant, and Grant turned in at the doorway and climbed the dim stairs smelling of the charwoman's Monday-morning ministrations. The stairs came to a pause at a wide landing, and Grant knocked at the door which had Sorrell's name on it. As he expected, there was no answer. He tried the door, and found it locked. He was about to turn away, when there was a stealthy sound from inside. Grant knocked again loudly. In the subsequent pause he could hear the loud hum of the distant traffic and the footsteps of the people below on the street, but no sound came from inside the room. Grant bent to the keyhole. There was no key in it, but the view he obtained was not extensive – the corner of a desk and the top of a coal-scuttle. The room he was looking into was the back one of the two which had evidently constituted Sorrell's offices. Grant stayed where he was for a little, motionless and expectant, but nothing living crossed the small still-life picture that the keyhole framed. He rose to go away, but, before he had taken the first step, again there was that stealthy sound. As Grant cocked his head the better to listen, he became aware that over the banister of the floor above hung an inverted human head, grotesque and horrible, its hair spread round it by the force of gravity into a Struwwelpeter effect.

Finding itself observed, the head said mildly, 'Are you looking for someone?'

'The evidence points that way, doesn't it?' said Grant nastily. 'I'm looking for the man who has these offices.'

'Oh?' said the head, as if this were an entirely new idea. It disappeared, and a moment later appeared right way up in its proper place as part of a young man in a dirty painter's smock, who came down the last flight to the landing, smelling of turpentine and smoothing down his mop of hair with paint-covered fingers.

'I don't think that man's been here for quite a while now,' he said. 'I have the two floors above – my rooms and my studio – and I used to pass him on the stairs and hear his

– his – I don't know what you call them. He was a bookie, you know.'

'Clients?' suggested Grant.

'Yes. Hear what I presume were his clients coming sometimes. But I'm sure it's more than a fortnight since I saw or heard him.'

'Did he go to the course, do you know?' Grant asked.

'Where's that?' asked the artist.

'I mean, did he go to the races every day?'

The artist did not know.

'Well, I want to get into his offices. Where can I get a key?'

The artist presumed that Sorrell had the key. The agent for the property had an office off Bedford Square. He could never remember the name of the street or the number, but he could find his way there. He had lost the key of his own room or he would have offered it for a trial on Sorrell's door.

'And what do you do when you go out?' asked Grant, curiosity for a moment overcoming his desire to get behind the locked door.

'I just leave it unlocked,' said this happy wight. 'If anyone finds anything in my rooms worth stealing, they're cleverer than I am.'

And then suddenly, apparently within a yard of them and just inside the locked door, that stealthy sound that was hardly sound – merely a heard movement.

The artist's eyebrows disappeared in the Struwwelpeter hair. He jerked his head at the door and looked interrogatively at the inspector. Without a word Grant took him by the arm and drew him down the stairs to the first turn. 'Look here,' he said, 'I'm a plain-clothes man – you know what that is?' for the artist's innocence as to courses had shaken any faith he might have had in his worldly knowledge. The artist said, 'Yes, a bobby,' and Grant let him away with it. 'I want to get into that room. Is there a yard at the back where I can see the window of the room?'

There was, and the artist led him to the ground floor and through a dark passage to the back of the house, where they came out into a little bricked yard that might have been part of a village inn. A low outhouse with a lead roof was built against the wall, and directly above it was the window of Sorrell's office. It was open a little at the top and had an inhabited air.

'Give me a leg up,' said Grant, and was hoisted on to the roof of the outhouse. As he drew his foot from the painty clasp of his assistant, he said, 'I might tell you that you are conniving at a felony. This is housebreaking and entirely illegal.'

'It is the happiest moment of my life,' the artist said. 'I have always wanted to break the law, but a way has never been vouchsafed me. And now to do it in the company of a policeman is joy that I did not anticipate my life would ever provide.'

But Grant was not listening to him. His eyes were on the window. Slowly he drew himself up until his head was just below the level of the window-sill. Cautiously he peered over. Nothing moved in the room. A movement behind him startled him. He looked round to see the artist joining him on the roof. 'Have you a weapon?' he whispered, 'or shall I get you a poker or something?' Grant shook his head, and with a sudden determined movement flung up the lower half of the window and stepped into the room. Not a sound followed but his own quick breathing. The wan, grey light lay on the thick dust of a deserted office. But the door facing him, which led into the front room, was ajar. With an abrupt three steps he had reached it and thrown it open. And as he did so, out of the second room with a wail of terror sprang a large black cat. It cleared the rear room at a bound and was through the open window before the inspector recognised it for what it was. There was an agonised yell from the artist, a clatter and a crash. Grant went to the window, to hear queer choked moans coming from the yard below.

He slid hastily to the edge of the outhouse and beheld his companion in crime sitting on the grimy bricks, holding his evidently painful head, while his body was convulsed in the throes of a still more painful laughter. Reassured, Grant went back to the room for a glance at the drawers of Sorrell's desk. They were all empty – methodically and carefully cleared. The front room had been used as another office, not a living-room. Sorrell must have lived elsewhere. Grant closed the window and, sliding down the lead roof, dropped into the yard. The artist was still sobbing, but had got to the length of wiping his eyes.

'Are you hurt?' Grant asked.

'Only my ribs,' said Struwwelpeter. 'The abnormal excitation of the intercostal muscles has nearly broken them.' He struggled to his feet.

'Well, that's twenty minutes wasted,' said Grant, 'but I had to satisfy myself.' He followed the hobbling artist through the dark passage again.

'No time is wasted that earns such a wealth of gratitude as I feel for you,' said Struwwelpeter. 'I was in the depths when you arrived. I can never paint on Monday mornings. There should be no such thing. Monday mornings should be burnt out of the calendar with prussic acid. And you have made a Monday morning actually memorable! It is a great achievement. Sometime when you are not too busy breaking the law come back and I'll paint your portrait. You have a charming head.'

A thought occurred to Grant. 'I suppose you couldn't draw Sorrell from memory?'

Struwwelpeter considered. 'I think I could,' he said. 'Come up a minute.' He led Grant into the welter of canvases, paints, lengths of stuff, and properties of all kinds which he called his studio. Except for the dust it looked as though a flood had passed and left the contents of the room in the haphazard relationships and curious angles that only receding water can achieve. After some flinging about of things that might be expected to be concealing something, the artist produced a bottle of Indian ink, and after another search a fine brush. He made six or seven strokes with the brush on a blank sheet of a sketching block, considered it critically, and having torn it from the block handed it over to Grant.

'It isn't quite correct, but it's good enough for an impression,' he said.

Grant was astonished at the cleverness of it. The ink was not yet dry on the paper, but the artist had brought the dead man to life. The sketch had that slight exaggeration of characteristics that is half-way to caricature, but it lived as no photographic representation could have done. The artist had even conveyed the look of half-anxious eagerness in the eyes which Sorrell's had presumably worn in life. Grant thanked him heartfeltly and gave him his card.

'If there is ever anything I can do for you, come and see me,' he said, and went away without waiting to see the altering expression on Struwwelpeter's face as he took in the significance of the card.

Near Cambridge Circus are the palatial offices of Laurence Murray – Lucky-Folk-Bet-With-Laury Murray – one of the biggest bookmakers in London. As Grant was going past on the other side of the street, he saw the genial Murray arrive in his car and enter the offices. He had known Laury Murray fairly well for some years, and he crossed the street now and followed him into the shining headquarters of his greatness. He sent in his name and was led through a vast wilderness of gleaming wood, brass, and glass partitions and abounding telephones to the sanctum of the great man, hung round with pictures of great thoroughbreds.

'Well,' said Murray, beaming on him, 'something for the National, is it? I hope to goodness it isn't Coffee Grounds. Half Britain seems to want to back Coffee Grounds today.'

But the inspector denied any intention of losing money

even on such an attractive proposition as Coffee Grounds seemed to be.

'Well, I don't suppose you've come to warn me about ready-money betting?'

The inspector grinned. No; he wanted to know if Murray had ever known a man called Albert Sorrell.

'Never heard of him,' said Murray. 'Who is he?'

He was a bookmaker, Grant thought.

'Course?'

Grant did not know. He had an office in Minley Street.

'Silver ring, probably,' said Murray. 'Tell you what. If I were you, I should go down to Lingfield today, and you can see all the silver-ring men in one fell swoop. It'll save you a lot of touting around.'

Grant considered. It was by far the quickest and most logical method, and it had the additional advantage of offering him a knowledge of Sorrell's business associates which the mere obtaining of his home address would not have done.

'Tell you what,' Murray said again as he hesitated, 'I'll go down with you. You've missed the last train now. We'll go down in my car. I have a horse running, but I couldn't be bothered to go down alone. I promised my trainer I'd go, but it was such a beast of a morning. Have you had lunch?'

Grant had not, and Murray went away to see about a lunch basket while Grant talked to the Yard on his telephone.

An hour later Grant was having lunch in the country; a grey and sodden country truly, but a country smelling of clean, fresh, growing things; and the drizzle that had made town a greasy horror was left behind. Grey, wet-looking torn clouds showed blue sky in great rifts, and by the time they had reached the paddock the pale unhappy pools in the rock-garden were smiling uncertainly at an uncertain sun. It was ten minutes before the first race, and both rings from

Grant's point of view were impossible. He pushed down his impatience and accompanied Murray to the white rails of the parade ring, where the horses for the first race were walking sedately round, the looker-on in him loving their beauty and their fitness – Grant was a fairly competent judge of a horse – while his eyes wandered over the crowd in a business-like commentary. There was Mollenstein – Stone, he called himself now – looking as if he owned the earth. Grant wondered what bogus scheme he was foisting on a public of suckers now. He shouldn't have thought that anything as uncomfortable as a jumping meeting in March would have appealed to him. Perhaps one of his suckers was interested in the game. And Vanda Morden, back from her third honeymoon and advertising the fact in a coat of a check so aggressive that it was the most obvious thing in the paddock. Wherever one looked, it seemed, there was Vanda Morden's coat. And the polo-playing earl who had been shadowed in the hope that he was the Dago. And many others, both pleasant and unpleasant, all of whom Grant recognised and noted with a little mental remark.

When the first race was over, and the little eddy of lucky ones had surrounded the bookmakers and been sent gloating away, Grant began his work. He pursued his enquiries steadily until the ring began to fill again with eager inquirers after odds for the second race, when he returned to the paddock. But no one seemed to have heard of Sorrell, and it was a rather disconsolate Grant who joined Murray in the paddock before the fourth race – a handicap hurdle – in which Murray's horse was running. Murray was sympathetic, and as Grant stood with him in the middle of the parade ring he mixed adjurations to admire his horse with suggestions for the tracking of Sorrell. Grant whole-heartedly admired the magnificent bay that was Murray's property and listened with only half an ear to his suggestions. His thoughts were worried. Why did no one in the silver ring know Sorrell?

The jockeys began to filter into the ring, the crowd round

the rail thinned slightly as people moved away to points of vantage on the stands, lads kept ducking eager heads under their charges' necks in anxiety to intercept the summons that would mean mounting time.

'Here comes Lacey,' said Murray, as a jockey came stepping cat-like over the wet grass to them. 'Know him?'

'No,' said Grant.

'Flat-race crack really, but has a go over hurdles occasionally. Crack at that too.'

Grant had known that – there is very little between a Scotland Yard inspector and omniscience – but he had never actually met the famous Lacey. The jockey greeted Murray with a tight little smile, and Murray introduced the inspector without explaining him. Lacey shivered slightly in the damp air.

'I'm glad it's not fences,' he said, with mock fervour. 'I'd just hate to be emptied into the water today.'

'Bit of a change from heated rooms and all the coddling,' said Murray.

'Been in Switzerland?' asked Grant conversationally, remembering that Switzerland was the winter Mecca of flat-race jockeys.

'Switzerland!' repeated Lacey in his drawling Irish voice; 'not me. I've had measles. Measles – if you'd believe it! Nothing but milk for nine days and a whole month in bed.' His pleasant, cameo-like face twisted into an expression of wry disgust.

'And milk is so fattening,' laughed Murray. 'Talking of fat, did you ever know a man called Sorrell?'

The jockey's pale bright eyes trickled over the inspector like twin drops of icy water and came back to Murray. The whip, which had been swinging pendulum-wise from his first finger, swung slowly to a halt.

'I think I can remember a Sorrell,' he said, after some cogitation, 'but he wasn't fat. Wasn't Charlie Baddeley's clerk called Sorrell?'

But Murray could not recall Charlie Baddeley's clerk.

'Would you recognise a sketch?' asked the inspector, and took Struwwelpeter's impressionistic portrait from his pocket-book.

Lacey took it and looked at it admiringly. 'It's good, isn't it! Yes; that's old Baddeley's clerk, all right.'

'And where can I find Baddeley?' asked Grant.

'Well, that's rather a difficult question,' said Lacey, the tight smile back at his mouth. 'You see, Baddeley died over two years ago.'

'Oh! And you haven't seen Sorrell since?'

'No, I don't know what became of Sorrell. Probably doing office work somewhere.'

The bay was led up to them. Lacey took off his coat, removed a pair of goloshes, which he laid neatly side by side on the grass, and was thrown into the saddle. As he adjusted the leathers he said to Murray, 'Alvinson isn't here today' – Alvinson was Murray's trainer – 'he said you would give me some instructions.'

'The instructions are the usual ones,' said Murray. 'Do as you like on him. He should about win.'

'Very good,' said Lacey matter-of-factly, and was led away to the gate, horse and man as beautiful a picture as this weary civilisation can provide.

As Grant and Murray walked to the stands, Murray said, 'Cheer up, Grant. Baddeley may be dead, but I know who knew him. I'll take you down to talk to him as soon as this is over.' So it was with a real enjoyment that Grant watched the race; saw the colour that flickered and streamed against the grey curtain of the woods on the back stretch, while a silence settled eerily on the crowd – a silence so complete that he might have been there alone with the dripping trees, and the grey wooded countryside, and the wet grass; saw the long struggle in the straight and the fighting finish, with Murray's bay second by a length. When Murray had seen his horse again and congratulated Lacey, he led Grant into

Tattersalls and introduced him to an elderly man, with the rubicund face of the man who drives mail coaches through the snow on Christmas cards. 'Tracker,' he said, 'you knew Baddeley. What became of his clerk, do you know?'

'Sorrell?' said the Christmas-card man. 'He set up for himself. Has an office in Minley Street.'

'Does he come to the course?'

'No, don't think so. Just has an office. Seemed to be doing quite well last time I saw him.'

'How long ago was that?'

'Oh, long time.'

'Do you know his home address?' asked Grant.

'No. Who wants him? He's a good boy, Sorrell.'

The last irrelevance seemed to suggest suspicion, and Grant hastened to assure him that no harm was intended Sorrell. At that Thacker put his first and second fingers into either corner of his mouth and emitted a shrill whistle in the direction of the railings at the edge of the course. From the crowd of attentive faces which this demonstration had turned towards him he selected the one he wanted. 'Joe,' he said in stentorian tones. 'let me speak to Jimmy a minute, will you?' Joe detached his clerk, as one detaches a watch and chain, and presently Jimmy appeared – a clean, cherubic youth with an amazing taste in linen.

'You used to be pally with Bert Sorrell, didn't you?' asked Thacker.

'Yes, but I haven't seen him for donkey's years.'

'Do you know where he lives?'

'Well, when I knew him he had rooms in Brightling Crescent, off the Fulham Road. I've been there with him. Forget the number, but his landlady's name was Everett. He lived there for years. Orphan he was, Bert.'

Grant described the Dago, and asked if Sorrell was ever friendly with a man like that.

No, Jimmy had never known him in such company, but then, as he pointed out, he hadn't seen him for donkey's years. He had dropped out of the regular crowd when he started on his own, though he sometimes went racing for his own amusement – or perhaps to pick up information.

Through Jimmy, Grant interviewed two more people who had known Sorrell, but neither could throw any light on Sorrell's companions. They were self-absorbed people, these bookmakers, looking at him with a vague curiosity and obviously forgetting all about him the minute their next bet was booked. Grant announced to Murray that he had finished, and Murray, whose interest had waned with the finish of the handicap hurdle, elected to go back to town at once. But as the car slid slowly out of the press Grant turned with a benedictory glance at the friendly little course which had provided him with the information he sought. Pleasant place. He would came back some day when he had no business on his mind to bother him, and make an afternoon of it.

On the way up to town Murray talked amiably of the things he was interested in: bookmakers and their clannishness – 'They're like Highlanders,' he said. 'They may squabble among themselves, but if an outsider butts into the scrap, it's a case of tartan against all;' horses and their foibles; trainers and their morals; Lacey and his wit. Presently he said, 'How's the queue affair getting along?'

Very well, Grant said. They would make an arrest in a day or two if things continued to go as well as they were doing.

Murray was silent for a little. 'I say, you don't want Sorrell in connection with that, do you?' he asked diffidently.

Murray had been extraordinarily decent. 'No,' said Grant; 'it was Sorrell who was found dead in the queue.'

'Great Heavens!' said Murray, and digested the news in silence for some time. 'Well, I'm sorry,' he said at last.

'I never knew the fellow, but everyone seems to have liked him.'

And that was what Grant had been thinking too. Bert Sorrell, it seemed, had been no villain. Grant longed more than ever to meet the Dago.

CHAPTER 8

MRS EVERETT

Brightling Crescent was a terrace of red brick three-storey houses of the Nottingham lace and pot-plant type of decoration. Their stone steps were coaxed into cleanliness and hideousness by liberal applications of coloured pipeclay. Some blushed at finding themselves so conspicúous, some were evidently jaundiced by the unwelcome attention, and some stared in pallid horror as at an outrage. But all of them wore that *Nemo me impune lacessit* air. You might pull the bright brass bell-handles – indeed, their high polish winked an urgent invitation to do so – but you passed the threshold only at the cost of a wide-stepping avoidance of these constantly refurbished traps of pipeclayed step. Grant walked up the street that Sorrell had trodden so often, and wondered if the Dago knew it too. Mrs Everett, a bony, short-sighted woman of fifty or so, herself opened the door of ninety-eight to him, and Grant inquired for Sorrell.

Mr Sorrell was no longer there, she said. He had left just a week ago to go to America.

So that was the tale someone had told.

Who said he had gone to America?

'Mr Sorrell, of course.'

Yes, Sorrell might have told the tale to mask his suicide.

Had he lived alone there?

'Who are you, and what do you want to know for?' she asked, and Grant said that he was a plain-clothes officer and would like to come in and talk to her for a moment. She looked a little staggered, but took the news calmly, and ushered him into a ground-floor sitting room. 'This used to be Mr Sorrell's,' she said. 'A young lady teacher has it now, but she won't mind us using it for once. Mr Sorrell hasn't done anything wrong, has he? I wouldn't believe it of him. A quiet young man like him.'

Grant reassured her, and asked again if Sorrell had lived alone.

No, she said; he shared his rooms with another gentleman, but when Mr Sorrell had gone to America the other gentleman had had to look out for other rooms because he couldn't afford these alone, and a young lady had wanted to come into them. She was sorry to lose both of them. Nice young men, they were, and great friends.

'What was his friend's name?'

'Gerald Lamont,' she said. Mr Sorrell had been a bookmaker on his own account, and Mr Lamont was in his office. Oh no, not a partner, but they were great friends.

'What other friends had Sorrell?'

He had had very few, she said. He and Jerry Lamont went everywhere together. After some strenuous thinking she recollected two men who had once come to the house, and described them well enough to make it certain that neither was the Dago.

'Have you any photographs of Sorrell or his friend?'

She thought she had some snapshots somewhere, if the inspector wouldn't mind waiting while she hunted. Grant had had hardly enough time to examine the room before she came back with two amateur photographs of postcard size. 'These were taken last summer when they were on the river,' she said.

The snapshots had been taken obviously on the same occasion. They both showed the same willowy background of Thames bank and the same piece of punt. One was a photograph of Sorrell in flannels, a pipe in one hand and a cushion in the other. The other was also a photograph of a young man in flannels, and the man was the Dago.

Grant sat a long time looking at that dark face. The

photograph was a good one. The eyes were not a mere
shadow as in most snapshots; they were eyes. And Grant
could see again the sudden horror that had lit them as they
lighted on him in the Strand. Even in the pleasant repose
of the moment on the river the eyes had an inimical look.
There was no friendliness in the hard-boned face.

'Where did you say Lamont had gone?' he asked matter-
of-factly.

Mrs Everett did not know.

Grant examined her minutely. Was she telling the truth?
As if conscious of his suspicion, she supplemented her
statement with another. He had got rooms somewhere on
the south side of the river.

Suspicion filled him. Did she know more than she was
telling? Who had sent the money to bury Sorrell? His friend
and the Dago were one, and the Dago, who had had two
hundred and twenty-three pounds from him, had certainly
not sent the money. He looked at the woman's hard face.
She would probably write like a man; the handwriting
experts were not infallible. But then, the person who had
sent the money had owned the revolver. No, he corrected
himself; the person who had *posted* the money had had the
revolver.

Had either of the men owned a revolver? he asked.

No; she had never seen such a thing with either of them.
They weren't that type.

There she was again, harping on their quietness. Was it
mere partisanship, or was it a feeble attempt to head him
off the track? He wanted to ask if Lamont were left-handed,
but something held him back. If she were not being straight
with him, that question in relation to Lamont would alarm
her immediately. It would give away the whole extent of
his investigations. She would give warning and flush the
bird from cover long before they were ready to shoot. And
it was not vital at the moment. The man of the photograph
was the man who had lived with Sorrell, was the man who

had fled at sight of him in the Strand, was the man who had had all Sorrell's money, and was almost certainly the man of the queue. Legarde could identify him. It was more important at the moment to keep Mrs Everett in the dark as to how much they knew.

'When did Sorrell leave for America?'

'His boat sailed on the fourteenth,' she said, 'but he left here on the thirteenth.'

'Unlucky day!' said Grant, hoping to bring the conversation to a less formal and less antagonistic level.

'I don't believe in superstition,' she said. 'One day is very like another.'

But Grant was thinking hard. The thirteenth was the night of the murder.

'Did Lamont leave with him?' he asked.

Yes, they had left together in the morning. Mr Lamont was going to take his things to his new rooms and then to meet Mr Sorrell. Mr Sorrell was going down to Southampton with a boat train at night. She had wanted to go to see him off, but he had been very insistent that she shouldn't.

'Why?' asked Grant.

'He said it was too late, and in any case he didn't like being seen off.'

'Had he any relations?'

No, none that she had ever heard of.

And Lamont, had he any?

Yes, he had a father and mother and one brother, but they had emigrated to New Zealand directly after the War and he had not seen them since.

How long had the two men stayed with her?

Mr Sorrell had been with her for nearly eight years and Mr Lamont for four.

Who shared the rooms with Sorrell for the four years previous to Lamont's arrival?

There had been various people, but most of the time

it was a nephew of her own, who was now in Ireland. Yes, Mr Sorrell had always been on good terms with all of them.

'Was he always bright and cheerful?' asked Grant.

Well, no, she said; bright and cheery didn't describe Mr Sorrell at all. That was Mr Lamont, if he liked. Mr Lamont was the bright and cheery one. Mr Sorrell was quiet, but pleasant. Sometimes he'd be a bit mopy, and Mr Lamont would be extra bright to cheer him up.

Grant, remembering how grateful one is when someone deliberately attempts to take the black dog from one's back, wondered why it hadn't been the other way about, and Sorrell had murdered Lamont.

Did they ever quarrel?

No, never that she had known of, and she would have known quick enough.

'Well,' said Grant at last, 'I suppose you have no objections to lending me these snapshots for a day or two?'

'You'll let me have them back safe, will you?' she said. 'They're the only ones I have, and I was very fond of both of them.'

Grant promised, and put them carefully away in his pocket-book, praying that they were covered with valuable finger-prints.

'You're not going to get them into trouble, are you?' she asked as he was going. 'They never did a wrong thing in their lives.'

'Well, if that's so, they're quite safe,' Grant said.

He hurried back to Scotland Yard and, while the fingerprints on the photographs were being recorded, heard Williams' report of an unproductive day among the bookmaking offices of London. As soon as the snapshots were again in his possession, he repaired to Laurent's. It was very late and the place was deserted. A solitary waiter was absent-mindedly assembling the crumbs from a table, and the air smelt of rich gravy, wine, and cigarette smoke.

The distrait minion laid away the crumb-scoop and bent to hear his pleasure with that air of having hoped for nothing, and of having the melancholy pleasure of being right, which a waiter presents to the foolhardy one who attempts to dine when others have finished. As he recognised Grant he reassembled his features in a new combination intended to read, 'What a pleasure to serve a favourite customer!' but which in reality was unfortunately clear as 'Good heavens, that was a bloomer! It's that pet of Marcel's.'

Grant asked after Marcel, and heard that he had that morning departed for France in a hurry. His father had died and he was an only son, and there was, it was understood, a matter of a good business and a vineyard to be settled. Grant was not particularly desolated at the thought of not seeing Marcel again. The manners on which Marcel had always prided himself had left Grant invariably slightly nauseated. He ordered a dish, and asked if Raoul Legarde was on the premises and, if so, would he be allowed to come and speak to him for a moment. Several minutes later Raoul's tall figure, clad in white linen overall and cap, emerged from the screens by the door and followed the waiter diffidently to Grant's table. He had the air of a shy child going up for a prize which it knows it has earned.

'Good evening, Legarde,' Grant said amiably; 'you've been a great help to me. I want you to look at these and see if you can recognise any of them.' He spread twelve photographs roughly fan-wise on the table and left Raoul to examine them. The boy took his time – in fact, the pause was so long that Grant had time to wonder if the boy's statement that he would recognise the man he had seen had been merely a boast. But when Raoul spoke there was no hesitation about him.

'That,' he said, laying a slender forefinger on the photograph of Sorrell, 'is the man who was beside me in the queue. And that,' this time the forefinger descended on Lamont's photograph, 'is the man who came to talk to him.'

'Will you swear to that?' Grant asked.

Raoul knew all about swearing to a thing this time. 'Oh yes,' he said; 'I take my oath any time.'

That was all Grant wanted. 'Thank you, Legarde,' he said gratefully. 'When you are *maître d'hôtel*, I'll come and stay and bring half the aristocracy in Britain.'

Raoul smiled broadly at him. 'It may never come,' he said, '*the maître d'hôtel*. They offer very much on the movies, and it is easy just to be photographed and look' – he sought for a word – 'you know!' he said, and suddenly let his beautiful but intelligent face slip into an expression of idiotic languishing which was so unexpected that some of Grant's duck and green peas went the wrong way. 'I think I try that first,' he said, 'and after, when I grow'– he moved his hands to indicate a corporation – 'I can buy a hotel.'

Grant smiled benevolently as he watched the graceful figure making its way back to the spoons and the silver cleaning rags. Typically French he was, he thought, in his shrewd recognition of the commercial worth of his beauty, in his humour, in his opportunism. It was sad to think that *embonpoint* would ever mar his slenderness and good looks. Grant hoped that in the midst of his adipose tissue he would keep his humour. When he himself got back to the Yard it was to obtain a warrant for the arrest of Gerald Lamont for the murder of Albert Sorrell, outside the Woffington Theatre, on the evening of the thirteenth of March.

When she closed the door behind the inspector, the woman in Brightling Crescent remained for a long time motionless, her eyes on the brown patterned linoleum that covered the floor of the lobby. Her tongue came out and ran along her thin lips in a contemplative way. She did not appear agitated, but her whole being seemed concentrated in an effort of thought; she vibrated with thought as a dynamo vibrates. For perhaps two minutes she stood there quite motionless, still as a piece of furniture, in the clock ticking silence. Then she turned and went back to the sitting-room. She plumped up the cushions which had been depressed by the inspector's weight – she herself had taken the wholly instinctive precaution of seating herself on a hard chair – as if that were the most immediately important thing in her life. She took a white tablecloth from a drawer in the sideboard and began to set a meal, coming and going between the sitting-room and the kitchen in an unhurrying deliberation, laying knives and forks exactly parallel in a painstaking fashion that was evidently habit. Before she had finished a key rattled in the lock, and a drab woman of twenty-eight or so let herself in, her grey-drab coat, fawn-drab scarf, timidly fashionable green-drab hat, and unexpectant air proclaiming her profession. She removed her goloshes in the hall and came into the sitting-room, with an artificially cheerful remark about the wet day. Mrs Everett agreed and said, 'I was thinking, as it's cold supper, you mightn't mind if I left it set and went out. I'd like to run over and see a friend, if it makes no difference to you.'

Her boarder assured her that it made no difference whatever, and Mrs Everett thanked her and retired to the kitchen. There she took from the larder a roast of beef, from which she cut thick slices, and proceeded to make sandwiches. She wrapped them neatly in white paper and put them into a basket. Into the basket with them she put some cooked sausage, some meat lozenges, and a packet of chocolate. She stoked the fire, filled the kettle, and set it on the side of the hearth so that it would be hot when she came back, and proceeded upstairs. In her bedroom she made a deliberate toilet for the street, tucking stray strands of hair carefully under her uncompromising hat. She took a key from one drawer and opened another, withdrew a roll of notes and counted them, and put them into her purse. She opened a blotter worked in canvas and silks and wrote

a short note, which she sealed in an envelope and put into
her pocket.

She came downstairs again, pulling on her gloves, and
taking the small basket from the kitchen table, let herself out
at the back door, locking it behind her. She went down the
street, looking neither to right nor left, her flat back, lifted
chin, and resolute walk proclaiming the citizen with a good
conscience. In the Fulham Road she waited at a bus-stop
and took such casual interest in her fellow-attendants as
does a woman who knows what is what and keeps herself
to herself. So entirely orthodox was she that when she left
the bus, only the bus conductor, whose power of observation
was entirely instinctive, could have said that she had been
a passenger. And in the bus that took her to Brixton she
was equally inconspicuous; her fellow-travellers noticed her
no more than if she had been a sparrow or a lamp-post.
Sometime before Brixton became Streatham Hill she got
off the bus and disappeared into the foggy evening, and
no one remembered that she had been there; no one had
been disturbed by the terrific pent urgency that her passive
exterior hid.

Up a long street where the street-lamps hung like misty
moons she went, and down another its exact replica – flat
fronts, foggy lamplight. deserted roadway; along another
and yet another. Half-way along this last she turned
abruptly and walked back to the nearest lamp-post. A
girl hurried past her, late for some appointment, and a
small boy came jingling two pennies in his joined palms.
But no one else. She made a pretence of looking at her watch
in the light and went on again in the original direction. To
her left was a terrace of the high, imposing-looking houses
which the social descent of Brixton has left high and dry,
the plaster peeling in large flakes from the walls, and the
variegated window-curtaining proclaiming the arrival of the
flat-dweller. Nothing could be seen at this hour of the detail
of the mass; only a chink of light here and there and the

recurrent fanlights of the doors told of human habitation.
Into one of these she disappeared, the door closing softly
behind her. Up two flights of stairs, dimly lighted and
shabby, she went, and came to the third flight, where
there was no light. She glanced up into the dark above
and listened. But only the stealthy creaking of the old wood
sounded in all the house. Slowly, feeling her way step by
step, she climbed, negotiated the turn without a stumble,
and came to rest at the top of the house on an unlighted
landing, breathless. With the assurance of one who knows
her way, she put out her hand to locate the invisible door,
and having found it, knocked gently. There was no answer,
and no streak of light below the door betrayed a presence
beyond. But she knocked again and said softly, with her
lips to the crack where the door met the upright, 'Jerry!
it's me.' Almost immediately something was kicked away
from inside the door, and it opened to show a lamp-lit
room, with a man's figure silhouetted crucifix-wise against
the light.

'Come in,' said the man, and drew her quickly in and shut
the door and locked it. She set her basket on the table by
the curtained window and turned to face him as he came
from the door.

'You shouldn't have come!' he said. 'Why did you?'

'I came because there was no time to write to you, and
I had to see you. They've found out who he was. A man
from Scotland Yard came this evening and wanted to know
all about you both. I did everything I could for him. Told
him everything he wanted to know, except where you were.
I even gave him snaps of you and him. But he knows you are
in London, and it's only a matter of time if you stay here.
You've got to go.'

'What did you give him the photographs for?'

'Well, I thought about it when I went away to pretend
to look for them, and I knew I couldn't go back and say I
couldn't find them and make him believe me. I mean, I was

afraid I wouldn't do it well enough. And then I thought, since they had got so far – finding out all about you two – a photograph wouldn't make much difference one way or another.'

'Wouldn't it?' said the man. 'Tomorrow every policeman in London will know exactly what I look like. A description's one thing – and that's bad enough, God knows – but a photograph is the very devil. That's torn it!'

'Yes, it might have if you were going to stay in London. But if you stayed in London, you'd be caught in any case. It would only be a matter of time. You've got to get out of London tonight.'

'There's nothing I'd like better,' he said bitterly, 'but how, and where to? If I leave this house, it's fifty to one I walk straight into the police, and with a mug like mine it wouldn't be very easy to convince them that I wasn't myself. This last week's been ten thousand hells. God, what a fool I was! – and for so little reason. To put a rope round my neck for next to nothing!'

'Well, you've done it,' she said coolly. 'Nothing can alter that. What you've got to consider now is how to get away. And as quickly as you can.'

'Yes, you said that before – but how, and where to?'

'Have some food and I'll tell you. Have you had a proper meal today?'

'Yes, I had breakfast,' he said. But he did not appear to be hungry, and his angry, feverish eyes watched her unwaveringly.

'What you want,' she said, 'is to get out of this district, where everyone's talking about the thing, to a place where no one's ever heard of it.'

'If you mean abroad, it isn't the slightest good trying. I tried to get taken on a boat as a hand four days ago, and they asked if I was Union or something, and wouldn't look at me. And as for the Channel boats, I might as well give myself up.'

'I'm not talking about abroad at all. You're not as famous as you think. I'm talking about the Highlands. Do you think the people in my home on the West Coast have ever heard of you or what happened last Tuesday night? Take my word for it, they haven't. They never read anything but a local paper, and local papers report London affairs in one line. The place is thirty-six miles from a railway station, and the policeman lives in the next village, four miles away, and has never seen anything more criminal than a salmon poacher. That's where you are going. I have written a letter saying that you are coming because you are in bad health. Your name is George Lowe, and you are a journalist. There is a train for Edinburgh from King's Cross at ten-fifteen and you are catching that tonight. There isn't much time, so hurry.'

'And what the police are catching is me at the platform barrier.'

'There isn't a barrier at King's Cross. I haven't gone up and down to Scotland for nearly thirty years without knowing that. The Scotch platform is open to anyone who wants to walk on. And even if there are detectives there, the train is about half a mile long. You've got to risk *something* if you're going to get away. You can't just stay here and let them get you! I should have thought that a gamble would have been quite in your line.'

'Think I'm afraid, do you?' he said. 'Well, I am. Scared stiff. To go out into the street tonight would be like walking into no-man's-land with Fritz machine-gunning.'

'You've either got to pull yourself together or go and give yourself up. You can't sit still and let them come and take you.'

'Bert was right when he christened you Lady Macbeth,' he said.

'Don't!' she said sharply.

'All right,' he muttered. 'I'm sort of crazy.' There was a thick silence. 'All right, let's try this as a last stunt.'

'There's very little time,' she reminded him. 'Put some-thing into a suitcase quickly – a suitcase that you can carry yourself – you don't want porters.'

He moved at her bidding into the bedroom that led off the sitting-room, and began to fling things into a suitcase, while she put neat parcels of food into the pockets of the coat that hung behind the door.

'What's the good?' he said suddenly. 'It's no use. How do you think I can take a main-line train out of London without being stopped and questioned?'

'You couldn't if you were alone,' she said, 'but with me it's a different matter. Look at me. Do I look the sort who would be helping you to get away?'

The man stood in the doorway contemplating her for a moment, and a sardonic smile twisted his mouth as he took her in, in all her upright orthodoxy. 'I believe you're right,' he said. He gave a short, mirthless laugh and thereafter put no difficulties in the way of her plans. In ten minutes they were ready for departure.

'Have you any money?' she asked.

'Yes,' he said; 'plenty.'

She seemed about to ask a question.

'No, not that,' he said. 'My own.'

She carried a rug and an extra coat – 'You mustn't suggest hurry in any way; you must look as though you were going a long journey and didn't care who knew it' – and he carried the suitcase and a golf-bag. There was to be no hole-and-corner business. This was bluff, and the bigger the bluff, the more chance there was of carrying it off. As they stepped into the foggy road, she said, 'We'll go to Brixton High Street and get a bus or a taxi.'

As it happened, it was a taxi that offered itself first. It swelled out of the dark before they had reached a main thoroughfare, and as the man heaved what they were carrying aboard, the woman gave the address of their destination.

'Cost you something, lady,' said the driver.

'Well, well,' she said, 'it isn't every day my son has a holiday.'

The driver grunted good-naturedly. 'That's the stuff! Feast and famine. Nothing like it.' And she climbed in, and the taxi ceased its agitated throbbing and slid into action.

After a silence the man said, 'Well, you couldn't do more for me if I were.'

'I'm glad you're not!' she said. There was another long silence.

'What is your name?' she asked suddenly.

He thought for a moment. 'George Lowe,' he said.

'Yes,' she said; 'but don't think next time. There is a train north to Inverness that leaves Waverley at ten o'clock tomorrow morning. You'll have to spend tomorrow night in Inverness. I have written down on a paper what you do after that.'

'You seem to be perfectly sure that nothing's going to happen at King's Cross.'

'No, I'm not,' she said. 'The police are not fools – that Scotland Yard man didn't believe half I said – but they're just human. All the same, I'm not going to give you that bit of paper until the train's going.'

'I wish I had that revolver now!' he said.

'I'm glad you haven't. You've made a big enough fool of yourself already.'

'I wouldn't use it. It would just give me courage.'

'For goodness' sake, be sensible, Jerry. Don't do anything silly and spoil things.'

They fell to silence again, the woman sitting upright and alert, the man shrunk in the corner, almost invisible. Into the west of London they went like that, through the dark squares north of Oxford Street, out into the Euston Road and with a sharp left-handed turn into King's Cross. The moment had come.

'You pay the taxi and I'll get the ticket,' she said.

As Lamont paid the taxi-man the shadow of his turned-down hat hid his face, so that his retreating back was all that the incurious gaze of the driver noted. A porter came and took his things from him, and he surrendered them willingly. Now that the time had come, his 'nerves' had gone. It was neck or nothing, and he could afford to play the part well. When the woman joined him from the booking-office, the change in him was evident in the approbation on her cold face. Together they went on to the platform and followed the porter down it, looking for a corner seat. They made a sufficiently convincing picture – the man with the rug and the golf-bag and the wraps, and the woman in attendance with the man's extra coat.

The porter dived into a corridor and came out again saying, 'Got you a corner, sir. Probably have the side to yourself all the way. It's quiet tonight.'

Lamont tipped him and inspected his quarters. The occupant of the other side had staked his claims, but was not present other than in spirit. He went back to the doorway with the woman and talked to her. Footsteps came down the corridor at his back, and he said to her, 'Have they any fishing, do you think?'

'Only sea-fishing in the loch,' she said, and continued the subject until the steps had moved on. But before they faded out of earshot they stopped. Lamont cast as casual a glance as he could achieve down the corridor, and found that the owner of the steps had halted at the open door of his compartment and was examining the luggage on the rack. And then he remembered, too late, that the porter had put his suitcase up with the initials outside. The G. L. was plain for all the world to read. He saw the man stir preparatory to coming back. 'Talk!' he said quickly to the woman.

'There's a burn, of course,' she said, 'where you can catch what they call "beelans." They are about three inches long.'

'Well, I'll send you a beelan,' he said, and managed a

low laugh that earned the woman's admiration just as the man stopped behind him.

'Excuse me, sir, is your name Lorrimer?'

'No,' said Lamont, turning round and facing the man squarely. 'My name is Lowe.'

'Oh, sorry!' the man said. 'Is that your luggage in the compartment, then?'

'Yes.'

'Oh, thank you. I am looking for a man Lorrimer, and I was hoping that it might be his. It's a cold night to be hanging round for people who aren't here.'

'Yes,' said the woman; 'my son's grumbling already at the thought of his first night journey. But he'll grumble a lot more before he's in Edinburgh, won't he?'

The man smiled. 'Can't say I've ever travelled all night myself,' he said. 'Sorry to have bothered you,' he added, and moved on.

'You should have let me take that other rug, George,' she said as he moved out of earshot.

'Oh, rug be blowed!' said George, as to the manner born. 'It will probably be like an oven before we've been going an hour.'

A long, shrill whistle sounded. The last door was banged.

'This is for expenses,' she said, and put a packet into his hand, 'and this is what I promised you. The man's on the platform. It's all right.'

'We've left out one thing,' he said. He took off his hat and bent and kissed her.

The long train pulled slowly out into the darkness.

CHAPTER 9

GRANT GETS MORE INFORMATION
THAN HE EXPECTED

Grant was studying the morning papers with his habitual
half-careless thoroughness. That is not a paradox; Grant
apparently skimmed the paper, but if you asked him about
any particular happening afterwards, you would find that
he had acquired a very efficient working knowledge of it.
He was feeling pleased with himself. It was only a matter
of hours before he got his man. It was a week today that
the murder had been committed, and to locate the murderer
from among a mass of conflicting clues in such a short time
was good work. He had been favoured by luck, of course; he
acknowledged that freely. If it weren't for luck on someone's
part, half the criminals in the world would go unpunished.
A burglar, for instance, was hardly ever convicted except
through an outrageous piece of luck on the part of the police.
But the queue affair had not been a picnic by any means.
There had been spade-work galore; and Grant felt as nearly
complaisant as it was in him to feel as he thought of the
crowd of men working the south of London at this minute,
as eager as hounds in cover. He had had his suspicions of
Mrs Everett, but on the whole he had decided that she was
telling the truth. The man put on to watch her had reported
that no one had come or gone from the house from eight
o'clock last night, when he went on duty, until this morning.
Moreover, she had produced photographs of the men when
there had been no necessity to, and it was quite possible
that she did not know her late boarder's address. Grant
knew very well the queer indifference that London breeds in

people who have lived long in it. The other side of the river
to a Fulham Londoner was as foreign a place as Canada,
and Mrs Everett would probably be no more interested in
an address at Richmond than she would have been in a
12345 Something Avenue, Somewhere, Ontario. It would
convey as little to her. The man Lamont was the one who
had been least time with her, and her interest in him was
probably less than that which she had for the dead man. He
had probably promised in the friendly if insincere warmth of
parting to write to her, and she had been content with that.
On the whole, he thought that Mrs Everett was genuine.
Her finger-prints were not those on the revolver and the
envelope. Grant had noticed where her left thumb and
forefinger had held the photographs tightly by the corner,
and the marks when developed proved to be quite new in
the case. So Grant was happy this morning. Apart from
the kudos arising from the apprehension of a badly-wanted
man, it would afford Grant immense satisfaction to lay
his hands on a man who had stuck another in the back.
His gorge rose at the contemplation of a mind capable of
conceiving the crime.

In the week since the queue murder its sensational value
to the Press had been slightly minimised by other important
happenings, and though Grant's chief interest seemed to be
devoted to apparently unimportant and irrelevant scraps
of information like the theft of bicycles, he was amusedly
and rather thankfully aware that the most important things
in Britain today, judging by the size of the heading that
announced them and the amount of space allotted them,
were the preparations for the Boat Race, the action of
a society beauty-doctor against a lady who had been
'lifted', and the departure of Ray Marcable to the United
States. As Grant turned over the page of the illustrated
paper and came face to face with her, he was conscious
again of that queer, uneasy, unpolice-like movement in his
chest. His heart did not jump – that would be doing him

an injustice; C.I.D. hearts are guaranteed not to jump, tremble, or otherwise misbehave even when the owner is looking down the uncompromising opening of a gun-barrel – but it certainly was guilty of unauthorised movement. It may have been resentment at his own weakness in being taken aback by a photograph, but Grant's eyes were very hard as he looked at the smiling face – that famous, indeterminate smile. And though his mouth may have curved, he was not smiling as he read the many captions: 'Miss Ray Marcable, a studio photograph'; 'Miss Marcable as Dodo in *Didn't You Know*?'; 'Miss Marcable in the Row'; and lastly, occupying half the centre page, 'Miss Marcable departs from Waterloo *en route* for Southampton'; and there was Ray, one dainty foot on the step of the Pullman, and her arms full of flowers. Arranged buttress-wise on either side of her were people well enough known to come under the heading 'left to right.' In either bottom corner of the photograph were the eager heads of the few of the countless multitudes seeing her off who had been lucky enough to get within hailing distance. These last, mostly turned to look into the camera, were out of focus and featureless, like a collection of obscene and half-human growths. At the end of the column describing the enthusiastic scenes which had attended her departure, was the sentence: 'Also sailing by the *Queen Guinivere* were Lady Foulis Robinson, the Hon. Margaret Bedivere, Mr Chatters-Frank, M.P., and Lord Lacing.'

The inspector's lips curved just a little more. Lacing was evidently going to be managed by that clear, cold will for the rest of his life. Well, he would live and die probably without being aware of it; there was some comfort in that. Nothing but a moment of unnaturally clear sight had presented the knowledge of it to himself, and if he went into any London crowd, Rotherhithe or Mayfair, and announced that Ray Marcable, under her charm and her generosity, was hard as flint, he would be likely to be either lynched or excommunicated. He flung the paper away, and was about to take up another when a thought occurred to him, prompted by the announcement of the sailing of the *Guinivere*. He had decided to accept Mrs Everett's statement as being correct, but he had not investigated her statement that Sorrell was going to America. He had taken it for granted that the America story had been a blind by Sorrell to mask his intended suicide, and the Dago – Lamont – whether he believed the tale or not, had not sought to alter the supposition of Sorrell's departure. Had he been wise in not investigating it further? It was, at least, unbusinesslike. He sent for a subordinate. 'Find out what liners sailed from Southampton last Wednesday,' he said; and remained in thought until the man came back with the news that the Canadian Pacific liner *Metalinear* had sailed for Montreal, and the Rotterdam-Manhattan liner *Queen of Arabia*, for New York. It seemed that Sorrell had at least taken the trouble to verify the sailings. Grant thought that he would go down to the Rotterdam-Manhattan offices and have a chat, on the off chance of something useful coming to light.

As he stepped from the still drizzling day into the cathedral-like offices of the Rotterdam-Manhattan a small boy in blue leaped genie-like from the tessellated pavement of the entrance-hall and demanded his business. Grant said that he wanted to see someone who could tell him about the sailings for New York last week, and the urchin, with every appearance of making him free of mysteries and of knowing it, led him to an apartment and a clerk, to whom Grant again explained his business and was handed on. At the third handing-on Grant found a clerk who knew all that was to be known of the *Queen of Arabia* – her internal economy, staff, passengers, capacity, peculiarities, tonnage, timetable, and sailing.

'Can you tell me if anyone booked a passage on the *Queen of Arabia* this trip and did not go?'

Yes, the clerk said, two people had failed to occupy their berths. One was a Mr Sorrell and the other was a Mrs James Ratcliffe.

Grant was speechless for a moment; then he asked the date of the bookings. They had been booked on the same day – seven days before the murder. Mrs Ratcliffe had cancelled hers at the last minute, but they had had no further word from Mr Sorrell.

Could he see the plan of the cabins?

Certainly, the clerk said, and brought them out. Here was Mr Sorrell's, and here, three along in the same row, was Mrs Ratcliffe's.

Were they booked separately?

Yes, because he remembered the two transactions quite well. He thought the lady was Mrs Ratcliffe, and he was sure from his conversation with him that the man was Sorrell himself. Yes, he thought he would recognise Mr Sorrell again.

Grant produced the Dago's photograph and showed it to him. 'Is that the man?' he asked.

The clerk shook his head. 'Never saw him before to my knowledge,' he said.

'That, then?' asked Grant, handing over Sorrell's photograph, and the clerk immediately recognised it.

'Did he inquire about his neighbours in the row?' Grant asked. But the clerk could recall no details like that. It had been a very busy day that Monday. Grant thanked him, and went out into the drizzle, quite unaware that it was raining. Things were no longer reasonable and understandable; cause and effect, motive and action decently allied. They were acquiring a nightmare inconsequence that dismayed his daytime brain. Sorrell had intended to go to America, after all. He had booked a second-class passage and personally chosen a cabin. The amazing and incontrovertible fact did not fit in anywhere. It was a very large wrench thrown into the machinery that had begun to run so smoothly. If

Sorrell had been as penniless as he seemed, he would not have contemplated a second-class journey to New York, and in view of the booking of the passage, contemplated suicide seemed a poor explanation for the presence of the revolver and absence of belongings. It shouted much more loudly of his first theory – that the lack of personal clues had been arranged in case of a brush with the police. But Sorrell had, to all accounts, been a law abiding person. And then, to crown things, there was Mrs Ratcliffe's reappearance in the affair. She had been the only one of the people surrounding Sorrell to show marked distress at the time of the murder or afterwards. It was she and her husband who had avowedly been next behind Sorrell in the queue. Her husband! A picture of James Ratcliffe, that prop of British citizenship, swam into his mind. He would go and have another, and totally unheralded, interview with Mr Ratcliffe.

The boy took in his card, and he waited in the outer office for perhaps three minutes before Mr Ratcliffe came out and drew him in with a welcoming affability.

'Well, Inspector,' he said, 'how are you getting on? Do you know, you and dentists must be the most unhappy people in the world. No one sees you without remembering unpleasant things.'

'I didn't come to bother you,' Grant said. 'I just happened to be round, and I thought you'd perhaps let me use your telephone to save me going to a post office.'

'Oh, certainly,' said Ratcliffe. 'Carry on. I'll go.'

'No, don't go,' said Grant. 'There'll be nothing private. I only want to know whether they want me.'

But no one wanted him. The scent in South London was weak, but the hounds were persevering and busy. And he hung up with a relief which was rather surprising when one considered the eager frame of mind in which he had set out from the Yard. Now he did not want an arrest until he had time to think things over for a bit. The nightmare of a Scotland Yard officer's whole life is Wrongful Arrest. He

turned to Ratcliffe, and allowed him to know that an arrest
was imminent; they had located their man. Ratcliffe was
complimentary, and in the middle of the compliments Grant
said, 'By the way, you didn't tell me that your wife had
intended sailing for New York the night after the murder.'

Ratcliffe's face, clear in the light of the window, was both
blank and shocked. 'I didn't know,' he began, and then with
a rush – 'I didn't think it was of any importance or I should
have told you. She was too much upset to go, and in any
case there was the inquest. She has a sister in New York,
and was going over for a month just. It didn't make any
difference, did it? Not knowing, I mean? It had no bearing
on the crime.'

'Oh no,' Grant said. 'I found it out quite accidentally. It
is of no consequence. Is your wife better?'

'Yes, I think so. She has not been at home since the
inquest. She is at Eastbourne with the other sister – the
one you met, I think.'

Still more puzzled, Grant made his way back to the
Yard. He pressed the button on his desk and said to the
man who answered it, 'I want someone for special work.
Is Simpson in?'

'Yes, sir.'

'Send him in.'

A fair and freckled man of medium height arrived; he had
the pleased, alert air of a terrier who is waiting for someone
to throw a stone. To him Grant said:

'At fifty-four Lemonora Road, Golder's Green, live a Mr
and Mrs Ratcliffe. I want to know what terms they are
on – with each other, I mean. Also anything else you
can learn about the household. The gossipier the better.
I know all about his business, so you needn't waste time
on that. It's his home affairs that I want to know about.
You can use any method you like as long as you keep
within the law. Report to me tonight whether you have
got anything or not. Is Mullins in the Yard just now?'

Yes, Simpson had seen him as he came up. 'Well, send him to me.'

Mullins was not freckled, and he looked rather like a verger. 'Good morning, sir,' he said, and waited.

'Good morning, Mullins. From now until further notice you are a pedlar. You make an excellent Italian, but I think perhaps you had better be British. It is less conspicuous. I'll give you a chit to Clitheroe in Lowndes Street, and he will give you the kind of stock I want. Don't sell more than you can help. And I don't want you to come back here. Meet me in the alley by Clitheroe's in an hour from now. Can you manage it in an hour?'

'I think so, sir. Am I young or old?'

'It doesn't matter. Young to middle-aged. Greybeards are too theatrical. Don't overdo anything. Respectable enough to travel on a bus if need be.'

'Very good, sir,' said Mullins, as though his instructions had been to post a letter.

When Grant stumbled across him in the alley in Lowndes Street an hour later, he said, 'You're a wonder, Mullins – simply a wonder. I should never believe you had ever written a report in your life if I didn't know first-hand.' He looked appreciatively at the pedlar before him. It was incredible that that slightly drooping figure was one of the most promising men at the Yard. It is very seldom that the C.I.D. resort to disguise, but when they do, they do it well. Mullins had the supreme touch – that faculty of looking as though he could not possibly be other than he was at the moment. His clothes, even, though obviously third-hand, had not that uneasy fit that newly donned garments have. They lay to his shoulders as a much-worn garment does, however ill-fitting.

'Like a trinket, sir?' said Mullins, the pedlar, opening the lid of his wicker tray. On the baize lining lay a collection of articles mostly of cheap Italian manufacture – paper-knives, painted wood ornaments of all

sorts, useful and useless, papier-mâché bowls, stucco fig-
ures.

'Good!' said Grant. He took from his pocket a thin thing
wrapped in tissue paper. As he unrolled the paper he said,
'I want you to go to ninety-eight Brightling Crescent, off the
Fulham Road, and find out if the woman who lives there
has ever seen this before.' He laid a silver dagger with an
enamelled handle down among the painted wood and the
stucco. 'Needless to say, it isn't for sale. What's the price
of this?' he added, picking up an article.

'Give that to a gentleman like you for one-and-nine-
pence,' said Mullins, without hesitation.

As the passer-by went beyond hearing, Grant continued
cheerfully as if there had been no parenthesis: 'When you've
disposed of the woman in Brightling Crescent – and keep
your eyes open generally – go to fifty-four Lemonora Road
and see if anyone there recognises it. Report as soon as you
have finished.'

When the pedlar of Italian goods reached the back door
of 54 Lemonora Road about tea-time, a pretty but capless
maid said, 'Goodness, here's another!'

'Another wot?' said the pedlar.

'Another man selling things.'

'Oh? Bin a lot? Bet they hadn't anything like mine,' he
said, and opened the tray.

'Oh!' she said, obviously enraptured. 'Are they dear?'

'Not them. 'Sides, a girl with wages like yours can easy
afford something nice.'

'What do you know about my wages, mister?'

'Well, I don't *know* anything. I'm just dedoocing. Pretty
girl, nice house, good wages.'

'Oh, the wages are good enough,' she said in a tone that
indicated other shortcomings.

'Wouldn't the lady of the house like to have a look at
them?' he said.

'There's no lady,' she said. 'I'm the lady of the house

just now. The missus is at Eastbourne. You been in the Army?'

'I was in the Army during the War. That's the only time bin in the Army counts. France? I was four years in France, miss.'

'Well, you can come in and have some tea, and let me see the things properly. We're just in the middle of it.'

She led him into the kitchen, where the table was spread with butter, bread, several kinds of jam, and cake. At the table, with an enormous cup of tea halfway to his mouth, was a freckled fair man with a blue muffler and a discharged soldier's silver badge on his lapel. Beside him on the table was a pile of cheap writing-pads.

'This is another ex-service man,' the maid said. 'He's selling writing-paper. I shouldn't think there's much sale for it now. It's ages since I seen someone round selling pads.'

'How do, mate?' said the freckled one, meeting the quizzical regard of the pedlar with complete equanimity. 'How's trade?'

'Fair. Just fair. You seem to be very comfortable.'

'Well, I needed it. Haven't sold a pad today. This country's going to the dogs. It's something to come across someone now and again who has a heart.'

'Have some jam,' said the maid, pushing his cup of tea across to the pedlar, and he helped himself liberally.

'Well, I'm glad the missus isn't at home in one way, but I'm sorry in another. I thought as how she might buy something, too.'

'Well, I'*m* not sorry,' she said. 'It's a blessed relief. What with her airs and her tantrums, life isn't worth living.'

'Got a temper, has she?'

'Well, I call it temper, but she calls it nerves. And ever since this murder affair – she was in the queue that night the man was murdered, you know. Yes, stood right up against him. And oh, what a to-do! And then she had to go to the inquest and give evidence. If she'd done the murder herself she couldn't have kicked up a bigger fuss about going. The night before she was screaming and howling and saying she couldn't stand it. And when the poor master tried to quiet her down she wouldn't let him go near her. Hurling names at him you wouldn't use to a dog. I tell you it wasn't half a relief when she went off to Eastbourne with Miss Lethbridge – that's her sister.'

'Yes, the best thing they can do when they're like that is to go away for a bit,' said the freckled man. 'Does she go often?'

'Not so often as I'd like, believe me. She was going to Yorkshire the day after the murder, and then was so upset that she couldn't go. Now she's gone to Eastbourne instead, and long may she stay there, say I. Let's see your stuff,' she said to the pedlar.

He jerked his head at the tray. 'Have a look for yourself. Anything you fancy you can have cheap. It's a long time since I had tea like this. Wot say, Bill?'

'Ar,' agreed his fellow-itinerant through a large mouthful of cake. 'It's isn't often people has a heart.'

She gloated over the bright-coloured collection a while. 'Well, the missus is missing something,' she said. 'She's mad on curios and such-like things that hold the dust. Artistic, she is. What's this for?' she said, holding up the dagger. 'Murdering people with?'

'An't you ever seen one like that before?' the pedlar said in astonishment. 'That's a paper-knife. Same as the wooden ones.'

She tried the point absently on a finger-tip, and with a queer little shudder of disgust that was quite involuntary she put it down again. In the end she chose a little painted bowl, quite useless but very gay to look upon. The pedlar let her have it for sixpence, and in her gratitude she produced cigarettes of Mr Ratcliffe's, and while they smoked enlivened them with talk of what was obviously uppermost in her mind – the murder.

'We had an inspector of police here, if you'd believe it. Quite nice-looking he was. You'd never say he was a policeman. Not coarse like a bobby. But it wasn't nice, all the same, having him round. Of *course* he was suspicious, with her carrying on like that and not wanting to see him. I heard Miss Lethbridge say to her, "Don't be a fool, Meg. The only way to stop him is to see him and *convince* him. You've got to do it."'

'Well, Eastbourne's a nice place,' said the freckled man. 'She'll have company there to forget her troubles.'

'Ah, she's not one for company much. Always having crazes for someone or other, and then she runs them to death and has someone new. Boys, as often as not. She's queer, she is.'

When her talk began to be repetitive instead of informative the freckled man stood up and said, 'Well, miss, I an't had such a tea not in years, and I'm real grateful to you.'

'You're welcome,' she said. 'If you take my advice, you'll give up the writing-pad business. There's nothing in it nowadays. It's old-fashioned. Try stuff like him there – novelty stuff like they sell in the shops at Christmas-time.'

The freckled man's glance fell sardonically on the dagger among the 'Christmas goods.' 'You going up the road or down?' he said to the pedlar.

'Up,' said the pedlar.

'Well, cheerio, I'll be going. Many thanks again for the tea, miss.' And the door closed behind him. Five minutes later the pedlar took his leave.

'If I was you, miss, I wouldn't be so free with my teas,' he said. 'There's lots of decent chaps on the road, but there's lots of the other kind, too. You can't be too careful when you're alone in the house.'

'Are you jealous of the freckly man?' she asked coquettishly and quite unimpressed. 'You needn't be. I didn't buy a pad, you know.'

'Well, well,' said the pedlar, frustrated in his good intentions, and went lagging down the path to the gate.

By sheer chance he found the freckled man occupying the front outside seat of the bus he boarded.

'Well?' said that worthy cheerily. 'Had a good day, mate?'

'Rotten,' said the pedlar. 'Just rotten. How you been doing?'

'Fair. Isn't it amazing,' he said, seeing that the bus-top behind them was deserted, 'what fools these girls are! Why, we could have polished her off and made away with every thing in the house, and it never seemed to occur to her.'

'I said as much to her when I was going, but she though I was jealous of you.'

'Of me? It should be the other way about. She didn't buy a pad!'

'So she pointed out.'

'That was a good stock you had. The boss choose it?'

'Yes.'

'Thought so. He's a daisy. What's he nosing out there?'

'Don't know.'

'The girl din't fall for the knife, I noticed.'

'No.' The pedlar was not communicative.

The freckled one resigned himself. 'Chatty bird!' he remarked, and drawing two cigarettes from the recesses of his person he handed one to his companion. The pedlar cast an idle glance at the maker's name and recognised it as one of Mr Ratcliffe's. His stern features relaxed into a smile.

'Scrounger!' he said, and held his cigarette to the offered match.

But there was nothing of the freebooter in the reports which Mullins and Simpson presented to Grant an hour later. Simpson said that Mr and Mrs Ratcliffe lived on ami-cable terms, with intervals of very severe squall. Simpson was unable to say whether the squall was started by

Mr Ratcliffe's shortcomings or by Mr Ratcliffe's resentment of his wife's, since the maid was never present at the beginning of a quarrel. What she heard she heard through a shut door usually. The biggest row had occurred when they came home on the night of the murder. Since then they had not been on friendly terms. Mrs Ratcliffe had intended to go to Yorkshire the day after the murder, but was too upset to go; and after the inquest she and her sister had gone down to Eastbourne, where she was now at the Grand Parade Hotel. She was a person who took sudden and violent likings for people, and during the time she liked them would be quite unreasonable about them. She had a little money of her own, and was rather independent of her husband.

Mullins said that at ninety-eight he had had difficulty in making Mrs Everett interested enough to allow him to open his tray. She had insisted that she wanted nothing. When he did uncover his wares, the first thing her eyes had lighted on was the dagger. She had immediately cast a glance full of suspicion at him and had said, 'Go away!' and shut the door in his face.

'What do you think? Did she know it?'

Mullins could not say, but it was the sight of it that had made her shut the door like that. She had been going to put up with him until she saw the knife. The maid at Lemonora Road had never seen it before. That he was sure of.

When he had dismissed Mullins and locked away the knife in its drawer again, Grant sat thinking for a long time. This was an unlucky day. There had been no arrest – though he was inclined to think of that as a mixed blessing – there had been the stunning discovery that Sorrell had really meant to go to America, and there had been no trace of the bank-notes handed over to Lamont with the rest of the two hundred and twenty-three pounds, of which the twenty-five sent by the unknown friend had been part. It was seven days since the murder, and the notes had been handed out ten days before that, and not one of them, apart from the twenty-five in their possession, had been traced. Moreover, his two scouts had brought in nothing of importance. In no way could he account for a connection between Mrs Ratcliffe and Sorrell. He was inclined to think it sheer coincidence that had put their names together in a ship's list and had placed them together in the queue. Her husband's appearance of shock when Grant had mentioned the departure for New York might have been merely the result of the recollection that he had omitted to tell the inspector of his wife's intended departure. As for Mrs Everett, her sudden withdrawal spoke more of intelligence than guilt. Mullins had said that she looked at him suspiciously. She had made no attempt to carry off the situation with a high hand by ignoring the dagger or by wantonly calling attention to it. She had been merely suspicious. He decided to give the Everett woman a few more marks for intelligence and to acquit her of complicity. As for the Ratcliffes, he would temporarily cut them out. They didn't fit, and there was no evidence. Things often fit to the police satisfaction when there is no evidence whatever, but here things neither fitted nor were backed by evidence, and consequently would have to stand aside. Presently he would find out why Mrs Ratcliffe had told her maid that she was going to Yorkshire when she intended to go abroad.

The telephone buzzed. Grant took it up with an eagerness of which he was not conscious. It was Williams.

'We've located him, sir. Would you like to come, or shall we carry on?'

'Where is it?' Williams told him. 'Have you got the exits all secured? No chance of failure if we hang on for a little?'

'Oh no, sir. We've got him all right.'

'In that case meet me at the Brixton Road end of Acre Lane in half an hour.'

When he joined his subordinate he asked for details, and

Williams supplied them as they went along. He had found his man through the house-agents. Lamont had engaged a furnished top flat – two small rooms – three days before the murder, and had moved in on the actual day of the murder, in the morning.

Yes, thought Grant, that fitted Mrs Everett's story. 'What name did he give?' he asked.

'His own,' Williams said.

'What! His own name?' repeated Grant incredulously, and was silent, vaguely troubled. 'Well, you've done well, Williams, to run him down so soon. Shy bird, is he?'

'He is,' said Williams, with emphasis. 'Even yet I can't get anyone to say that they've seen him. Shy's the word. Here we are, sir. The house is the fourth in the terrace from here.'

'Good,' said Grant. 'You and I will go up. Got a shooter in your pocket, in case? All right, come on.'

They had no latch-key, and there was apparently no bell for the third floor. They had to ring several times before the inhabitants of the ground floor came grumbling to their rescue and admitted them. As they ascended the increasingly shabby stairs in the last of the daylight. Grant's spirits rose, as they always did at the point of action. There would be no more pottering round. He was about to come face to face with the Dago, the man he had seen in the Strand, the man who had stuck Sorrell in the back. He knocked abruptly at the door in the shadows. The room beyond sounded hollow and empty; there was no answer. Again Grant knocked, with no result.

'You might as well open it, Lamont. We're police officers, and if you don't open it we'll have to burst it.'

Still a complete silence. 'You're sure he's here?' Grant asked Williams.

'Well, he was here yesterday, sir, and no one's seen him since. The house has been under observation since three this afternoon.'

'We'll burst the lock, then,' Grant said, 'and don't forget to stand back when the door goes in.' With their combined weight they attacked the door, which gave up the unequal struggle with a groaning crash, and Grant, with his right hand in his pocket, walked into the room.

One glance round him told him the truth, and he suddenly knew that ever since he had arrived on the landing outside he had had a conviction that the rooms were empty. 'The bird's flown, Williams. We've missed him.'

Williams was standing in the middle of the floor, with the expression of a child from whom a sweet has been taken. He swallowed painfully, and Grant, even in the middle of his own disappointment, found time to be sorry for him. It wasn't Williams' fault. He had been a little too sure, but he had done well to locate the man so quickly.

'Well, he went in a hurry, sir,' said Williams, as if that fact were a palliative to his own hurt pride and disappointment. And certainly there was every evidence of haste. Food was left on the table, drawers were half open and obviously ransacked, clothing had been left behind, and many personal possessions. It was not a methodical get-away, it was a flight.

'We'll go through what he has left behind,' Grant said. 'I'll test for finger-prints before we have to light the lights. There seems to be nothing but the lamp for illumination.' He went round the two rooms with his light powder, but there were few surfaces in the flat on which a print was likely to show clear and unmistakable, and these were so patterned over with prints as to be unproductive. But fairly high up on the varnished wood of the door, where a person's left hand would rest as his right took a coat from the hooks nailed there, were two good prints. A little consoled, Grant lit the lamp and went through the things Lamont had left behind. An exclamation from Williams in the bedroom took him there. Williams was holding a wad of Bank of England notes.

'Got them at the back of this drawer, sir. He did go in a hurry!' Balm was flowing on Williams' excoriated soul. 'Won't he be biting himself!'

But Grant was searching in his pocket-book, and presently produced a list of numbers, which he compared with those on the notes. Yes, there was no doubt about it, these were the notes that Lamont had drawn with the cheque he had had from Sorrell. And Lamont had been so hurried in his flight that he had actually forgotten a thing so vital. The whole amount was there, except for the twenty-five pounds sent for Sorrell's burial. That was rather extraordinary. Why had the Dago, as Grant continued to think of him, spent none of it in the ten days between the time he had received it and the murder? There had been no need of fear then, surely. The value of the notes was large, but that was no explanation. The man had drawn the money himself, and could have had the whole amount in Treasury notes if he had so wanted. Why had he spent none of it?

There was little else in the flat to interest them. The man had a catholic taste in literature, Grant thought, looking along the single row of books that adorned the mantelpiece: Wells, O. Henry, Buchan, Owen Wister, Mary Roberts Rinehart, Sassoon's poems, many volumes of the annual edition of *Racing Up-to-Date*, Barrie's *Little Minister*. He took down one and opened it. On the fly-leaf, in the writing he had seen on the cheque at the bank, was the owner's name: Albert Sorrell. He took down the others one by one. Nearly all of them had belonged to Sorrell. They had evidently been bequeathed to Lamont by Sorrell on his departure for the United States. Up to the last minute, then, these two men had been friendly. What had happened? Or was it only an outward friendship? Had Lamont always been a snake in the grass?

And now there was the new problem of Lamont's present hiding-place. Where would he be likely to go? He was in a hurry – a desperate hurry. It was no planned affair. That

meant that he had probably had to take what refuge came
his way. There was no need for them to consider any such
possibility as an escape abroad in an elaborate disguise. He
had not done that, certainly. He had almost certainly not
gone out of London. He would, as he had done before, stick
rat-like to the place he knew.

Grant left instructions that the search was to go on as
before, and went back to the Yard trying to put himself
in the wanted man's place in the hope of working out
a line of flight. It was very late at night, and he was
very weary, when at last he found light on the matter.
The photographs of the prints he had found on the door
were sent to him, and the prints were Mrs Everett's! There
was no doubt of it. That first finger that had left a mark
at the back of Sorrell's photograph in the little room at
Brightling Crescent belonged to the hand that had leaned
against the door in the effort of reaching for something in
Lamont's room. Mrs Everett. Good Heaven! Talk of snakes
in the grass! And he, Grant, should really retire. He had
got to the stage of trusting people. It was incredible and
humiliating, but he had believed Mrs Everett was being
straight with him. His putting a man to watch her had been
the merest form. Well, it was a bad break, but he had his line
on Lamont now. He would get him through Mrs Everett.
He did not doubt for a moment that it was information
furnished by Mrs Everett that had stirred Lamont into
flight. She had probably gone straight to him after he
had left her yesterday evening. She was gone before the
watcher arrived, but he should have seen her come back;
that would have to be looked into; Andrews was careless.
And in all probability she had either suggested or provided
the new hiding-place. He did not believe that a woman of
her intelligence would be fool enough to believe that she
could keep Lamont hidden at Brightling Terrace, therefore
he had now to find out all about Mrs Everett and all the
ramifications of the Everett family. How should he do it?

What was the best avenue of approach to a woman of Mrs Everett's moated and castellated type. No back-door business, anyhow. She was not a door-gossiper, evidently, and now she was on her guard. That effort to stampede her into a show of emotion had been both futile and ill-advised. He might have known that she wasn't the woman to give anything away in a back-door conversation. Well, what then? In what kind of society, on what kind of occasion, if any, did Mrs Everett open out? He visualised her in various surroundings, and found her invariably grotesque. And then he suddenly had it. Church! The woman shrieked church-worker. She would be greatly respected by all the congregation, but very slightly unpopular because she kept herself to herself, a quality little beloved by the earnest members of work-parties and such Christian activities who, having provided a titbit such as a rumoured bankruptcy among the flock, expect to be offered a decently-sized and tolerably luscious titbit in return. 'Church' had placed her, and since she was most certainly not over-popular, her fellow-worshippers would be all the more ready to talk about her.

As Grant's eyes closed in sleep, he was deciding whom to send to investigate Mrs Everett.

CHAPTER 10

THE BURST TO THE NORTH

'Simpson,' said Grant, 'what were you yesterday when you were gathering information about the Ratcliffes?'

'I was an ex-service man with writing-pads, sir.'

'Oh, well, you can be an ex-service man again today. Very self-respecting, clean, with a collar, not a muffler, and out of a job. I want to know about a Mrs Everett who lives at ninety-eight Brightling Crescent, off the Fulham Road. I don't want any door-to-door business. She's shy of that, and you must be very careful. She looks as if she attends church. Try that. I think you should find it useful. Bar a club, it's the gossipiest community I know of. I want to know, above all, where her friends and relations live. Never mind her correspondence. I can keep an eye on that myself, and, in any case, I have an idea that that isn't likely to be useful. Mrs Everett was not born yesterday. Get that into your head and remember it. Don't work faster than you can with safety. If she spots you, it will mean that someone else will have to take over, and a promising line of investigation will be spoiled. The minute you get something, let me know, but don't come back here until you've talked to me on the telephone first.'

That was how Mr Caldicott, the clergyman of the Brightlingside Congregational Church, pushing damply at the mower which jibbed at the tough grass of his front lawn and finding the March sun too prodigal of its blessing, became aware that his labours were being viewed by a stranger with a queer mixture of sympathy and envy.

Seeing that he had been discovered, the stranger made a sketchy motion towards his cap, in deference evidently to the cloth, and said, 'That's hot work on a day like this, sir. Will you let me take a hand?'

Now the clergyman was young and very fond of showing that he was not above a good day's work. 'Do you think I'm not able to do a job like that myself?' he asked, with a strong, brotherly smile.

'Oh no, sir. It isn't that at all. It's only that I'd be very glad to earn a copper or two for doing it for you.'

'Oh?' said Mr Caldicott, his professional instincts aroused. 'Are you looking for work?'

'That's about it,' said the man.

'Married?'

'No, sir.' Simpson was about to add a pious thanksgiving, but stopped himself in time.

'What kind of work are you looking for?'

'Anything.'

'Yes, but have you a trade?'

'I can make shoes, sir,' said Simpson, thinking he might as well stick to the truth as far as it served him.

'Well, perhaps it *would* be more sensible if you did the grass and I attended to other duties. Come in and have lunch with me at one o'clock.'

But that was not at all what Simpson wanted. The kitchen was his objective, not the parsonical conversation of the dining-room. With a masterly confusion he turned hesitatingly from the mower on which he had already laid zealous hands, and stammered, 'If it's all the same to you, sir, I'd rather have a bite in the kitchen. You see – I'm not used to the other kind.'

'Come, come,' began Mr Caldicott in brotherly rallying, and Simpson, fearful that his chance of precious gossip was going to be taken from him, could have hit the reverend gentleman.

'*Please*, sir, if you don't mind—' he said, with such

a wealth of conviction in his tone that the clergyman gave way.

'Well, well,' he said half-testily – had he not exhibited broad-mindedness and the true spirit of brotherhood and had them discounted? – 'if you really would prefer it.' He went away, but before very long he came back, and under pretext of hearing Simpson's history – he catalogued his visitor in a completely unbrotherly fashion as a very respectable fellow – he remained on the pathway until lunch-time, gossiping cheerfully about the things that interested him. He talked about the War – he had been a C.F. at Rouen – about seedlings, and London soot, and shoe-leather – this last as being of possible interest to his listener – and the difficulty he experienced in getting young men to come to church. When Simpson found that his last sermon had proved conclusively that God disapproved of betting, and that those who betted committed a sin against themselves, against their neighbour, and against God, he was not particularly surprised at the paucity of Mr Caldicott's youthful following.

'Now you are young,' Mr Caldicott said. 'Can you tell me why young men do not like church?' But Simpson had no intention of leaving the clergyman's house before evening if he could help it, so he refrained from instructing him, and merely shook his head sadly to indicate mournful disapproval. A consciousness of the weekly half-crown that went to enrich the bookmakers instead of the managers of the local Empire made him attack his work with a new zeal, but he was glad when a gong sounded in the house and the clergyman dismissed him with his blessing to the back regions. More than any meal to Simpson was the pursuit of the game he was engaged in.

The clergyman – who, he learned, was a most eligible bachelor – had two maids: a cook-housekeeper and a 'help,' who looked just like every stage and cinema Tweeny. They were delighted to welcome such a presentable male to their board, and in the hour that he took to his meal, Simpson learned more of lower-class suburbia than he had known in a whole lifetime spent among it. But beyond hearing that Mrs Everett was a stuck-up widow who gave herself airs because her father had been a clergyman, he learned nothing that he wanted to know. When he asked if her father had been clergyman here, they said oh no, that it had been somewhere in the North. Some one-horse place, he might be sure. Mrs Everett went to all the church meetings and things, the cook opined, not because she was keen on church, but just to keep everyone in mind that her father had been a clergyman. Revolving this really striking elucidation of human motive, Simpson went back to the garden to resume the mowing which was very nearly finished, and presently the clergyman joined him again. They were having a social meeting in the church hall that evening – would Simpson care to come? Simpson thanked him, and said with sincerity that he would be delighted. In that case there were chairs and such impedimenta to be carried from the church into the church hall – would Simpson like to help with them? If he went down after tea, he would find the ladies' committee preparing for the event. A ladies' committee was the thing above all that Simpson wanted to meet at the moment, and he again expressed his complete willingness, and the clergyman departed.

After an afternoon of border-trimming and gossiping alternately with the cook and the 'help,' who invented excuses to come and talk to him without apparently caring whether he believed the excuses or not, and a kitchen tea which, though more productive than the previous day's one in Lemonora Road, lacked the spice provided by his colleague's presence, Simpson betook himself to the church. The church he had already located – a red-brick building of a hideousness so complete that it was difficult to believe that it was accidental. The yellowish-brown and ultramarine blue of the stained-glass windows was now decently shrouded by the kindly dusk, but evening had its own horror in the brightly lit church hall, where two or three women were rushing about in the aimless, excited fashion of hens, talking much and achieving little, since none of their number did a thing without one of the others suggesting an amendment, which resulted in the committee immediately going into session. Their debates were protracted beyond the limits of an ordinary man's patience by their constant and insincere deferrings to each other, and after Simpson had watched them from the door for a little, very much as he had watched Mr Caldicott's efforts with a lawn-mower; he came slowly forward, cap in hand, and called attention to himself. 'Are you looking for someone?' one of them said, and he explained that Mr Caldicott had sent him down to assist. He was an immediate success. In fact, he was so sought-after that he began to feel inordinately pleased with himself – a state of mind which has no business in a member of the Criminal Investigation Department, and which died a sudden death when later in the evening he met his rivals. Reporting them afterwards *in camera* to Mullins, he used a picturesqueness of phrase which I regret I cannot reproduce, but which left no doubt in Mullins' mind as to the type of men who had attended that 'social.' Altogether Simpson was rather bitter about that evening, though why he should have been, I cannot fathom. His red-fair hair and freckles were his passport to happiness – no one could resist them; the pink wash that adorned the walls – it was raspberry, with a touch of cochineal – did not presumably hurt him as it might have hurt more sensitive souls; he was by far the most popular male present; and the information he had come to seek was lying about in chunks waiting to be picked up. But the fact remains that, when the play was all over and Mullins said to him, 'The boss is pleased with you about Brightling Crescent,' Simpson's pleasant face twisted in a sneer that did not go with red hair and freckles, and he snarled, yes snarled, 'Well, I sweated for it!'

The 'social' broke up at the eminently respectable hour of nine-forty-five, and Simpson once more helped the committee to play the game of robbing Peter to pay Paul, and then 'saw home' the most gossiping of the females who had been nice to him. So that it was the following morning that Grant interviewed him and heard all that was to be known of Mrs Everett.

Mrs Everett was Scotch. Her lack of accent was explained by the fact that she had been for twenty-five years in London, and that initially she came from the West Coast. Her father had been the minister of a Wee Free church in a village on the west coast of Ross, and now her brother was a minister there. Her name was Logan. She had been a widow for fifteen years and had no children. She was not very popular because she kept herself to herself, but she was greatly respected. Not even the fact that she let her rooms to two bookmakers had been sufficient to degrade her in the eyes of the Brightlingside Congregational Church. Sorrell had gone to her on coming out of the Army, and he had not been a bookmaker then, so perhaps she was absolved from any charge of deliberately choosing depravity as a boarder. The two men had not been known personally to any of the church community. They had been regarded from afar, Grant understood, as moral lepers without equal, but the subject of them seemed to have that never-palling attraction that thorough-paced wickedness has for virtue, and no detail of their lives was hidden from people whom the two men had quite certainly not known by sight. The two men, as Mrs Everett had said – Mrs Everett, Grant thought, would not lie about something that could be verified! – went everywhere together. Neither had had a 'girl.' They were both very smart according to Brightlingside standards, and Mrs Everett waited hand-and-foot on them. Mrs Everett had no relations in London that anyone knew of, but once a year usually she went to Scotland, and if her boarders

happened not to be away, engaged and paid someone to
look after them.

When Simpson had taken his burnished presence out of
the room, Grant sent for the men who had been on duty
at King's Cross and Euston on Monday night, and asked
them to describe the suspects they had examined. At the
King's Cross man's tale of a young man with his mother,
he halted. 'Describe the mother,' he said, and the man did,
quite accurately.

'Were there no other possibles on that train?'

Oh yes, the man said, several. He inferred bitterly that
the original home of thin, dark men with high cheek-bones
must be the north of Scotland. They swarmed on all
north-bound trains.

'What made you think he wasn't the man you wanted?'

'His manner, sir. And the woman's. And his case was on
the rack, with the initials, outside for anyone to see – G. L.
And he had a golf-bag, and altogether looked too casual.'

Well done, Mrs Everett! thought Grant. It wasn't the
man who left the notes in the drawer who thought of the
golf-bag. He wondered if leaving the case like that had been
deliberate. He could hardly credit that anyone would risk
unnecessarily the whole success of the thing on such an
enormous bluff. It was probably accident.

Where was he going.?

There were no labels on his luggage, but the ticket
collector had said he was going to Edinburgh.

It did not take Grant long to find out Lamont's probable
destination. There were not many Logans in the Church of
Scotland, and only one had a church in Ross-shire. He was
minister of the United Free church in Carninnish – having
evidently ratted from the stern faith of his fathers – and
Carninnish was a village at the head of a loch on the west
coast of the county.

Grant went in to Barker and said, 'I'm going fishing in
Scotland for a day or two.'

'There are more comfortable places than Scotland for hiding your diminished head,' said Barker, who knew all about the arrest that had side-slipped.

'May be, but the fishing isn't so good. That's my approximate address. Two days will do me, I expect.'

'Taking anyone along?'

'No.'

'I think you'd better. Think for a moment what a Highland rural policeman is like.'

'He can always kill the fish by falling on it – but I don't think it will come to that. I may want someone to take the fish to London, though.'

'All right. When are you going?'

'I'm going with the seven-thirty from King's Cross tonight, and I'll be in Inverness before ten tomorrow morning. After that I'll advise you.'

'Right!' said Barker. 'Good fishing! Don't get stuck on your own hooks.'

Grant spent a considerable time arranging for the prosecution of the search in his absence. He had no guarantee that the man who had gone to Carninnish was Lamont. He was going after the suspect himself because he was the only man among the searchers who had actually set eyes on the Dago. But the search in London would go on as usual. The whole departure for Carninnish might be a huge bluff. Grant had a great respect for Mrs Everett.

As he was getting his fishing tackle together and looking out his old clothes, Mrs Field came in with sandwiches and commiseration, neither of which Grant felt to be appropriate. He refused the former on the ground that he would have a very good dinner on the train and a very good breakfast, again on the train, in the morning.

'Yes,' she said; 'that's all very well, but look at the long night there'll be. You never know the minute you'll waken up hungry and be glad of the sandwiches even if it's only to pass the time. They're chicken, and you don't know when you'll have chicken again. It's a terribly poor country, Scotland. Goodness only knows what you'll get to eat!'

Grant said that Scotland nowadays was very like the rest of Britain, only more beautiful.

'I don't know anything about beauty,' said Mrs Field, putting the sandwiches resolutely away in the rug-strap, 'but I do know that a cousin of mine was in service there once – she went for the season with her people from London – and there wasn't a house to be seen in the whole countryside but their own, and not a tree. And the natives had never heard of teacakes, and called scones "skons."'

'How barbaric!' said Grant, folding his most ancient tweed lovingly away in his case.

As the train steamed out of King's Cross he settled down to the study of a one-inch survey map of the Carninnish district. It gave him a pleasant feeling to be studying a map again. There was quite a distinctive thrill in hunting your man in open country. It was more primitive and more human, less mechanised than the soulless machinery that stretched and relaxed noiseless steel tentacles on Thames bank. It was man against man. There would be a telephone only where there was a post office. And there would be no calling out of reserves to head off anyone making a break for it. It was your wit against his – perhaps your gun against his. But Grant hoped that it would not come to that. There would be little satisfaction in bringing a dead man to justice. And the police, in any case, do not look with favour on summary methods in their detectives. He would have to go about it quietly. After all, he was only two days behind the fair. The man could not have arrived at his destination before last night. The longer he had to settle down in, the less suspicious he would become. At first every boulder would hide a detective for him, but as he grew used to the country – and Grant knew the type of country – its complete severance from any outside interests would have its inevitable effect of giving him a false sense of security.

Grant studied the map. The village of Carninnish lay along the south bank of a river – the Finley – where the river joined the sea in Loch Finley. About four miles to the south, a second loch ran into the land, and on the north shore of it was a village slightly larger apparently than Carninnish, called Garnie. That is, Carninnish lay on the north side of a peninsula and Garnie on the south, the distance between them over the peninsula being about four miles by a hilly and third-class road. Grant decided that he would stay at Garnie – there was an hotel there which he knew from hearsay contained a bath – and from there he would keep an eye on Carninnish under pretence of fishing the Finley. Until late at night he pored over the map, until the country grew as familiar to him as if he had known it. He knew from bitter experience that the very best map-reader had to suffer some severe shocks when he comes face to face with reality, but he had the comfortable knowledge that he now knew the district probably much better than the man he was hunting.

And morning brought him nothing but exhilaration. As he opened his eyes on the daylight, through the open chink at the top of his window he could see the brown moors sliding slowly past, and the chug-chug of the hitherto racing train told of its conquest of the Grampians. A clear, cold air that sparkled, greeted him as he dressed, and over breakfast he watched the brown barrenness with its back-ground of vivid sky and dazzling snow change to pine forest – flat black slabs stuck mathematically on the hillsides like patches of woolwork – and then to birches; birches that stepped down the mountain-sides as escort for some stream, or birches that trailed their light draperies of an unbelievable new green in little woods carpeted with fine turf. And so with a rush, as the train took heart on the down grade, to fields again – wide fields in broad straths and little stony fields

tacked to hillsides – and lochs, and rivers, and a green
countryside. He wondered, standing in the corridor as the
train rattled and swerved and swung in its last triumphant
down-rush to Inverness, what the fugitive had thought of
it all – the Londoner torn from his streets, and the security
of buildings and bolt-holes. Sundays on the river would not
have prepared him for the black torrents that waited him in
the west, nor the freedom of a Surrey common for the utter
unnerving desolation of those moors. Had he regretted his
flight? He wondered what the man's temperament was. He
had been the bright and cheerful one – at least, according
to Mrs Everett. Was he anything more than bright and
cheerful? He had cared sufficiently for something to stab a
man in the back for it, but that did not argue sensitiveness.
To a sensitive man, the horror of being alone and helpless
and hunted in a country like this would probably be worse
than a cell of familiar bricks and mortar. In the old days
in the Highlands, to take to the hills had been synonymous
with flying from justice – what the Irish call being on the
run. But civilisation had changed that completely. Not one
criminal in a thousand now fled to the Highlands or to
Wales for refuge. A man demanded the means of food and
shelter in his retreat nowadays, and a deserted bothy or a
cave on the hillside were out of date. If it had not been
for Mrs Everett's promise of sanctuary, not even her will
would have got Lamont out of London – Grant felt sure
of that. What had Lamont felt when he saw what he had
come to?

At Inverness he left the comfort of the through train
and crossed the wind-swept platform into a little local
affair that for the rest of the morning trundled from the
green countryside back into a brown desolation such as
had greeted Grant on waking. West and still farther west
they trailed, stopping inexplicably at stations set down
equally inexplicably in the middle of vast moors devoid of
human habitation, until in the afternoon he was bundled

out on to a sandy platform, and the train went away into the desolation without him. Here, he was told, he took the mailcar. It was thirty-six miles to Carninnish, and with any luck he'd be there by eight the night. It would all depend on how many things they met on the road. It wasn't but a fortnight back that Andy had had the right wheel in the front taken clean off of him by another motor-car, and him with the left wheel half into the ditch and all. Grant was led through a booking-office, and in the gravelled space behind the station beheld the contraption in which he was to spend the next five hours, and which would, with luck on the road, duly deposit him in Garnie. It was quite literally a charabanc. Behind the driving-seat were three benches, their penitential qualities inadequately mitigated by cushions, stuffed, apparently, with sawdust and covered in American cloth. There were, amazing as it seemed to him, five other candidates for seats on this conveyance. Grant made inquiries about hiring a car to do the journey, and the expressions on the faces of his audience conveyed to him not only the futility of his quest, but the fact that he had been guilty of a grave error of taste. One did not scorn the mail-car. It was the one significant thing in each day to the dwellers in the thirty-six miles between him and the sea. Grant resigned himself to discomfort, and hoped that comedy would save the journey from boredom. So far comedy had been absent from him. He bagged a seat by the driver and hoped for the best.

As they went along the narrow roads, torn here and there where burns had swept across them in their downward path in spate from the hills, he realised the force of the man's remark about meeting things. There was no room in most places for even a perambulator to pass.

'How do you manage when you meet something?' he asked the driver.

'Well, sometimes we back – and sometimes they back,' he said. After about five miles Grant saw this new rule of

the road demonstrated when they came face to face with a
traction-engine. It was a diminutive specimen of its kind,
but formidable enough in the circumstances. On one side
was the hill, and on the other a small rocky ravine. With
the greatest good humour the driver reversed, and backed
his unwieldy vehicle until he could run it into the bank
in a siding for road metal. The traction-engine chuffed
complacently past, and the journey was resumed. In all
the thirty-six miles they met only two more obstacles,
both motors. In one case they grazed past by a mutual
withdrawing of skirts, the near wheel of the mail-car being
in a ditch and the near wheel of the other in a bank of
heather and boulders. In the other case the car proved to
be a Ford, and with the mongrel adaptability of its kind took
without parley to the moor, and with complete insouciance
swept bumping past the stationary mail-car what time the
drivers exchanged unintelligible greetings. This display of
amphibiousness seemed to astonish no one, and though the
car was now full to overflowing, no remark was made. It
was evidently a daily occurrence.

With the laden state of the car in his mind, Grant
wondered what would happen to the people along the road
who would have no means of travelling. The same fear had
occurred to a little old woman who had been waiting by
a roadside cottage for the car. As it slowed down and the
driver descended to her assistance she looked scaredly at
the crowded benches and said, 'How are you going to make
room, Andy?'

'Be quiet,' said Andy cheerfully; 'we never left anyone
yet.' 'Be quiet,' Grant learned, was not a reproof in this
country, and had nothing to do with its English meaning. It
was an expression of half-jocose refutal, and, on occasions,
of straightforward admiration tinged with disbelief. On
Andy's lips it meant that the old lady was what a Lowlander
would call 'haivering.' And certainly he was as good as his
word. Room was found, and no one seemed to suffer very

badly, unless it was the hens in the coop at the back, which had been rolled slightly sideways. But they were still vociferously alive when their proud owner, waiting at the head of a track that led apparently nowhere, claimed them and bore them away in a wheelbarrow.

Several miles before Garnie, Grant smelt the sea – that seaweedy smell of the sea on an indented coast. It was strange to smell it so unpreparedly in such unsea-like surroundings. It was still more strange to come on it suddenly as a small green pool among the hills. Only the brown surge of the weed along the rocks proclaimed the fact that it was ocean and not moor loch. But as they swept into Garnie with all the éclat of the most important thing in twenty-four hours, the long line of Garnie sands lay bare in the evening light, a violet sea creaming gently on their silver placidity. The car decanted him at the flagged doorway of his hostelry, but, hungry as he was, he lingered in the door to watch the light die beyond the flat purple outline of the islands to the west. The stillness was full of the clear, faraway sounds of evening. The air smelt of peat smoke and the sea. The first lights of the village shone daffodil-clear here and there. The sea grew lavender, and the sands became a pale shimmer in the dusk.

And he had come here to arrest a man who had committed murder in a London queue!

CHAPTER 11

CARNINNISH

Grant had got little information from Andy, the mail-car driver, not because the driver was ignorant – after all, he had presumably driven Lamont these thirty-six miles over the hills only two days before – but because Andy's desire to find out all about himself was, surprisingly enough, just as strong as his to find out about Lamont, and he brushed aside Grant's most hopeful leads with a monosyllable or a movement of his head, and produced instead leads of his own. It was a game that soon palled, and Grant had given him up long before he had resigned himself to knowing no more of Grant. And now the landlord of the Garnie Hotel, interviewed in the porch after breakfast, proved equally unhelpful, this time through genuine ignorance. Where the mail-driver would have been intensely interested in whatever happened at Carninnish, which was his home and his resting-place each night, the landlord was interested only in Garnie, and in Garnie only as it affected his hotel.

'Come for some fishing, sir?' he said, and Grant said yes, that he had thoughts of fishing the Finley if that were possible.

'Yes,' the man said; 'that's just four mile at the back of the hill beyond. Perhaps you'll know the country?' Grant thought it best to disclaim any knowledge of the district. 'Well, there's a wee village the other side, on Loch Finley, but you're better here. It's a wee poky place of an hotel they have there, and they have nothing but mutton to eat.' Grant said they might do worse. 'Yes, you'd think that the first day, and maybe the second, but by the end of a week the sight of a sheep on the hill'd be too much for you. We can send you over in the Ford every day if you're not fond of walking. You'll have a permit, I suppose?' Grant said that he had thought there would be some water belonging to the hotel. 'No; all that water belongs to the gentleman who has Carninnish House. He is a Glasgow stockbroker. Yes, he's here – at least he came a week ago, if he's not gone again.'

'Well, if I can have the Ford now, I'll go over and see him.' Fishing was the only excuse which would allow him to wander the country without remark. 'What did you say his name was?' he asked, as he stepped into a battered Ford alongside a hirsute jehu with a glaring eye.

'He's a Mr Drysdale,' the landlord said. 'He's not over-generous with the water, but perhaps you'll manage it.' With which cold comfort Grant set off on a still colder drive over the hills to the Finley valley.

'Where is the house?' he asked the hirsute one, whose name he learned was Roddy, as they went along.

'At Carninnish.'

'Do you mean right in the village?' Grant had no intention of making so public an appearance at this early date.

'No; it's the other side of the river from the village.'

'We don't go through the village?'

'No; the bridge is before you come to the village at all.'

As they came to the edge of the divide the whole new valley opened map-like before Grant's fascinated gaze several hundreds of feet below. There were no fields, no green at all except on the border of the river that ran, a silver thread, through scattered birch to the distant sea-loch. It was a brown country, and the intensity of the sea's blue gave it a foreign air – faery lands forlorn, with a vengeance, Grant thought. As they ran seawards down the side of the hill he noticed two churches, and took his opportunity.

'You have enough churches for the size of the village.'

'Well,' said Roddy, 'you couldn't be expecting the Wee

Frees to go to the U.F. That's the U.F. down there –
Mr Logan's.' He pointed down to the right over the edge
of the road, where a bald church and a solid four-square
manse sheltered in some trees by the river. 'The Wee Free
is away at the other end of the village, by the sea.'

Grant looked interestedly out of the corner of his eyes
at the comfortable-looking house that sheltered his quarry.
'Nice place,' he said. 'Do they take boarders?'

No, Roddy thought not. They let the house for a month in
the summer. The minister was a bachelor, and his widowed
sister, a Mrs Dinmont, kept house for him. And his niece,
Mrs Dinmont's daughter, was home for holidays just now.
She was a nurse in London.

No word of another inmate, and he could not pursue
the subject without making the always curious Highlander
suspicious. 'Many people at the hotel here?'

'Three,' said Roddy. As befitted the retainer of a rival
concern there was nothing he did not know about the inn
at Carninnish. But though all three were men, none of them
was Lamont. Roddy had the history and predilections of all
of them at his fingertips.

Carninnish House lay on the opposite side of the river
from the village, close to the sea, with the high road to
the north at its back. 'You'd better wait,' Grant said, as
Roddy pulled up before the door; and with what dignity
Roddy's method of coming to a halt had left him, he
descended on to the doorstep. In the hall was a lean, rather
sour-looking man in good tweeds. The stockbroker's got a
party, thought Grant. He had quite unconsciously pictured
the stockbroking gentleman as round and pink and too tight
about the trouser-legs. It was therefore rather a shock when
the lean man came forward and said, 'Can I do anything
for you?'

'I wanted to see Mr Drysdale.'

'Come in,' said the man, and led him into a room
littered with fishing-tackle. Now Grant had intended quite

shamelessly to try sob-stuff on the broker of his imagination, appealing to his generosity not to spoil his holiday; but the sight of the real man made him change his mind. He took out his professional card, and was gratified at the man's surprise. It was a compliment to the perfection of the disguise which his old fishing clothes afforded.

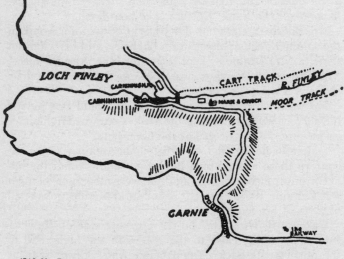

'Well, Inspector, what can I do for you?'

'I want you to be good enough to let me fish in the Finley for a little. Two days at most, I think. I think a man I want is in this neighbourhood, and the only way I can go about without attracting notice is to fish. I thought the hotel at Garnie would have some fishing of their own, but it appears they haven't. I won't catch any fish, but I have fished a good deal, and I won't frighten everything in the river.'

To his surprise a smile had come over the dour face of Mr Drysdale. 'Inspector,' he said, 'I don't think you can have any idea how unique this occasion is, how utterly unique you are. Even in the "forty-five" they didn't come here looking for anyone, and no one, certainly, has done it since. It's simply incredible. A criminal in Carninnish, and a C.I.D. inspector looking for him! Why, drunk and incapable is the most horrible crime that this neighbourhood has known since the flood.'

'Perhaps my man thought of that,' said the inspector dryly. 'Anyhow, I promise I shan't bother you long if you give me the permission to fish.'

'Certainly you can fish. Anywhere you like. I'm going up the river now. Would you care to come with me, and I'll introduce you to the best pools? You might as well have a decent day's fishing if you're going to fish at all. Send that madman back to Garnie' – Roddy was giggling with a maid in high-pitched Gaelic outside the open window, quite indifferent to the probable proximity of 'the gentlemen' – 'and tell him he needn't come back. I'll send you over in the evening whenever you want to go.'

Delighted at the unexpected graciousness on the part of the ill-favoured and reputedly ungenerous one, Grant dismissed Roddy, who received his congé with the grave respect of an A.D.C., but departed in a flurry of high unintelligible cackle flung between himself and the maid. It sounded like the protesting row of an alarmed hen as she rockets over a fence to safety. When the noises had died away, Drysdale began in silence to collect his tackle for the river. He asked no more questions, and Grant was again grateful to him. To break the silence which Drysdale had evidently no intention of breaking, he asked about the state of the river, and soon they were talking fishing with the freedom of two enthusiasts. They proceeded up the right bank of the river – that is, the opposite bank from the village and the manse – and Drysdale pointed out the pools and their peculiarities. The whole tawny, narrow, boulder-strewn river was not more than six miles long. It ran from a hill loch in an impetuous scramble, broken by still pools, to the sea at Carninnish.

'I expect you'd like to be near the village,' Drysdale said, and suggested that the inspector should be left the lower half of the river while he went up to the hill end, where he would probably spend the day; and to that Grant gratefully agreed. As they passed opposite the manse, Grant said, 'That the manse? Scotch clergymen seem to be very comfortable.'

'They are,' said Drysdale, with emphasis, but did not pursue the subject. Grant remarked on the apparent size of the house, and asked if they took boarders. It would be a good place to stay. Drysdale said that as far as he knew they did not take anyone and he repeated Roddy's tale of the summer letting. He took leave of Grant with the abruptness of a shy man, and departed into the landscape, leaving Grant with the comfortable knowledge that he had an ally after his own heart if the need for one should arise.

Grant decided that he would start fishing perhaps two hundred yards above the manse and work slowly down, taking his bearings and keeping an eye on the traffic to and from the house. On his side of the river there was a cart-track that was almost a road, but on the other side there was, as far as he could see, only the path like a sheep-track made by the feet of fishermen and gillies, so that anyone coming up-river would come on his side. The manse was surrounded by a stone wall, and faced away from him towards the high-road on the other side of the river. Inside the wall was a row of scraggy firs which effectually hid the detail of the house. Only gleams of whitewash and its eight chimneys advertised its presence. At the back the garden wall ran down to the river bank, and in the middle of the wall flanking the river was a small iron gate of the strictly utilitarian pattern popular in the Highlands. Though he could not see the high-road immediately in front of the house he had an uninterrupted view of the road on either side. No one could come or go from the house without his being aware of it. And he could stay where he was all day unquestioned and unremarkable. It was an ideal situation. Grant sent the first cast hissing over the brown shining water and felt that life was good. It was too sunny for fishing, and his prospects of catching anything were meagre in the extreme; but a bigger catch lay to his hand. No one had mentioned that a stranger had arrived at the manse, but just as he had known on the Brixton stair-landing that the rooms were empty, Grant now had a feeling that his man was here.

It was eleven before he began to fish, and for an hour or more no human activity other than his own broke the perfect peace of the morning. The two chimneys of the manse continued to smoke lazily into the bright air. The river babbled its eternal nursery-rhyme song at his feet, and the water slid under his eyes with a mesmeric swiftness. Away to his right beyond the distant bridge the whitewashed houses by the shore showed over the slight rise of the moor, placid and sunlit as a stage setting. Grant began to feel that the whole thing was a picture, like the illustration from which he had first learned French in his youth, and that he was merely stuck down there by the river so that the picture might be complete. He was not Grant of the C.I.D.; he was *pêcheur*, to be pointed at with a wooden wand that tickled, for the education of someone unknown. A postman coming from the village, leaning heavily and alternately on the pedals of a push-bike, broke the spell. It was still a picture, but he no longer belonged to it. It was a stage setting – one of the tiny exhibition ones – and he was the giant who was going to upset the whole box of tricks. And, even as he thought it, the iron gate in the low wall of the manse swung open, and a girl came out, followed by a man. They shut the gate with difficulty and some laughter, and turned in single file down the footpath towards the bridge. Grant was still nearly a hundred yards above the house, and neither of them had noticed him. The man was dressed in flannel trousers, an old trench coat, and

a cap, and, except for his slightness, was as unlike the figure
that had flung itself into the maelstrom of the Strand traffic
as might well be. Grant was conscious of slight surprise.
Revolving the matter during his long journey north, he had
taken for granted that the man would look out of place. A
London bookmaker's clerk would not be thrown into the
western Highlands at a moment's notice and look like an
habitué. Well, it might not be the man, after all. He hoped
that they were making for the bridge and his side of the
river, and not for the village. Surely if they had set out for
the village, they would have gone out by the front way and
walked along the high road?

He watched in suspense until he saw the girl turn to
the bridge. But there was still a chance that they were
going straight on by the high-road past Carninnish House.
Grant expelled a thankful breath as once more the girl
turned riverwards and her companion joined her. They
were coming up the river to him. They would pass only
a few yards at his back. Industriously he flung a gleaming
cast to the far side of the pool. He must not look their way
again. In a minute or two they would have spotted him.
He felt grateful to the ancient hat that collapsed more than
drooped over his face, and to the shapeless garments that
clothed him. His boots, too, were convincing even to the
most suspicious eye. It had been no case of dressing the
part this time; he was the genuine article, and he was glad
of it. There would be no amateurish cast to attract the
practised eye of Miss Dinmont – it must be Miss Dinmont.
No suggestion of 'towniness' about his clothes to call forth
comment and her partner's instant interest.

Suddenly above the swirl of the water he could hear their
voices, raised because of the river's accompaniment. They
were still laughing and animated, and apparently very good
friends. Grant did not look round as they passed, nor did
he look round immediately they had passed. If he glanced
round now, a curious look from the man would have found

his face revealed. But as they retreated up-river he watched them. Was it Lamont? He tried to picture the man's walk again. Short of developing a limp, it is almost impossible to disguise a walk successfully. But he could not be sure. And then the man looked back suddenly. Grant was too far away to see his face, but the movement told him all he wanted to know. It was so vivid that, before his reason had time to note it, his mind was back at the bottom of Bedford Street. There was no doubt of it – the man was Lamont. Grant's heart sang. Had Lamont known him? He thought not. How could he? It was mere bad conscience that had made him turn. If he asked Miss Dinmont about him, he would hear that no one who was not staying at Carninnish House was allowed to fish the water, and he would be reassured.

And now what? Go to the house when he returned and arrest him straight away? He had the warrant in his pocket. But suddenly he wanted to be assured – assured beyond the possibility of doubt – that Lamont was the man who had murdered Sorrell. They knew that he was the man who had quarrelled with Sorrell before his death. But that was not proof. The link that connected him with the knife was still missing. Before he would risk executing the warrant he wanted to find out if Lamont's left hand bore the scar made by the knife. If it did not, then his case fell to pieces. However certain he himself might be, there must be no gaps in the evidence that would be put before a jury, and as long as there was a possible gap in the evidence, Grant had no intention of arresting anyone. He must get himself invited to the manse. It should not be difficult. If all else failed, he could fall into the river and appeal to them to dry him.

He was eating the sandwiches provided by the Garnie Hotel, on a boulder half in and half out of the water, when the couple came back. They went swinging past him down to the bridge and into the village, and presently he saw them reappear and come back to the manse by the high-road. It was lunch-time. They were safely occupied for an hour at least, and directly under his eye.

He was carefully wrapping up the remaining sandwiches against a lean time to come, when the local policeman appeared from up-river pushing a punctured push-bicycle. He slowed down when he saw Grant – if his previous leisurely progress could admit of any retarding without bringing him to a stop – and as Grant looked up, the last semblance of progression ceased.

'Having any luck, sir?' asked the policeman. He had a face like a very pink waxwork, round and devoid of expression, and one glance at him made Grant thankful for the discovery of Drysdale. His pale blue eyes were fringed like a doll's, with fine black lashes, and an unconvincing moustache of silky black made a line on his upper lip. His fat, soft body could neither hurry nor take cover; that slow brain would be of no use whatever in an emergency.

Grant admitted that he had caught nothing, but added that he had hardly expected to on such a bright morning

'Yes, that's so,' said the man; 'but it won't be long like that. There's never a day but there's some rain here. You'll catch a fish before night.'

Grant recognised this as the Highlander's usual desire to say the thing he thinks will be acceptable to his hearer. 'You haven't had the best of luck yourself,' he said, indicating the tyre.

'Indeed, I have not. These ro'ds are the very ruin on tyres. Not but that I get an allowance for them, you know, but there's others isn't so lucky. Mr Logan, the minister' – he jerked his head over at the manse – 'was just saying to me the other day that ministers should have a tyre allowance as well as the pollis. He had three tyres of his car punctured in one week. It would put even a minister in a temper.'

'Are there many motors in Carninnish?'

'Well, Mr Drysdale has two, as I expect you know, and

Mr Logan has one, but that's all. The other minister has a side-car.'

But when someone wanted to hire, what did they do?

Oh, as to that, the hotel had a Ford for visitors. They hired out that when they weren't needing it themselves. A Ford in the constable's opinion evidently did not come under the heading 'cars'.

Presently the constable said, 'There's Mr Logan away to see the new twins east at Arkless,' and Grant saw a rather heavy figure appear on the high-road on the Garnie side of the manse and proceed up-river at a business-like pace.

'I thought that road led only over the hill to Garnie,' Grant said.

'Oh yes, the high-road. But where the high-road begins to go up the hill there's a track goes off along the river to the crofts you can see from the ro'd. That's where he's going evernow, Mr Logan. And that's why he's walking. He's not very fond of walking.'

The constable stayed for a long time quite contentedly watching Grant fish, evidently glad to find interest for his eyes in a spot usually vacant, and Grant revolved the problem of what he would do if the Logan car appeared suddenly on the high-road beyond the manse, bound for Garnie and the south. He would have no guarantee that Lamont was the passenger. It was too far away to identify anyone. He would have to make certain of that before he did anything. And then it would be a choice between getting busy on a telephone or giving chase. The hotel Ford, he supposed. Or perhaps Drysdale would lend his car? But the afternoon wore on, the light took that white, hard unsympathetic look that it does about four o'clock, the constable trundled his bicycle away to the village where he could procure the patching materials which he had evidently forgotten, and still no one came from the manse. At five o'clock Grant ate his remaining sandwiches, and began to consider what other possibilities there were of cadging an entrance to the manse. The thought of a dip in the river – even if it was only a momentary one – became less and less pleasant as the evening wore on. His thoughts were interrupted and his difficulties miraculously solved by heavy footsteps behind him. He looked round to see Mr Logan at his back.

The minister gave him a hearty good evening, and his heavy red face with its hooked nose beamed benevolently. 'It doesn't look as if you have had much luck,' he said.

No, Grant said; he had been at it for a whole day, and had had nothing. They would laugh at him when he got back to Garnie.

'Oh, you're not staying at Carninnish House?'

No, Grant said; he was staying at the hotel at Garnie, but Mr Drysdale had very kindly given him permission to fish the Finley for a day or two.

'Are the Garnie people sending for you?'

No, Grant said; he had intended to walk back when he was tired of fishing. It was only four miles or so, and any fish he caught would, of course, be left with Mr Drysdale.

'It's very cold work, and disheartening when you've got nothing,' said the minister. 'Won't you come in and have a hot cup of tea at the manse? My name is Logan. Tea is between half-past five and six, and it should be ready now.'

Grant thanked him, and tried not to show an indecent degree of joy at the invitation. Fate was playing into his hands. Once inside the manse and it would be for him to call the tune. It was difficult not to bundle his things together, grab the minister by the arm, and run him the half-mile down the river and back to the house. As it was, he packed up with extra deliberation, dawdled at the minister's pace, which had slackened considerably since the early afternoon, down the track, across the bridge, and along the high-road to the front of the manse. As the minister led him down the broad path, cut in stretches of grass to the door, Grant's heart quickened perceptibly, and for once he did not smile at himself for a weakness. Ten days ago Barker had handed over this case to him, and he had been presented with a handkerchief, a revolver, and a bloodstained knife. Now, at the other end of the kingdom, he was about to come face to face with the man he wanted.

They divested themselves of their coats and hats in the hall, and Grant could hear through the closed door the chatter and clink of people at tea. Then Mr Logan stepped over to the door and preceded him into the room.

CHAPTER 12

CAPTURE

It was a dining-room, and there were three people having tea at the table: an elderly woman with a faint resemblance to Mrs Everett, a girl with reddish hair and a pale skin, and the Dago. Grant had time to note them all from behind the minister's bulk before his host's making way for him brought him into their view, and he had the exquisite pleasure of seeing his quarry recognise him. For a second Lamont's eyes widened at him, then the blood rushed to his face and as suddenly receded, leaving it deathly pale. The looker-on in Grant thought how Danny Miller would have sneered at such an exhibition – Danny, who would kill a man and not bother to remember it. The Dago was certainly an amateur at the game – a murderer by accident more than design, perhaps.

'I have brought you a visitor,' the minister was saying. 'This is Mr Grant. I found him fishing, but catching nothing, so I brought him in to get some hot tea. My sister, Mrs Dinmont, My niece, Miss Dinmont. And a friend of ours, Mr Lowe. Now, where will you sit?'

Grant was given a seat beside Miss Dinmont and facing Lamont. Lamont had bowed to him when introduced, but so far gave no sign of ill-meditated action. Either he was paralysed or he was going to take things quietly. And then as he sat down Grant saw the thing that made his heart leap. Lamont's cup was on the wrong side of his plate. The man was left-handed.

'I am so glad you didn't wait, Agnes,' Mr Logan said in a tone which clearly said, 'I think you might have waited.' 'It was such a fine evening that I crossed by the swing bridge and came home by the other side of the river.'

'Well, we're glad you did,' said his niece, 'because you've brought Mr Grant, and that makes an uneven number, and so we can put it to the vote. We've been having a fight as to whether a mixture of race in a person is a good thing or not. I don't mean black and white, but just different stocks of white. Mother says that a single-stock person is the best, of course, but that is because she is solid Highland, back to the flood and before. Logans are Maclennans, you know, and there never was a Maclennan who hadn't a boat of his own. But my father was a Borderer and my grandmother English, and Mr Lowe's grandmother was an Italian, so we are very firmly on the other side. Now, Uncle Robert is sure to side with Mother, being a pure-bred Highlander and having in a pure-bred degree all the stubbornness and stinking pride of his race. So we are looking to you for support. Do say that your ancestry is tartan.'

Grant said, quite honestly, that he thought a mixed strain of more value than a pure-bred one. That was, talking of pure-bred as it can exist today. It gave a man a many-sidedness instead of giving him a few qualities in excess, and that was a good thing. It tended to cleverness and versatility, and consequently broad-mindedness and wide sympathies. On the whole, he endorsed Miss Dinmont's and Mr – er – Lowe's point of view.

In view of the lightness of the conversation Grant was astonished at the vehemence and seriousness with which Mr Logan contradicted him. His race was a fetish with him, and he compared it at length with most of the other nations in Western Europe, to their extreme detriment. It was only towards the end of tea that Grant found, to his intense amusement, that Mr Logan had never been out of Scotland in his life. The despised Lowlanders he had met only during his training for the ministry some thirty years ago, and the other nations he had never known at all.

Frustrated in his effort – nobly seconded by Miss Dinmont
– to make light conversation, Grant played the part of a
Greek chorus to Mr Logan, and let his thoughts deal with
Lamont.

The Dago was beginning to look a little better. He met
Grant's eyes squarely, and except for the antagonism in his
own, there was nothing remarkable about him. He made
no attempt to hide the small scar on his thumb, though he
must have known, as he knew about his tell-tale cup, that it
was damning evidence. He had evidently decided that the
game was up. It remained to be seen, though, whether he
would come quietly when the time came. At least Grant
was glad to see that flicker of antagonism in his eyes. It is
an unlovely job to arrest a craven. A police officer would
much sooner be hacked on the shins than clasped about the
knees. There would quite obviously be no knee-clasping on
this occasion.

One thing caused Grant's heart to harden against the
man: the strides he seemed to have made in Miss Dinmont's
regard in the three days of his stay. Even yet his quick smile
came out to answer hers, and his eyes sought hers oftener
than those of anyone else at table. Miss Dinmont looked a
girl who would be quite able to take care of herself – she
had all a red-haired person's shrewdness and capability –
but that did not excuse Lamont's lack of decent feeling.
Had he merely been preparing an ally? A man on the
run for murder does not usually have the spare interest
for lovemaking – more especially if he is an amateur in
crime. It was a blatant and heartless piece of opportunism.
Well, he should have no chance of appealing to his ally;
Grant would see to that. Meanwhile he kept his place in
the conversation, and did justice to the fried trout which
was the *pièce de resistance* of five-thirty tea at the manse.
The Dago ate, too, and Grant caught himself wondering
what degree of effort was required to swallow each of these
mouthfuls. Did he care, or had he got past that? Was his

impudent 'Don't you think so Mr Grant?' a bluff or the real thing? His hands were quite steady – that thin, dark left hand that had put an end to his friend's life – and he did not shirk his part in the conversation. There was obviously to the others no difference between the man who sat there now and the man who had sat there at lunch. The Dago was doing it well.

At the end of tea, when they began to smoke, Grant offered Miss Dinmont a cigarette, and she raised her eyebrows in mock horror.

'My dear man,' she said, 'this is a Highland manse. If you like to come out and sit on a stone by the river, I'll have one, but not under this roof.'

The 'under this roof' was obviously a quotation, but her uncle pretended not to hear.

'There's nothing I'd like better,' Grant said, 'but it's getting late, and as I am walking to Garnie, I think I'd better start. I'm so grateful to you all for the good ending to my day. Perhaps Mr Lowe would walk a bit of the way with me? It's early yet and very fine.'

'Certainly,' said the Dago, and preceded him into the hall. Grant's adieux to his hostess were cut short by the fear that Lamont would have disappeared, but he found him in the hall calmly hoisting himself into the trench-coat he had worn that morning. And then Miss Dinmont came out to join her uncle, who was seeing them off the premises, and Grant had a sudden fear that she was going to offer to accompany them. Perhaps the resolute way in which Lamont kept his back turned to her daunted her a little. It would have been so natural for him to say, 'Won't you come along too?' But he said nothing. Kept his back turned though he knew she was there. That could only mean that he didn't want her, and the suggestion she had been on the point of making died on her lips. Grant breathed again. He had no desire for a scene with a hysterical female, if it could be avoided. At the gate both men turned to acknowledge

the presence of the two at the door. As Grant was replacing
his battered hat he saw Lamont's salutation. It was a mere
doffing his cap and donning it again, but Grant had not
known that any gesture could be so eloquent of farewell.

They walked in silence up the first slight ascent of road
until they were well out of sight of the house, at the parting
of the ways where the high-road went up the hill and the
track to the crofts branched off along the river. There Grant
halted and said, 'I think you know what I want you for,
Lamont?'

'What exactly do you mean?' asked Lamont, facing him
calmly.

'I am Inspector Grant from Scotland Yard, and I have a
warrant for your arrest for the murder of Albert Sorrell in
the Woffington queue on the night of the thirteenth. I must
warn you that anything you say may be used in evidence
against you. I want to see that you have nothing on you.
Will you take your hands out of your pockets a moment
and let me run you over?'

'You've made a mistake, Inspector,' the man said. 'I said
I'd go a bit of the way with you, but I didn't say how far.
This is where I get off.' His left hand shot out of his pocket,
and Grant, expecting a revolver, knocked his hand up as it
lifted, but, even as his eyes closed instinctively, he saw and
recognised the blue pepper-pot from the manse tea-table.
Helpless, half blind, coughing and sneezing, he heard the
man's flying feet on the moor-track, and desperately tried
to control himself so that he could hear the direction of the
retreating sounds. But it was at least two minutes before he
could see well enough to be able to follow. A remembrance
of that evening in the Strand came to him, and he decided to
take his time. No man, even as lightly built as the Dago was,
could run for more than a limited time. There was a radius
of possibility bounded by the circumference of exhaustion
point. And judging by the direction he had chosen, when
he reached that exhaustion point, the Dago would be in

a country that offered him little means of escape. And, of course, he would be shrewd enough to recognise that. Therefore, the more likely procedure would be that he should repeat the tactics of the Strand evening: lie hidden, probably till darkness made it safe to move, and then return to a better means of escape.

Well, Grant thought, the man who has the higher ground commands the situation. A few yards farther on, a small trickle of water came down the hill-side. The valley it made was not deep enough to afford him cover standing up, but, if he bent, it hid his progress up the hill-side from anyone farther along the moor-track. With as keen a scrutiny round him as his still smarting eyes would permit, he took to the small gully and, bent double, scrambled up it, stopping every few yards to make sure that nothing was in sight and that he himself was still in adequate cover. Farther up, the gully was bordered by stunted birch, and still farther up it ran through a small plateau thinly wooded with larger birch. Birch in its first mist of green is not ideal cover, but the plateau afforded a first-rate outlook, so Grant decided to risk it. Circumspectly he raised himself from the sandy bank of the stream to the fine turf of the plateau, and crawled across it to the fringe of thick heather that bordered a drop of several feet in the face of the hill-side. From this vantage he had the whole immediate sweep of the valley before him, with the exception of a slab to his right, which was hidden by one of the rectangular patches of firwood so typical of the country. The sight of the firwood reassured him. The firwood would be to Lamont what the door on the other side of Bedford Street had been. He had not the faintest doubt that Lamont was lying there now, waiting for him to declare himself on the road somewhere. What puzzled him was what Lamont thought was going to take the place of the buses and the taxis. What hope had he other than the darkness? And he must realise that, if he waited till dark, Grant would have given the

alarm. Already the light was beginning to go. Should he
abandon his hiding-place and give the alarm, or was that
the very thing that Lamont wanted? Would he be playing
into Lamont's hands now if he abandoned the watch and
went back to raise beaters? He wished he could make up
his mind – could see Lamont's play. The more he thought
of it, the surer he felt that Lamont was counting on his
going back to give the alarm. It was the obvious thing to
do. He had given Lamont his chance of going quietly, and
he had not taken it, even though his resistance had meant
the publication of his true standing; most assuredly, then,
he would expect the inspector to be squeamish no longer
about his or other people's feelings, and to go back for help
in his capture. That being so, Grant would stay where he
was and keep an eye on the country.

For a long time he lay there in the dampish, withered
heather, looking through the parted fronds at a tranquil
strath. Once the brakes of a car squealed away to his
left, where the high-road came down the hill, and later
he saw the car cross the bridge before the village, run
like a small black spider along the road at the back of
Carninnish House, and disappear up the coast road to the
north. A sheep bleated far away on the hill, and a late lark
sang high in the air, where the sun still was. But nothing
moved in the valley but the river, and the slow northern
twilight began to settle on it. And then something moved.
Down by the river it was. Nothing more definite than the
sudden flash of water in the river itself, there and gone
again. But it was not the river; something had moved.
Breathlessly he waited, his heart, pressed against the turf,
beating time with the blood in his ears. He had to wait
awhile, but what he saw, he saw distinctly this time. From
behind a huge twelve-foot boulder by the river his quarry
slid into sight and disappeared again under the bank. Grant
waited again patiently. Was he going to ground there, or
was he making for somewhere? Even in his anxiety he

was conscious of that amused indulgence with which a human being watches an unconscious wild animal busy about its own affairs – that 'tickled' feeling that all human beings have when they are spying. And presently a gentle movement farther downstream advertised the fact that Lamont was not stationary. He was heading somewhere. And for a townsman he was making a wonderful job of cover. But then, of course, there had been the War – Grant had forgotten that Lamont was old enough to have seen active service. He probably knew all that was to be known about the art of taking cover. Grant had seen nothing that second time – he had merely been conscious of movement. He would probably have seen nothing the first time if there had been a better method of getting from that rock to the shelter of the bank than coming into the open. There was no further sign of movement, and Grant remembered that the left bank of the river would afford good shelter nearly all the way. It was time that he abandoned his seat on the dais and went down into the arena. What could Lamont's plan be? If he held to his present course, he would be back at the manse in a quarter of an hour. Was that where he was making for? Was he going to take advantage of the tenderness he had aroused so far-seeingly in the Dinmont girl? A pretty enough plan. If he, Grant, had done as Lamont had suspected, and gone back for help, the last place anyone would look for him would be in the manse itself.

Grant swore, and let himself down the gully again as quickly as the going and his desire to remain in cover would allow. He regained the moor-track and hesitated, wondering which was the better plan. Between him and the river stretched a piece of moor, boulder-strewn certainly, but without cover for anything bigger than a rabbit. Only the fir-wood farther on had enabled Lamont to reach the river unobserved by him. Well, what about going back now and giving the alarm? And catch the man being hidden by the minister's niece? asked the looker-on in him. Well, why not? he demanded angrily of himself; if she hides him, she deserves all that's coming to her. But there's no need for publicity even yet, urged his other half. Make sure it is to the manse he has gone, and then follow and arrest him there.

That seemed sensible enough, and Grant, hoping that no one as far down the river as Lamont was could see him, crossed the little moor to the river at the double. What he wanted was to cross the river. To follow the man down the river-bed was to court certain discovery. He did not want the man to run; he wanted him to go peacefully to ground in the manse, so that he could be pounced upon comfortably. If by any chance he could cross the river, he could keep an eye on the man's progress from the high ground on the other side, could even move parallel with him, if he could come up with him, without the man's being aware that he was being stalked. He looked at the torrent. Time was precious, and a wetting was nothing now. It is one thing to dip oneself in icy water in the cold blood of a high resolution and quite another to plunge into a flood in the heat of a chase. Grant chose a spot where the river was divided into three parts by two large boulders. If he could succeed in negotiating the first one, he could take the second and the bank in a flying leap, and it would not matter very much if he missed the bank as long as his hands caught at it. He would be across. He stepped back a pace or two and measured the distance to the first boulder with his eye. The first was the flatter of the two, and offered a landing-place; the second was pointed, and must be taken on the run.

With an inarticulate prayer he launched himself into space, felt his nailed boots slip as they met the stone, recovered himself, felt the stone heeling over to the black pool beneath, leaped again, but knew even as he leaped that the slipping stone had lacked purchase for his spring, met the second stone sideways, and felt his hands on the far bank just in time to prevent himself going in further than to his waist. Thankful and breathless, he pulled himself out, hastily wrung as much of the water from his heavy tweed trousers as would prevent him from being hampered by its weight, and made for the high ground beyond. Never had the moor appeared so treacherous. Dry tussocks of grass melted under his foot into bog, dead brambles clung with a living tenacity to his wet tweed, hidden branches of birch rose and hit him as he stepped on the nearer end, holes waited for his feet among the heather. It was more like a music-hall turn, he thought ferociously, than a serious attempt to overtake a criminal. Panting, he came to a turn of the river, and flung himself down to reconnoitre. There was his man, about fifty yards above the manse, moving very slowly and cautiously. It occurred to Grant that it was he, the pursuer, who was having the rough time of it, while the pursued kept a pleasant and well-planned course in the open. Well, it wouldn't be for long. The minute the man turned into that little back gate that they were laughing so serenely over this morning he, Grant, would be out of the heather and doubling down the cart-track by the river as hard as he could go. He had a small automatic in his pocket and a pair of handcuffs, and this time he would use them – both if necessary. His man wasn't armed or he wouldn't have stolen the pepper-pot from the tea-table, but he wasn't taking risks any longer. No one's feelings would be considered any more in this case – his own least of all. Let every female from here to Land's End have hysterics at once – he wouldn't care.

Grant was still fuming and glowering and promising himself all sorts of fancy retributions when the man passed the gate. I have always wished that I could have seen Grant's face at that moment – seen the disgruntled anger and resentment of a man who has tried to do things decently, only to have had his decency taken advantage of, change to the sheer unbelieving astonishment of a small boy beholding his first firework. He blinked hard, but the picture remained the same; what he saw was real. The man had passed the gate. He was now at the end of the manse wall, and making for the bridge. What was the fool doing? Yes, Grant thought of him as a fool. He had worked out a perfectly good way of escape for him – to appeal to Miss Dinmont and lie doggo at the manse – and the fool wasn't taking advantage of it. He was near the bridge now. What was he doing? What was in his head? There was purpose in every movement. It was not an aimless or even a particularly furtive progress. He seemed to be too wrapped up in the thought of the business ahead to pay much attention to his present circumstances, beyond an occasional glance behind him up the river-bed. Not that there would be much good looking for cover so near the village. Even at this deserted hour, when everyone was eating his evening meal and no one was abroad until an hour later, they came to smoke pipes in the dusk at the bridge-end, there was always the chance of a passer-by, and any appearance of deliberate hiding would defeat its own ends. The man climbed on to the road beside the bridge, but went neither north to the right nor left towards the village. He crossed the road and disappeared on to the river-bank again. What could he get there? Was he going to work round to the hotel, which stood on the point where the river joined the sea, and try to steal the Ford? But he had obviously expected Grant to give the alarm. He would never venture up from the shore to the garage after waiting so deliberately to let Grant give warning. The shore?

Shore! Good heavens, he'd got it! The man had gone for a boat. They would be lying on the deserted shore, out of sight of the village. The tide was in – just on the ebb, in fact – and not a soul, child or adult, would be abroad to witness his departure. Grant hurled himself down the hillside, cursing in a reluctant admiration of the man's ingenuity. Grant knew the West Coaster, and he had a shrewd idea how often these boats were used. If you stay in a west-coast village, you find that the scarcest commodity of all is fresh fish. It might be literally days before anyone discovered that MacKenzie's boat was missing, and even then they would decide that someone had borrowed it, and would save up 'the rough side of their tongues' – a course which involved no expenditure of energy – for the borrower when he should put it back. Had Lamont sat and thought all that out at the tea at the manse? Grant thought, as his feet touched the cart-track, or was it a Heaven-sent inspiration in the moment of need? If he had planned it, he thought, racing down the road to the bridge that seemed so strangely distant, then he had also planned that murder in the queue. When one came to think of it, even if one's grandmother was an Italian, one doesn't carry daggers about on the offchance of their being useful. The man was a more accomplished villain than he had given him credit for, in spite of his lack of self-control on two occasions.

Long before Grant had reached the cart-track in his first avalanche down the hill-side he had decided on his course of action. This morning, when he had emerged from Carninnish House with Drysdale, he had noticed a boat-house just beyond the house itself, and protruding from it, alongside the little jetty that led from its shelter to the sea, was what Grant in retrospect was sure was the stern of a motorboat. If he was right, and Drysdale was at home, and the light held, then Lamont was as good as caught. But there were three 'ifs' in the affair.

By the time he had reached the bridge he was very nearly winded. He had come from the other side of the valley, and now down this one, in his heavy fishing boots, with his wet tweeds weighing him down. Keen as he was, it required a real effort of will to make him double that last hundred yards up the north road to the gates of Carninnish House. Once there, the worst was over; the house lay only a few yards inside the gate, in the narrow strip between the road and the sea. When Drysdale's butler beheld a damp and breathless man at the door, he immediately jumped to conclusions.

'Is it the master?' he said. 'What's wrong? Is he drowned?'

'Isn't he here?' said Grant. 'Damn! Is that a motor-boat? Can I have a loan of it?' He waved a none too accurate hand towards the boat-house, and the butler looked suspiciously at him. None of the servants had been present at Grant's arrival in the morning.

'No, you cannot, my lad,' said the butler, 'and the sooner you get out of this, the better it will be for you. Mr Drysdale will make you look pretty small when he comes, I can tell you.'

'Is he coming soon? When is he coming?'

'He'll be here any minute.'

'But any minute's too late!'

'Get out!' said the butler. 'And have one less next time.'

'Look here,' said Grant, gripping him by the arm, 'don't be a fool. I'm as sober as you are. Come down here where you can see the sea.'

Something in his tone arrested the man's attention, but it was with obvious fear of personal violence that he approached the sea in company with the madman. Out in the middle of the loch was a rowing-boat, being rapidly propelled seawards down the narrow estuary on the ebbing tide.

'Do you see that?' Grant asked. 'I want to overtake that boat, and I can't do it in a rowing boat.'

'No, you can't,' said the man. 'The tide goes out there like a mill stream.'

'That's why I must have the motor-boat. Who runs the motor? Mr Drysdale?'

'No; I do usually when he goes out.'

'Come on, then. You'll have to do it now. Mr Drysdale knows all about me. I've been fishing the river all day. That man has a stolen boat, to begin with, and we want him very badly for other reasons, so get busy.'

'Are you going to take all the responsibility of it if I go?'

'Oh yes; you'll have the law on your side all right. I promise you that.'

'Well, I'll just have to leave a message' – and he darted into the house.

Grant put out a hand to stop him, but was too late. For a second he was afraid that he was not, after all, convinced, and was merely making his escape, but in a moment he was back and they were running across the long, narrow lawn to the boat-house, where *Master Robert* floated. Drysdale had evidently christened the boat after the horse whose winning of the National had provided the money for her purchase. As the butler was fiddling with the engine, which uttered tentative spurts, Drysdale came round the end of the house with his gun, evidently just back from an afternoon on the hill, and Grant hailed him joyfully, and hurriedly explained what had happened. Drysdale said not a word, but came back to the boat-house with him and said, 'It's all right, Pidgeon; I'll see to that, and take Mr Grant out. Will you see that there is a good dinner waiting for two – no, three – when we get back?'

Pidgeon came out of the boat with an alacrity he took no trouble to hide. He gave *Master Robert* a push, Drysdale set the engine going, and with a roar they shot away from the jetty out into the loch. As they swerved round into their course down the loch, Grant's eyes fixed themselves on the dark speck against the pale yellow of the western sky. What would Lamont do this time? Come quietly? Presently the dark speck altered its course. It seemed to be making in to the land on the south side, and as it went away from the lighted skyline it became invisible against the background of the southern hills.

'Can you see him?' Grant asked anxiously. 'I can't.'

'Yes; he's making in to the south shore. Don't worry; we'll be there before he makes it.'

As they tore along, the south shore came up to meet them in a fashion seemingly miraculous. And in a moment or two Grant could make out the boat again. The man was rowing desperately for the shore. It was difficult for Grant, unacquainted with distances on water, to measure how far he was from the shore and how far they were from him, but a sudden slackening in *Master Robert's* speed told him all he wanted to know. Drysdale was slowing up already. In a minute they would have overhauled him. When the boats were about fifty yards apart, Lamont suddenly stopped rowing. Given it up, thought Grant. Then he saw that the man was bending down in the boat. Does he think we're going to shoot? thought Grant, puzzled. And then, when Drysdale had shut down the engine and they were approaching him with a smooth leisureliness, Lamont, coatless and hatless, sprang to his feet and then to the gunnel, as if to dive. His stockinged foot slipped on the wet gunnel, his feet went from under him. With a sickening crack that they heard quite distinctly, the back of his head hit the boat and he disappeared under water.

Grant had his coat and boots off by the time they were up to him.

'Can you swim?' asked Drysdale calmly. 'If not, we'll wait till he comes up.'

'Oh yes,' Grant said, 'I can swim well enough when there is a boat there to rescue me. I think I'll have to go for him if I want him. That was a terrific crack he got.' And he went over the side. Six or seven seconds later a dark head broke the surface, and Grant hauled the unconscious man to the boat, and with Drysdale's help pulled him in.

'Got him!' he said, as he rolled the limp heap on the floor.

Drysdale secured the rowing-boat to the stern of *Master Robert* and set the engine going again. He watched with interest while Grant perfunctorily wrung his wet clothes and painstakingly examined his capture. The man was completely knocked out, and was bleeding from a cut on the back of the head.

'Sorry for your planking,' Grant apologised as the blood collected in a little pool.

'Don't worry,' Drysdale said. 'It will scrub. This the man you wanted?'

'Yes.'

He considered the dark, unconscious face for a while. 'What do you want him for, if it isn't an indiscreet question?'

'Murder.'

'Really?' said Drysdale, very much as though Grant had said sheep-stealing. He considered the man again. 'Is he a dago?'

'No; a Londoner.'

'Well, at the moment he looks very much as if he would cheat the gallows after all, doesn't he?'

Grant looked sharply at the man he was tending. Was he as bad as that? Surely not!

As Carninnish House swam up to them from across the water Grant said, 'He was staying with the Logans at the manse. I can't very well take him back there. The hotel is the best place, I think. Then the Government can bear all the bother of the business.'

But as they floated swiftly in to the landing-stage, and Pidgeon, who had been on the look-out for their return, came down to meet them, Drysdale said, 'The man we went for is a bit knocked out. Which room was the fire lit in for Mr Grant?'

'The one next yours, sir.'

'Well, we'll carry this man there. Then tell Matheson to go over to Garnie for Dr Anderson, and tell the Garnie Hotel people that Mr Grant is staying the night with me, and bring over his things.'

Grant protested at this unnecessary generosity. 'Why, the man stuck his friend in the back!' he said.

'It isn't for him I'm doing it,' Drysdale smiled, 'though I wouldn't condemn my worst enemy to the hotel here. But you don't want to lose your man now that you've got him. Judging entirely by appearances, you had a very fine time getting him. And by the time they had lit a smoking fire in one of the glacial bedrooms over there' – he indicated the hotel on the point across the river – 'and got him to bed, your man would be as good as dead. Whereas here there is the room you would have had to wash in, all warm and ready. It is far easier and better to dump him there. And Pidgeon!' as the man was turning away, 'keep your mouth entirely closed. This gentleman met with an accident while boating. We observed it, and went to his assistance.'

'Very good, sir,' said Pidgeon.

So Grant and Drysdale, between them, carried the limp head upstairs, and rendered first aid in the big firelit bedroom; and then, between them, Pidgeon and Grant got him to bed, while Drysdale wrote a note to Mrs Dinmont explaining that her guest had met with a slight accident and would stay here for the night. He was suffering from slight concussion, but would they not be alarmed.

Grant had just changed into some things of his host's, and was waiting at the bedside until dinner should be announced, when there was a knock at the door, and in answer to his 'Come in,' Miss Dinmont walked into the room. She was bareheaded and carried a small bundle under her arm, but appeared to be completely self-possessed.

'I've brought down some things of his,' she said, and went over to the bed and dispassionately examined Lamont. For the sake of saying something, Grant said that they had sent for the doctor, but it was in his – Grant's – opinion a simple concussion. He had a cut on the back of the head.

'How did it happen?' she asked. But Grant had been facing this difficulty all the time he was changing out of his own wet things.

'We met Mr Drysdale, and he offered to take us out. Mr Lowe's foot slipped on the edge of the jetty, and the back of his head came in contact with it as he fell.'

She nodded. She seemed to be puzzling over something

and not to be able to make herself articulate. 'Well, I'm going to stay and look after him tonight. It's awfully good of Mr Drysdale to take him in.' She untied her bundle matter-of-factly. 'Do you know, I had a presentiment this morning when we were going up the river that something was going to happen. I'm so glad it's this and nothing worse. It might have been somebody's death, and that would have been incurable.' There was a little pause, and, still busy, she said over her shoulder, 'Are you staying the night with Mr Drysdale too?'

Grant said 'Yes,' and on the word the door opened and Drysdale himself came in.

'Ready, Inspector? You must be hungry,' he said, and then he saw Miss Dinmont. From that moment Grant always considered Drysdale a first-class 'intelligence' man wasted. He didn't 'bat an eyelid.' 'Well, Miss Dinmont, were you anxious about your truant? There isn't any need, I think. It's just a slight concussion. Dr Anderson will be along presently.'

With another woman it might have passed muster, but Grant's heart sank as he met the Dinmont girl's intelligent eye. 'Thank you for having him here,' she said to Drysdale. 'There isn't much to do till he comes round. But I'll stay the night, if you don't mind, and look after him.' And then she turned to Grant and said deliberately, 'Inspector of what?'

'Schools,' said Grant on the spur of the moment, and then wished he hadn't. Drysdale, too, knew that it was a mistake, but loyally backed him up.

'He doesn't look it, does he? But then inspecting is the last resort of the unintellectual. Is there anything I can get you before we go and eat, Miss Dinmont?'

'No, thank you. May I ring for the maid if I want anything?'

'I hope you will. And for us if you want us. We're only in the room below.' He went out and moved along the corridor, but, as Grant was following, she left the room with him and drew the door to behind her.

'Inspector,' she said, 'do you think I'm a fool? Don't you realise that for seven years I have worked in London hospitals? You can't treat me as a country innocent with any hope of success. Will you be good enough to tell me what the mystery is?'

Drysdale had disappeared downstairs. He was alone with her, and he felt that to tell her another untruth would be the supreme insult. 'All right, Miss Dinmont, I'll tell you the truth. I didn't want you to know the truth before because I thought it might save you from – from feeling sorry about things. But now it can't be helped. I came from London to arrest the man you had staying with you. He knew what I had come for when I came in at tea-time, because he knows me by sight. But when he came with me as far as the top of the road he bolted. In the end he took to a boat, and it was in diving from the boat when we followed that he cut his head open.'

'And what do you want him for.'

It was inevitable. 'He killed a man in London.'

'Murder!' The word was a statement, not a question. She seemed to understand that, if it had been otherwise, the inspector would have said manslaughter. 'Then his name is not Lowe?'

'No; his name is Lamont – Gerald Lamont.'

He was waiting for the inevitable feminine outburst of 'I don't believe it! He wouldn't do such a thing!' but it did not come.

'Are you arresting him on suspicion, or did he do the thing?'

'I'm afraid there isn't any doubt about it,' Grant said gently.

'But my aunt – is she – how did she come to send him here?'

'I expect Mrs Everett was sorry for him. She'd known him some time.'

'I only met my aunt once in the time I've been in London – we didn't like each other – but she didn't strike me as a person to be sorry for a wrongdoer. I'd be much more likely to believe she did the thing herself. Then he isn't even a journalist?'

'No,' Grant said; 'he's a bookmaker's clerk.'

'Well, thank you for telling me the truth at last,' she said. 'I must get things ready for Dr Anderson now.'

'Are you still going to look after him?' Grant asked involuntarily. Was the outburst of disbelief coming now?

'Certainly,' said this remarkable girl. 'The fact that he is a murderer doesn't alter the fact that he has concussion, does it? – nor does the fact that he abused our hospitality alter the fact that I'm a professional nurse. And even if it weren't for that, perhaps you know that in the old days in the Highlands a guest received hospitality and sanctuary even if he had his host's brother's blood on his sword. It isn't often I boost the Highlands,' she added, 'but this is rather a special occasion.' She gave a little catch of her breath that might have been a laugh or a sob, and was probably half one, half the other, and went back into the room to look after the man who had so unscrupulously used herself and her home.

CHAPTER 13

MARKING TIME

Grant did not sleep well that night. There was every reason why he should have slept in all the sublime peace of the righteous man of good digestion. He had finished the work he had come to do, and his case was complete. He had had a hard day in the open, in air that was at once a stimulant and a narcotic. The dinner provided by Drysdale had been all that either a hungry man or an epicure could have wished for. The sea outside his window breathed in long, gentle sighs that were the apotheosis of content. The turf fire glowed soothingly as no flickering bonfire of wood or coals ever does. But Grant slept badly. Moreover, there was discomfort in his mind somewhere, and like all self-analytical people, he was conscious of it and wanted to locate it, so that he could drag it out to the light and say, 'Goodness, is that all!' and find relief and comfort as he had so often done before. He knew quite well how that uneasiness which ruined the comfort of his twelve mattresses of happiness proved on investigation to be merely the pea of the fairy-tale. But, rout round as he would, he could find no reason for his lack of content. He produced several reasons, examined them, and threw them away. Was it the girl? Was he being sorry for her because of her pluck and decency? But he had no real reason to think that she cared for the man other than as a friend. Her undeniable interest in him at tea might have been due merely to his being the only interesting man from her point of view in a barren countryside. Was he over-tired, then? It was a long time since he had had a whole day's fishing followed by a burst across country at a killing pace. Or was it fear that his man would even yet slip through his fingers? But Dr Anderson had said that there was no fracture and the man would be able to travel in a day or two. And his chances of escape now weren't worth considering, even as hypothesis.

There was nothing in all the world, apparently, to worry him, and yet he had that vague uneasiness in his mind. During one of his periodical tossings and turnings he heard the nurse go along the corridor, and decided that he would get up and see if he could be of any use. He put on his dressing-gown and made for the wedge of light that came from the door she had left ajar. As he went, she came behind him with a candle.

'He's quite safe, Inspector,' she said, and the mockery in her tone stung him as being unfair.

'I wasn't asleep, and I heard you moving and thought I might be of some use,' he said, with as much dignity as one can achieve in the *déshabillé* of the small hours.

She relented a little. 'No, thank you,' she said; 'there's nothing to do. He's still unconscious.' She pushed open the door and led him in.

There was a lamp at the bedside, but otherwise the room was dark and filled with the sound of the sea – the gentle 'hus – s – h' which is so different from the roar of breakers on an open coast. The man, as she said, was still unconscious, and Grant examined him critically in the light of the lamp. He looked better, and his breathing was better. 'He'll be conscious before morning,' she said, and it sounded more like a promise than a statement.

'I can't tell you how sorry I am,' Grant said suddenly, 'that you should have had all this – that you should have been brought into this.'

'Don't worry, Inspector; I'm not at all fragile. But I'd like to keep my mother and uncle from knowing about it. Can you manage that?'

'Oh, I think so. We can get Dr Anderson to prescribe south treatment for him.' She moved abruptly, and he was conscious of the unhappiness of his phrase, but could see no way of remedying it, and was silent.

'Is he a bad lot?' she asked suddenly. 'I mean, apart from—'

'No,' said Grant, 'not as far as we know.' And then, afraid that the green growth he had burned out last night might begin to shoot again, and more pain be in store for her, he added, 'But he stuck his friend in the back.'

'The man in the queue?' she said, and Grant nodded. Even yet he was waiting momentarily for the 'I don't believe it.' But it did not come. He had at last met a woman whose common sense was greater than her emotions. She had known the man only three days, he had lied to her every hour of these days, and the police wanted him for murder. That was sufficient evidence in her clear eyes to prevent her taking any brief in his favour.

'I have just put the kettle on the gas-ring in the bathroom for tea,' she said. 'Will you have some?' and Grant accepted and they drank the scalding liquid by the open window, the sea heaving below them in the strangely balmy west-coast night. And Grant went to bed again quite sure that it was not Miss Dinmont's emotions that worried him, but still uneasy about something. And now, writing triumphant telegrams to Barker in the golden morning, with the comfortable smell of bacon and eggs contending amiably with the fragrance of seaweed, he was still not as happy as he should have been. Miss Dinmont had come in, still in the white overall that made her look half-surgeon, half-religieuse, to say that her patient was conscious, but would Grant not come to him until Dr Anderson had been? – she was afraid of the excitement; and Grant had thought that eminently reasonable.

'Has he just come round?' he asked.

No, she said; he had been conscious for some hours,

and she went serenely away, leaving Grant wondering what had passed between patient and nurse in those few hours. Drysdale joined him at breakfast, with his queer mixture of taciturnity and amiability, and arranged that he should have a real day's fishing as an offset to the distracted flogging of the water which had occupied him yesterday. Grant said that, once Anderson had been and he had heard a report of his man, he would go. He supposed any telegrams could be sent down to him.

'Oh yes; there's nothing Pidgeon likes like being important. He's in his element at the moment.'

Dr Anderson, a little man in ancient and none too clean tweeds, said that the patient was very well indeed – even his memory was unimpaired – but he would advise Grant, whom he took to be the man's nearest friend, not to see him until this evening. It would be best to give him a day to be quiet in. And since Miss Dinmont seemed determined to look after him, they need have no fear about him. She was an excellent nurse.

'When can he travel?' asked Grant. 'We're in a hurry to get south.'

'If it is very important, the day after tomorrow, perhaps.' And seeing Grant look disappointed, 'Or even tomorrow, if the journey were made comfortable. It all depends on the comfort of the travel. But I wouldn't recommend it till the day after tomorrow at the earliest.'

'What's the hurry?' Drysdale said. 'Why spoil the ship for a ha'p'orth of tar?'

'Afraid of loose moorings,' Grant said.

'Don't worry. The excellent Pidgeon will dote on being head warder.'

Then Grant turned to the surprised doctor and explained the truth of the situation. 'There's no chance of his getting away if we let him stay here till he is stronger?'

'He's safe enough today,' Anderson said. 'The man isn't fit to lift a little finger at the moment. He'd have to be carried if he escaped, and I don't suppose there's anyone here who would be willing to carry him.'

So Grant, conscious of being entirely unreasonable and at sea with himself, agreed, wrote a second report to Barker to supplement the one he had written on the previous night, and departed to the river with Drysdale.

After a day of wide content, broken only by the arrival of Pidgeon's subordinate, a youth with a turned-up nose and ears that stuck out like handles, with telegrams from Barker, they came back to the house between tea and dinner; and Grant, after a wash, knocked at the door that sheltered Lamont. Miss Dinmont admitted him, and he met the black eyes of the man on the bed with a distinct feeling of relief; he was still there.

Lamont was the first to speak. 'Well, you've got me,' he said, drawling a little.

'Looks like it,' said Grant. 'But you had a good run for your money.'

'Yes,' agreed the man, his eyes going to Miss Dinmont and coming back at once.

'Tell me, what made you dive off the boat? What was the idea?'

'Because swimming and diving is the thing I'm best at. If I hadn't slipped, I could have got to the rocks under water and lain there, with only my nose and my mouth out, until you got tired looking for me, or the dark came. But you won – by a head.' The pun seemed to please him.

There was a little silence, and Miss Dinmont said in her clear, deliberate voice: 'I think, Inspector, he's well enough to be left now. At least, he won't need professional services any longer. Perhaps someone in the house would look after him tonight?'

Grant deduced that this was her way of saying that the man was strong enough now to have a more adequate guard, and thankfully agreed. 'Do you want to go now?'

'Just as soon as someone can take my place without anyone being upset.'

Grant rang, and explained the situation to the maid that came. 'I'll stay if you would like to go now,' he said when the maid had gone, and she agreed.

Grant went to the window and stood looking out at the loch, so that, if she wanted to say anything to Lamont, the way was clear, and she began to collect her things. There was no sound of conversation, and, looking round, he saw that she was apparently quite absorbed in the task of leaving nothing behind her, and the man was watching her unblinkingly, his whole being waiting for the moment of her leave-taking. Grant turned back to the sea, and presently he heard her say, 'Shall I see you again before you go?' There was no answer to that, and Grant turned round to find that she was addressing himself.

'Oh yes, I hope so,' he said. 'I'll call at the manse if I don't see you otherwise – if I may.'

'All right,' she said, 'then I needn't say good-bye just now.' And she went out of the room with her bundle.

Grant glanced at his captive and looked away at once. It is indecent to pry too far into even a murderer's soul. When he looked back again, the man's eyes were closed and his face was a mask of such unspeakable misery that Grant was unexpectedly moved. He had cared for her, then – it had not been merely opportunism.

'Can I do anything for you, Lamont?' he asked presently.

The black eyes opened and considered him unseeingly. 'I suppose it *is* too much to expect anyone to believe that I didn't do it,' he said at length.

'It is, rather,' said Grant dryly.

'But I didn't, you know.'

'No? Well, we hardly expected you to say you did.'

'That's what *she* said.'

'Who?' asked Grant, surprised.

'Miss Dinmont. When I told her I hadn't done it.'

'Oh? Well, it's a simple process of elimination, you see. And everything fits in too well for the possibility of a mistake. Even down to this,' and picking up Lamont's hand from where it lay on the counterpane, he indicated the scar on the inside of his thumb. 'Where did you get that?'

'I got it carrying my trunk up the stairs to my new rooms in Brixton – that morning.'

'Well, well,' said Grant indulgently, 'we won't argue the affair now, and you're not well enough to make a statement. If I took one now, they'd hold it up to me that I had got it from you when you weren't *compos mentis*.'

'My statement'll be the same whenever you take it,' the man said; 'only, no one will believe it. If they would have believed it, I wouldn't have run.'

Grant had heard that tale before. It was a favourite gambit with criminals who had no case. When a man plays injured innocence, the layman immediately considers the possibility of a mistake; but the police officer, who has a long acquaintance with the undoubtedly guilty, is less impressionable – in fact, is not impressed at all. A police officer who was impressed with a hard-luck story, however well told, would be little use in a force designed for the suppression of that most plausible of creatures, the criminal. So Grant merely smiled and went back to the window. The loch was like glass this evening, the hills on either side reflected to their last detail in the still water. *Master Robert* rode below the boat-house – 'a painted ship', only that no paint could reproduce the translucence of the sea as it was now.

Presently Lamont said, 'How did you find where I had come to?'

'Finger-prints,' said Grant succinctly.

'Have you got finger-prints of mine?'

'No, not yours. I'm going to take them in a minute.'

'Whose, then?'

'Mrs Everett's.'

'What has Mrs Everett got to do with it?' the man said, with the first hint of defiance.

'I expect you know more about that than I do. Don't talk. I want you to be able to travel tomorrow or the next day.'

'But look here, you haven't done anything to Mrs Everett, have you?'

Grant grinned. 'No; I think it's what Mrs Everett's done to us.'

'What do you mean? You haven't arrested her, have you?'

There was obviously no hope of the man being quiet until he knew how they had traced him, so Grant told him. 'We found a finger-print of Mrs Everett's in your rooms, and as Mrs Everett had told us she didn't know where your new rooms were, it was a fair conclusion that she had a finger in the pie. We found that her relations stayed here, and then we found the man you fooled at King's Cross, and his description of Mrs Everett made things sure. We only just missed you at the Brixton place.'

'Mrs Everett won't get into trouble over it, will she?'

'Probably not – now that we've got you.'

'I was a fool to run, in the first place. If I'd come and told the truth in the beginning, it couldn't be any worse than it is now, and I'd have been saved all the hell between.' He was lying with his eyes on the sea. 'Funny to think that, if someone hadn't killed Bert, I'd never have seen this place or – or anything.'

The 'anything' the inspector took to be the manse. 'M'm! And who do you think killed him?'

'I don't know. There wasn't anyone I know of who'd do that to Bert. I think perhaps someone did it by mistake.'

'Not looking what they were doing with the needle, as it were?'

'No; in mistake for someone else.'

'And you're the left-handed man with a scar on his thumb

who quarrelled with Sorrell just before his death, and who has all the money Sorrell had in the world, but you're quite innocent.'

The man turned his head wearily away. 'I know,' he said. 'You don't need to tell me how bad it is.'

A knock came to the door, and the boy with the protruding ears appeared in the doorway and said that he had been sent to relieve Mr Grant, if that was what Mr Grant wanted. Grant said, 'I'll want you in five minutes or so. Come back when I ring,' and the boy melted into the dark of the passage, grin last, like the Cheshire cat. Grant took something out of his pocket and fiddled with it at the washstand. Then he came over to the bedside and said, 'Finger-prints, please. It's quite a painless process, so you needn't mind.' He took prints of both hands on the prepared sheets of paper, and the man submitted with an indifference tinged with the interest one shows in experiencing something, however mild, for the first time. Grant knew even as he pressed the finger-tips on the paper that the man had no Scotland Yard record. The prints would be of value only in relation to the other prints in the case.

As he laid them aside to dry, Lamont said, 'Are you the star turn at Scotland Yard?'

'Not yet,' said Grant. 'You flatter yourself.'

'Oh, I only thought – seeing your photograph in the paper.'

'That was why you ran last Saturday night in the Strand.'

'Was it only last Saturday? I wish the traffic had done for me then!'

'Well, it very nearly did for me.'

'Yes; I got an awful jolt when I saw you behind me so soon.'

'If it's any comfort to you, I got a much worse one when I saw you arriving back in the Strand. What did you do then?'

'Took a taxi. There was one passing.'

'Tell me,' the inspector said, his curiosity getting the better of him, 'were you planning the boat escape all the time at the manse tea?'

'No; I had no plans at all. I thought of the boat afterwards only because I'm used to boats, and I thought you'd think of them last. I was going to try to escape somehow, but I didn't think of it until I saw the pepper-pot as I was going out. It was the only way I could think of, you see. Bert had my gun.'

'Your gun? Was that your gun in his pocket?'

'Yes; that's what I went to the queue for.'

But Grant did not want statements of that sort tonight. 'Don't talk!' he said, and rang for the boy. 'I'll take any statement you want to give me tomorrow. If there's anything I can do for you tonight, tell the boy and he'll let me know.'

'There isn't anything, thank you. You've been awfully decent – far more decent than I thought the police ever were to – criminals.'

That was so obviously an English version of Raoul's *gentil* that Grant smiled involuntarily, and the shadow of a smile was reflected on Lamont's swarthy face. 'I say,' he said, 'I've thought a lot about Bert, and it's my belief that, if it wasn't a mistake, it was a woman.'

'Thanks for the tip,' said Grant dryly, and left him to the tender mercies of the grinning youth. But as he made his way downstairs he was wondering why he had thought of Mrs Ratcliffe.

CHAPTER 14

THE STATEMENT

It was not at Carninnish, however, that Lamont gave his statement to the inspector, but on the journey south. Dr Anderson, on hearing what was mooted, pleaded for one more day's rest for his patient. 'You don't want the man to have inflammation of the brain, do you?'

Grant, who was dying to have a statement down in black and white, explained that the man himself was anxious to give one, and that giving it would surely harm him less than having it simmering in his brain.

'It would be all right at the beginning,' Anderson said, 'but by the time he had finished he would need another day in bed. Take my advice and leave it for the meantime.' So Grant had given way and let his captive have still longer time to burnish the tale he was no doubt concocting. No amount of burnish, he thought thankfully, would rub out the evidence. That was there unalterable, and nothing the man might say could upset the facts. It was as much curiosity on his part, he told himself, as fear for his case that made him so eager to hear what Lamont had to say. So he bullied himself into some show of patience. He went sea-fishing in *Master Robert* with Drysdale, and every chug of the motor reminded him of the fish he had landed two nights ago. He went to tea at the manse, and with Miss Dinmont's imperturbable face opposite him and an odd pepper-pot alongside the salt on the table, his thoughts were almost wholly of Lamont. He went to church afterwards, partly to please his host, but mainly to avoid what was evidently going to be a *tête-à-tête* with Miss Dinmont if he stayed behind, and sat through a sermon in which Mr Logan proved to his own and his congregation's satisfaction that the King of kings had no use for the fox-trot; and thought continually of the statement Lamont would give him. When the incredibly dreary noise of Highland 'praise' had faded into silence for the last time, and Mr Logan had pronounced an unctuous benediction, his one thought was that now he could go back and be near Lamont. It was rapidly becoming an obsession with him, and he recognised the fact and resented it. When Mrs Dinmont – Miss Dinmont had not come to church – reminded him as she was saying goodnight that on the morrow the car would stop at the manse gate to allow them to say good-bye to Mr Lowe, it came as a shock to him that there was more play-acting to be done before he departed from Carninnish.

But things proved easier than he had anticipated. Lamont played up as he had played up during the fateful tea, and neither his host nor his hostess suspected that there was anything more serious amiss than the matter of his health. Miss Dinmont was not present. 'Dandy said she had already said good-bye to you, and it is unlucky to say good-bye twice,' her mother said. 'She said you had been unlucky enough already. Are you a very unlucky person, then?'

'Very,' said Lamont, with an admirable smile, and as the car moved away, Grant took out the handcuffs.

'Sorry,' he said brusquely. 'It's only till we reach the railway.' But Lamont merely repeated the word 'Unlucky!' as if, surprisingly, he liked the sound of it. At the station they were joined by a plain-clothes man, and at Inverness had a compartment to themselves. And it was after dinner that night, when the last light was going on the hills, that Lamont, pale and rather ill-looking, offered again to tell them all he knew.

'It isn't much,' he said. 'But I want you to know.'

'You realise that what you say may be used against you?' Grant said. 'Your lawyer would probably want you to say nothing. You see, it's putting your line of defence into our hands.' And even while he was saying it, he was wondering 'Why am I so punctilious? I've told him already that anything he says may be used against him.' But Lamont wanted to talk, and so the constable produced his notebook.

'Where shall I begin?' Lamont asked. 'It's difficult to know where to start.'

'Suppose you tell us how you spent the day Sorrell was murdered — that's a week last Tuesday — the thirteenth.'

'Well, in the morning we packed — Bert was leaving for America that night — and I took my things to my new room in Brixton and he took his to Waterloo.'

Here the inspector's heart missed a beat. Fool! He'd forgotten all about the man's luggage. He had been so hot on the false scent of the Ratcliffes and then on the trail of Lamont that he hadn't had time to see the thing under his nose. Not that it was of supreme importance, in any case.

'That took us till lunch-time. We had lunch in the Coventry Street Lyons—'

'Whereabouts?'

'In a corner table on the first floor.'

'Yes; go on.'

'All the time we were having lunch we argued as to whether I was going to see him off or not. I wanted to go down to Southampton with him and see him sail, but he wouldn't let me come even to the boat-train at Waterloo. He said there wasn't anything in the world he hated like being seen off, especially when he was going a long way. I remember he said, "If a chap's not going far, then there's no need, and if he's going to the other side of the world, then there's no good. What's a few minutes more or less?" Then in the afternoon we went to the Woffington to see *Didn't You Know?*'

'What!' said Grant. 'You went to the show at the Woffington in the afternoon?'

'Yes; that was arranged a long time beforehand. Bert had booked seats. Stalls. It was a sort of final do – celebration. At the interval he told me that he was going to join the pit queue for the evening performance as soon as we got out – he had gone a lot to *Didn't You Know?*, it was a sort of craze; in fact, we both went a lot – and said that we'd say good-bye then. It seemed a poor way to me to say good-bye to a pal you'd known as well as I knew Bert, but he was always a bit unaccountable, and anyhow, if he didn't want me, I wasn't going to insist on being with him. So we said good-bye outside the front of the Woffington, and I went back to Brixton to unpack my things. I was feeling awfully fed up, because Bert and I had been such pals that I hadn't any others worth mentioning, and it was lonely at Brixton after Mrs Everett's.'

'Didn't you think of going with Sorrell?'

'I wanted to, all right, but I hadn't the money. I hoped for a while that he'd offer to lend me it. He knew that I'd pay him back all right. But he never did. I was a bit sore about that too. Every way I was pretty fed up. And Bert himself didn't appear to be happy about it. He hung on to my hand like anything when we were saying good-bye. And he gave me a little packet and said I was to promise not to open it till the day after tomorrow – that was the day after he sailed. I thought it was a sort of farewell present, and didn't think anything more about it. It was a little white packet done up in paper like jewellers use, and as a matter of fact I thought it was a watch. My watch was always going crazy. He used to say, "If you don't get a new watch, Jerry, you won't be in time for kingdom-come even."'

Lamont choked suddenly and stopped. He carefully wiped away the steam on the window and then resumed:

'Well, when I was unpacking my things in Brixton, I missed my revolver. I never used the thing, of course. It was just a war souvenir. I had a commission, though you mightn't think it. And I tell you straight I'd rather a thousand times be for it wire-cutting, or anything else like that, than be hunted round London by the police. It isn't so bad in the open. More like a game, somehow. But in London it's like being in a trap. Didn't *you* feel that it wasn't so deadly awful out in the country somehow?'

'Yes,' admitted the inspector; 'I did. But I didn't expect you to. I thought you'd be happier in town.'

'Happy! God!' said Lamont, and was silent, evidently living it over again.

'Well,' prompted the inspector, 'you missed your revolver?'

'Yes; I missed it. And though I didn't use it – it used to be kept locked in a drawer at Mrs Everett's – I knew exactly where I had put it when I was packing. Whereabouts in the trunk, I mean. And as it was only that morning I had packed, I was just taking things out in the reverse order from the way I'd put them in, and so I missed it at once. And then I grew frightened somehow – though even yet I can't tell you why. I began to remember how quiet Bert had been lately. He was always quiet, but lately he had been more so. Then I thought he might just have wanted a gun going to a strange country. But then I thought he might have asked for it. He knew I'd have given it to him if he asked for it. Anyway, I was sort of frightened, though I couldn't tell you just why, and I went straight back to the queue and found him. He had a good place, about a third of the way down, so I think he had had a boy to keep his place for him. He must have meant all the time to go back on his last night. He was sentimental, Bert. I asked him if he had taken my revolver, and he admitted it. I don't know why I grew so scared then all of a sudden. Looking back, it doesn't seem to be anything to be scared about – your pal having taken your revolver. But I was, and I lost my head and said, "Well, I want it back right now." And he said, "Why?" And I said, "Because it's my property and I want it." He said, "You're a mean skunk, Jerry. Can't I borrow anything of yours even when I'm going half round the world and you're going to stay in little safe old London?" But I stuck to having it back. Then he said, "Well, you'll have a sweet time unpacking my things for it, but I'll give you the key and the ticket." It was only then that it occurred to me that I had taken it for granted that he had the revolver on him. I began to feel small and to feel I'd made a fool of myself. I always did things first and thought afterwards, and Bert always thought for ages about a thing, and then would do exactly as he had intended to. We were opposites in lots of ways. So I told him to keep his ticket and the revolver too, and went away.'

Now there had been no cloakroom ticket found in Sorrell's possession.

'Did you see the ticket?'

'No; he only offered to give it to me.

'Next morning I was late because I wasn't used to doing for myself, and I had to make my own breakfast and tidy up, but I didn't hurry because I had no job. I was hoping to get a clerk's place when the "flat" started. It was nearly twelve when I went out, and I wasn't thinking of anything but Bert. I was so fed up with the way we'd parted and the fool I'd made of myself that I went to a post office and sent a wire to Bert addressed to the *Queen of Arabia*, saying, "Sorry. – JERRY."'

'What post office did you send the telegram from?'

'The one in Brixton High Street.'

'All right; go on.'

'I bought a paper and went back to my rooms and then I saw about the queue murder. It didn't give any description of the man except that he was young and fair, and I didn't connect him with Bert. When I thought of Bert, I always thought of him aboard ship by this time, d'you see? If the man had been shot, I'd have been alarmed at once. But stuck with a knife was different.'

At this stage Grant looked with incredulous astonishment

at Lamont. Was the man by any remotest possibility telling the truth? If not, he was the most cold-blooded wretch Grant had ever had the unhappy lot to meet. But the man appeared unconscious of Grant's scrutiny; he seemed wholly absorbed in his story. If this was acting, it was the best Grant had ever seen, and he deemed himself a connoisseur.

'On Thursday morning when I was clearing up I remembered Bert's parcel, and opened it. And inside was all Bert's cash. I was flabbergasted, and somehow I was scared again. If anything had happened to Bert, I'd have heard about it – I mean, I thought I would have – but I didn't like it. There was no note with it. He had said when he handed it over, "This is for you," and made me promise not to open it till the time he said. I didn't know what to do about it because I still thought of Bert as being on the way to New York. I went out and got a paper. They had all big headlines about the queue murder, and this time there was a full description of the man and his clothes and the contents of his pockets. That was in black type, and I knew at once it was Bert. I got on a bus, feeling sick all over, but meaning to go to Scotland Yard right away and tell them all I knew about it. On the bus I read the rest of the thing. It said that the murder had been done by someone left-handed, and wanted to know who had left the queue. Then I remembered that we had had an argument that anyone might have overheard, and that I had all Bert's money without a single thing to show how I got it. I got off the bus in an awful sweat, and walked about thinking what was to be done. The more I thought about it, the more it seemed that I couldn't go to Scotland Yard with a tale like that. I was torn between that and letting Bert lie there while the – skunk that killed him went free. I was about crazy that day. I thought that, if I didn't go, perhaps they'd get on to the track of the right man. And then I'd wonder if I was using that as an excuse for not going – funking, you know. My thoughts went round and round like that, and I couldn't come to any decision.

'On Friday they said the inquest was to be that day, and that no one had claimed to know Bert. There was one time during that day that I very nearly went to the police station, and then, just when the thought of Bert had got my courage up, I remembered what a thin yarn I had about myself. So instead I sent some of Bert's money to bury him. I'd have liked to say who he was, but I knew that would bring them all about me in a minute. And then next morning I saw they had my description. They were looking for me. I'd have gone then of my own accord. Only, in the description it said that the man had a scar on the inside of his finger or thumb. That tore it. I got that scar' – he extended his hand – 'as I told you – carrying my trunk up the stairs to my room. The buckle caught me as I was letting it down. But that tore it all right. Who would believe me now? I waited till it was late afternoon, and then I went to Mrs Everett. She was the only real friend I had, and she knew me. I told her every last thing about it. She believed me because she knew me, you see, but even she saw that no one who didn't know me would believe me. She called me a fool, or as good as, for not going straight away to tell what I knew. *She* would have. She ruled us both. Bert used to call her Lady Macbeth, because she was Scotch and used to screw us up to doing things when we were wavering about them. She said all I could do now was to lie low. If they didn't find me, there was always the chance of their getting on to the right man, and afterwards she would give me the money to go abroad. I couldn't use Bert's, somehow. When I left her I went all the way into town because I couldn't bear the thought of going back to my rooms with nothing to do but listen for feet on the stairs. I thought I would be safest in a movie show, and I meant to go up to the Haymarket. And then I looked back in the Strand and saw you behind me. You know that bit. I went back to my rooms at once, and didn't stir out of them till Mrs Everett came on Monday and told me you'd been to her. She came to King's Cross with me and gave me the introduction to the people at Carninnish. You know the rest. After I'd been a day in Carninnish I began to think I had a chance, until I saw you come into the room for tea.'

He lapsed into silence. Grant noticed that his hands were trembling.

'What made you think that the money you say Sorrell left with you was all he had?'

'Because it was the amount he had in his own private account at the bank. It was I who drew it for him more than a week before he was due to sail. He drew it all but a pound.'

'Were you in the habit of drawing money for him?'

'No; hardly ever. But that week he was terribly busy settling affairs at the office and clearing up generally.'

'Why did he draw it so soon if he did not need it to pay his fare, as he evidently didn't?'

'I don't know, unless he was afraid he wouldn't have enough in the business account to pay off all the accounts. But he had. He didn't leave a ha'penny owing.'

'Was business good?'

'Yes; not bad. As good as it ever is in the winter. We do very little National Hunt betting – did, I mean. During the "flat" it was good enough.'

'At the end of the winter would be a lean season with Sorrell, then?'

'Yes.'

'And you handed the money to Sorrell – when?'

'Directly I got back from the bank.'

'You say you quarrelled with Sorrell about the revolver. Can you prove the revolver was yours?'

'No; how can I? No one knew about it because it was locked up – no one but Bert, I mean. It was loaded, just the way it was when the Armistice came. It wasn't a thing to leave about.'

'And what do you suggest that Sorrell wanted it for?'

'I don't know. I haven't the remotest idea. I did think of suicide. It looked like that. But then there was no reason for it.'

'When you said to me at Carninnish that in your opinion a woman had killed Sorrell, what did you mean?'

'Well, you see, I knew all Bert's men friends, and he didn't have any girl ones — I mean girls that are more than acquaintances. But I always thought there might have been a woman before I knew him. He was very quiet about the things he cared about, and he wouldn't have told me in any case. I have seen him sometimes get letters in a woman's handwriting, but he never remarked about them, and Bert wasn't the kind you teased about that sort of thing.'

'Has a letter of that sort arrived for him lately — within the past six months, say?'

Lamont thought for a while and said yes, he thought so.

'What kind of writing?'

'Biggish, with very round letters.'

'You have read the description of the dagger that killed Sorrell. Have you ever handled one like it?'

'I not only never handled one but I never saw one.'

'Have you any suggestions as to who or what this hypothetical woman might have been?'

'No.'

'Do you mean to say that you were this man's intimate friend for years — actually lived with him for four years — and yet know nothing of his past?'

'I know quite a lot about his past, but not that. You didn't know Bert or you wouldn't expect him to tell me. He wasn't secretive in ordinary things — only in special things.'

'Why was he going to America?'

'I don't know. I told you I thought he hadn't been happy lately. He never was exactly bubbling over, but lately — well, it's been more of an atmosphere than anything you could give a name to.'

'Was he going alone?'

'Yes.'

'Not with a woman?'

'Certainly not,' said Lamont sharply, as if Grant had insulted him or his friend.

'How do you know?'

Lamont hunted round in his mind, evidently at a loss. He was quite obviously facing the possibility for the first time that his friend had intended to go abroad with someone and had not told him. Grant could see him considering the proposition and rejecting it. 'I don't know how I know, but I *do* know. He would have told me that.'

'Then you deny having any knowledge as to how Sorrell met his end?'

'I do. Don't you think, if I had any knowledge, I'd tell you all I knew?'

'I expect you would!' said Grant. 'The very vagueness of your suspicions is a bad feature in your line of defence.' He asked the constable to read out what he had written, and Lamont agreed that it coincided with what he had said, and signed each page with a none too steady hand. As he signed the last he said, 'I'm feeling rotten. Can I lie down now?' and Grant gave him a draught which he had cadged from the doctor, and in fifteen minutes the prisoner was sleeping the sleep of utter exhaustion, while his captor stayed awake and thought the statement over.

It was an extraordinarily plausible one. It fitted and dovetailed beautifully. Except for its fundamental improbability, it was difficult to fault it. The man had had an explanation for everything. Times and places, even motives fitted. His account of his supposed emotions, from the discovery of the loss of the revolver onwards, was a triumph of verisimilitude. Was it possible, even remotely possible, that the man's statement was true? Was this that

thousandth case where circumstantial evidence, complete
in every particular, was merely a series of accidents, completely unrelated and lying colossally in consequence? But
then, the thinness of the man's story – that fundamental
improbability! After all, he had had nearly a fortnight to
carve out his explanation, plane it, polish it, and make it fit
in every particular. It would be a poor wit that would not
achieve a tolerably acceptable tale with life itself at stake.
That there was no one to check the truth or otherwise of the
vital points was at once his misfortune and his advantage.
It occurred to Grant that the only way to check Lamont's
explanation was to unearth Sorrell's story, for story, Grant
felt, there must be. If he could discover that Sorrell really
intended suicide, it would go far to substantiate Lamont's
story of the purloined revolver and the gift of money. And
there Grant pulled himself up. Substantiate Lamont's story?
Was there a possibility of such a thing coming to pass? If
that were so, his whole case went up in smoke, Lamont
was not guilty, and he had arrested the wrong man. But
was there within the bounds of possibility a coincidence
which would put in one theatre queue two men, both
left-handed, both scarred on a finger of that hand, and
both acquaintances of the dead man, and therefore his
potential murderers? He refused to believe it. It was not
the credibility of the man's tale which had thrown dust in
his eyes, but the extraordinary credibility of the manner of
telling it. And what was that but plausibility!

His mind continued to go round and round the thing.
In the man's favour – there he was again! – was the fact
that the finger-prints on the revolver and those on the
letter containing the money were the same. If the prints he
had sent from Carninnish proved to be the same as these,
then the man's story was true to that extent. The tale of
Sorrell's letters from a feminine source could be checked by
application to Mrs Everett. Mrs Everett evidently believed
Lamont innocent, and had gone to considerable lengths in

support of her conviction, but then she was prejudiced, and therefore not a competent judge.

Supposing, then, that the man's tale was a concocted one, what combination of circumstances would explain his murdering Sorrell? Was it possible that he had resented his friend's departure without offering to help him, so much that he could commit murder for it? But he had Sorrell's money in his possession. If he had obtained that money before Sorrell died, he would have no reason for killing him. And if he had not, then the money would have been found in Sorrell's possession. Or suppose he had obtained the money by stealing his friend's pocket-book during that afternoon, he would still have no urge to murder, and there would have been every reason to keep away from the queue. The more Grant thought of it, the more impossible it became to invent a really good theory as to why Lamont should have murdered Sorrell. Most of all in his favour was that he should have come to so public a place as a theatre queue to expostulate with his friend about something. It was not a usual preliminary to intended murder. But perhaps the murder had not been intended. Lamont did not give the impression of a man who would intend murder for very long at a time. Had the quarrel been not over the revolver at all but about something more bitter? Was there a woman in the case after all, for instance?

For no reason Grant had a momentary recollection of Lamont's face when the Dinmont girl had gone out of the room as if he was not there, and the tones of his voice when he was telling of Sorrell's suspected romance, and he dismissed that theory.

But about business? Lamont had evidently felt his comparative poverty very keenly, and *had* resented his friend's lack of sympathy. Was his 'fed up' a euphuism for a smouldering resentment that had blazed into hatred? But – after having had two hundred and twenty-three pounds – no, of course, he didn't know about that until afterwards. That might have been true, that tale of the packet, and he had taken it for granted that it contained the expected watch. After all, one does not expect to be handed two hundred and twenty-three pounds by a departing friend whose whole fortune it is. That was possible to the point of probability. He had said good-bye, and afterwards – but what did he argue about? If he had come back to stab Sorrell, he would not have called attention to himself. And what had Sorrell intended to do? If Lamont's story were true, then the only explanation of Sorrell's conduct was intended suicide. The more Grant thought, the more certain he became that only light on Sorrell's history would elucidate the problem and prove Lamont's guilt or – incredible! – innocence. His first business when he was back in town would be to do what he had neglected in his hurry to get Lamont – find Sorrell's luggage and go through it. And if that yielded nothing, he would see Mrs Everett again. He would like to meet Mrs Everett once more!

He took a last look at the calmly sleeping Lamont, and said a last word to the stolidly wakeful constable, and composed himself to sleep, worried, but filled with resolution. This business was not going to be left where it was.

CHAPTER 15

THE BROOCH

After a hot bath, during which he had twiddled his toes in the wavering steam and tried to mesmerise himself into that habitually comfortable frame of mind of a detective officer who has got his man, Grant repaired to the Yard and went to interview his chief. When he came into the great man's presence Barker was complimentary.

'Congratulations, Grant!' he said; 'that was very smart work altogether.' And he asked for details of the capture which Grant had not, of course, included in his official report, and Grant provided him with a vivid sketch of the three days at Carninnish. The superintendent was highly amused.

'Well done!' he said. 'Rather you than me. Careering across bogs was never a sport of mine. It seems you were the right man in the right place this time, Grant.'

'Yes,' said Grant unenthusiastically.

'You don't let your emotions run away with you, do you?' said Barker, grinning at his unsmiling face.

'Well, it's been luck, mostly, and I made one bad break.'

'What was that?'

'I found out that Sorrell had really intended to go to America – at least, that he had booked a berth – and I forgot that his belongings would be lying at a terminus waiting to be examined.'

'That doesn't sound a very vital mistake to me. You knew who the man was and who his friends were. What more could you find out that would help you to Lamont?'

'Nothing about Lamont. It was because I was so hard on

Lamont's trail that I forgot about the luggage. But I want to know more about Sorrell. To tell you the truth,' he added in a sudden burst, 'I'm not very happy about this case.'

Barker's jaw dropped just a little. 'What's wrong?' he said. 'It's the clearest case the Yard has had for some time.'

'Yes; on the surface. But, if you dig a bit, there seems to be more than meets the eye.'

'What do you mean? – that there was more than one in it?'

'No; I mean that there's just the barest possibility that we've got the wrong one.'

For a little there was silence. 'Grant,' said Barker at last, 'I never knew you lose your nerve before. You need a holiday. I don't think scooting across moors can be good for you. Perhaps the jogging movement is addling to the brain. You certainly have lost your critical faculty.'

Grant could find nothing to say except 'Well, here's the statement he gave us last night,' and he handed it over. While Barker was reading it, he crossed to the window, gazed at the patch of green and the river in the sun, and wondered if he were making a complete fool of himself to be worrying when he had a good case. Well, fool or no fool, he would go along to Waterloo as soon as his chief had finished with him, and see what he could pick up there.

When Barker dropped the statement with a little flop on to the table, Grant turned eagerly to see what effect it had had on him. 'Well,' said that worthy, 'it leaves me with a strong desire to meet Mr Lamont.'

'Why?' asked Grant.

'Because I'd like to see in person the man who tried sobstuff on Inspector Grant and got away with it. The unimpressionable Grant!'

'That's how it strikes you, is it?' Grant said gloomily. 'You don't believe a word of it?'

'Not a word,' said Barker cheerfully. 'It's about the thinnest story I've known put up for some time. But

then I should think the man was hard put to it to find
any way out of the evidence at all. He did his damnedest
– I will say that for him.'

'Well, look at it from the other way, and can you think
of a reasonable explanation for Lamont's killing Sorrell?'

'Tut, tut, Grant, you've been at the Yard for I don't know
how many years, and you're looking at this late stage for
reasonable murders. You need a holiday, man. Lamont
probably killed Sorrell because the way he ate had got
on his nerves. Besides, it isn't any of our business to fit
psychology to people or to provide motives or anything of
that sort. So don't worry your head. Fit them with good
water-tight evidence and provide them with a cell, and
that's all we have to bother about.'

There was a short silence, and Grant gathered up his
papers preparatory to taking his leave and getting along
to Waterloo.

'Look here,' said Barker out of the silence, 'all joshing
apart – do you *believe* the man didn't do it?'

'I don't see how he could *not* have,' Grant said. 'There's
the evidence. I can't say why I'm uneasy about the thing,
but that doesn't alter the fact that I am.'

'Is this an example of the famous flair?' said Barker, with
a return to his former manner.

But Grant would not be other than serious this morning.
'No; I think it's just that I have seen Lamont and talked to
him when he was telling his story, and you haven't.'

'That's what I said to begin with,' Barker reminded him.
'Lamont has tried a sob-story on you and put it over . . .
Put it out of your head, Grant, until you get even a tittle of
evidence to substantiate it. Flair is all very well, and I don't
deny that you have been uncanny once or twice, but it has
always been more or less in accordance with the evidence
before, and in this case it most emphatically isn't.'

'That's the very thing that makes me worry most. Why
should I not be pleased with the case as it stands? What is

it that makes me *not* pleased? There is something, but I'm blowed if I can see what it is. I keep feeling that something is wrong somewhere. I want something that will either tighten up the evidence against Lamont, or loosen it.'

'Well, well,' said Barker good-humouredly, 'go ahead. You've done so well so far that you can afford to play yourself for a few days more. The evidence is good enough for the police court – or any other kind of court, for that of it.'

So Grant betook himself through the sunny, busy morning to Waterloo, trailing a little cloud of discontent behind him as he went. As he stepped from the warm pavement into the cool vault of the best but saddest of all London stations – the very name of it reeks of endings and partings – gloom sat on his face like a portent. Having obtained the necessary authority to open any luggage that Sorrell might have left, he repaired to the left-luggage room, where a highly interested official said, 'Yes sir, I know them. Left about a fortnight ago, they were,' and led him to the luggage in question. It consisted of two well-worn trunks, and it occurred to Grant that neither was labelled with the Rotterdam-Manhattan company's labels as they should have been if Sorrell had intended going aboard at Southampton. Nor were they addressed at all. On ordinary labels on each was written in Sorrell's writing, 'A. Sorrell,' but nothing else. With his own keys and a slight quickening of heart he opened them. Below the top garment in the first were Sorrell's passport and tickets for the voyage. Why had he left them there? Why not have taken them with him in a pocket-book? But alongside them were the labels supplied by the company for the labelling of passengers' luggage. Perhaps for some reason Sorrell had meant to open the trunk again before going down on the boat train, and had postponed labelling it till then. And had left his tickets and passport there as being safer than a pocket-book in a queue.

Grant continued his examination. There was no further
indication that Sorrell had not intended to go abroad as he
säid. The clothes were packed with a care and neatness that
surely argued a further use for them. There was method,
too, in the manner of their disposition. The articles which
would presumably be needed first were there to hand, and
the less necessary ones farther down. It was difficult, looking
at the packing, to believe that Sorrell had not intended
to take out the articles himself at some future time. And
there was no information, no letters, no photographs. That
last struck Grant as the only remarkable thing about the
luggage – that a man who was going abroad should have
no souvenirs of any sort with him. And then he came on
them, packed at the bottom between a pair of shoes – a little
bundle of snapshots. Hastily he untied the piece of string
that held them together, and looked them through. At least
half of them were photographs of Gerald Lamont, either
alone or with Sorrell, and the rest were old army groups.
The only women in the collection were Mrs Everett and
some V.A.D.'s who seemed to be incidental to the army
groups. Grant almost groaned aloud in his disappointment
– he had untied that string with such mighty if vague hopes
– but when he had tied up the bundle again, he put it
in his pocket. V.A.D.'s might be incidental in a group,
but individually they were women and, as such, not to
be despised.

And that was all! That was all he was going to get from
the luggage he had been banking so heavily on. Troubled
and disappointed, he began to put the things back as he
had found them. As he lifted a coat to fold it, something fell
from a pocket and rolled along the floor of the left-luggage
room. It was a small blue velvet case such as jewellers use
for their wares. No terrier is quicker on a rat than Grant
was on that small slowly revolving box, and no girl's heart
beat at the opening of a velvet case as Grant's heart beat
at the opening of that one. A press with his thumb and the

lid flew up. On the deep blue lining lay a brooch such as
women wear in their hats. It was made from small pearls
in the form of a monogram, and was very simple and rather
beautiful. 'M. R.,' said Grant aloud. Margaret Ratcliffe.

His brain had said it before his thoughts had time to
gather round it. He stared at the trinket for a little, took
it up from its velvet bed, turned it in his hand, and put
it back again. Was this his clue, after all? And did these
common-enough initials point to the woman who kept
stumbling into this case so persistently? It was she who
had stood behind Sorrell when he was killed; it was she
who had booked a berth on the same day on the same ship
to the same destination as Sorrell; and now the only thing
of value found among his belongings was a brooch with her
initials. He examined it again. It did not look the kind of
thing that is sold by the dozen, and the name on the box
was not that of a firm usually patronised by impecunious
young bookmakers. It was that of a Bond Street firm of good
reputation, with wares corresponding in price. He thought
that, on the whole, his best step would be to go and see
Messrs Gallio & Stein. He locked up the trunks, put the
brooch in his pocket with the snapshots, and departed from
Waterloo. As he mounted the stairs of a bus he remembered
that Lamont had said that the notes he had been given by
Sorrell had been wrapped in white paper such as jewellers
use. One more good mark for Lamont. But if Sorrell were
going abroad in the company of, or because of, Margaret
Ratcliffe, why should he hand over such a sum to Lamont?
Mrs Ratcliffe had money of her own, Simpson had reported,
but no man started out to live on the woman he was eloping
with, even if he was sorry to leave his friend in comparative
poverty.

The business of Messrs Gallio & Stein is conducted in a
small and rather dark shop in Old Bond Street, and Grant
found but one assistant visible. As soon as Grant opened
the blue box the man recognised the brooch. It was he who

had dealt with the customer about it. No; they did not have them in stock. It had been made to order for a Mr Sorrell, a young fair man. It had cost thirty guineas, and had been finished – he consulted a book – on the sixth, a Tuesday, and Mr Sorrell had called and paid for it and taken it away with him on that date. No; the assistant had never seen the man before. He had described what he wanted, and had made no fuss about the price.

Grant went away thinking deeply, but no nearer a solution. That a man in Sorrell's position had been willing to pay thirty guineas for an ornament argued infatuation of an extreme type. He had not presented it to the object of his devotion up to the time of his departure. That meant that it could be presented only after he had left Britain. It was packed deep in his trunk. He had no friends in America that anyone knew of. But – Margaret Ratcliffe was going out by the same boat. That woman! How she came into things! And her entry, instead of making things clearer, merely made the muddle worse than before. For muddle Grant was now convinced there was.

It was nearly lunch-time, but he went back to the Yard because he was expecting a message from the post office. It was there waiting for him. On the morning of the fourteenth (Wednesday) a telegram had been handed in at Brixton High Street post office addressed to Albert Sorrell on board the *Queen of Arabia*, and reading 'Sorry. – JERRY.' It had presumably been delivered, since there had been no word to the contrary, but it was not unlikely that, in the shoal of telegrams attending the departure of a big liner, if it had not been claimed, it might have been mislaid.

'So that's that!' said Grant aloud; and Williams, who was in attendance, said, 'Yes, sir,' accommodatingly.

And now what? He wanted to see Mrs Ratcliffe, but he did not know whether she had returned home. If he rang to inquire, she would be forewarned of his renewed interest in her. He would have to send Simpson again. Mrs Ratcliffe would have to wait for the moment. He would go and see Mrs Everett instead. He gave Simpson his instructions, and after lunch went down to Fulham.

Mrs Everett opened the door to him, with no sign of fear or embarrassment. Judging from the expression of her eyes, her hostility was too great to permit of her harbouring any other emotion. What line should he take with her? The stern official one would be useless both from the point of impressing her and from the point of extracting information; the dead man had done well to call her Lady Macbeth. And a magnanimous overlooking of the part she had played in Lamont's escape would also have no effect. Flattery would earn nothing but her scorn. It occurred to him that the only method of dealing with her to any advantage was to tell her the truth.

'Mrs Everett,' he said, when she had led him in, 'we have a case that will hang Gerald Lamont, but I'm not satisfied myself with the evidence. So far, I haven't caught Lamont out in a mis-statement, and there is just the faintest possibility that his story is true. But no jury will believe it. It is a very thin tale, and, told baldly in a court of law, would be beyond belief. But I feel that a little more information will tip the scales one way or another – either prove Lamont's guilt beyond a doubt or acquit him. So I've come to you. If he's innocent, then the chances are that the extra information will go to prove that, and not his guilt. And so I've come to you for the information.'

She examined him in silence, trying to read his motive through the camouflage of his words.

'I've told you the truth,' he said, 'and you can take it or leave it. It isn't any softness for Gerald Lamont that has brought me here, I assure you. It's a matter of my own professional pride. If there's any possibility of a mistake, then I've got to worry at the case until I'm *sure* I've got the right man.'

'What do you want to know?' she said, and it sounded like a capitulation. At least it was a compromise.

'In the first place, what letters habitually came for Sorrell, and where did they come from?'

'He got very few letters altogether. He had not many friends on these terms.'

'Did you ever know letters addressed in a woman's hand come for him?'

'Yes; occasionally.'

'Where were they posted?'

'In London, I think.'

'What was the writing like?'

'Very round and regular and rather large.'

'Do you know who the woman was?'

'No.'

'How long had the letters been coming for him?'

'Oh, for years! I don't remember how long.'

'And in all these years you never found out who his correspondent was?'

'No.'

'Did no woman ever come to see him here?'

'No.'

'How often did the letters come?'

'Oh, not often! About once in six weeks, perhaps, or a little oftener.'

'Lamont has said that Sorrell was secretive. Is that so?'

'No, not secretive. But he was jealous. I mean jealous of the things he liked. When he cared very much about a thing he would – hug it to himself, if you know what I mean.'

'Did the arrival of the letters make any difference to him – make him pleased or otherwise?'

'No; he didn't show any feeling that way. He was very quiet, you know.'

'Tell me,' said Grant, and produced the velvet case, 'have you ever seen that before?' He snapped it open to her gaze.

'M. R.,' she said slowly, just as Grant had done. 'No; I never saw it before. What has that got to do with Bertie?'

'That was found in the pocket of a coat in Sorrell's trunk.'

She put her worn hand out for it, looked at it with curiosity, and gave it back to him.

'Can you suggest any reason why Sorrell should commit suicide?'

'No, I can't. But I can tell you that about a week before he left to go – left here – a small parcel came by post for him. It was waiting for him when he came home one evening. He came home that night before Jerry – Mr Lamont.'

'Do you mean as small a parcel as this?'

'Not quite, but as big as that would be with wrapping round it.'

But the man in Gallio & Stein's had said that Sorrell had taken the brooch away with him. 'Can you remember what day that was?'

'I wouldn't swear to it, but I think it was the Thursday before he left.'

On Tuesday, Sorrell had taken the little parcel from the jeweller, and on Thursday evening the little parcel had been delivered at Sorrell's rooms. The inference was obvious. The woman had refused his offering.

'What was the writing on the parcel like?'

'It was addressed only on the label, and the address was printed.'

'Did Sorrell show any emotion on opening it?'

'I wasn't there when he opened it.'

'Then afterwards?'

'No; I don't think so. He was very quiet. But then he was always quiet.'

'I see. When did Lamont come and tell you what had happened?'

'On Saturday.'

'You knew before then that the man in the queue was Sorrell?'

'No; the description of the man wasn't published in full until Thursday, and I naturally thought that Bert had sailed on Wednesday. I knew that Jerry would have been with him up to the last minute, so I didn't worry. It was only when I saw the description of the man the police wanted that I put the two descriptions together and began to wonder. That was on Saturday.'

'And what did you think then?'

'I thought, as I think now, that there was a very bad mistake somewhere.'

'Will you tell me what Lamont told you? He has made a statement to us already.'

She hesitated a moment and then said, 'Well, I can't see that things can be worse than they are,' and told him the story Lamont had told her. To the smallest detail it coincided with what he had told Grant and the constable in the train coming south.

'And you didn't find anything fishy in such a story?'

'I don't know that I would have believed the story from a stranger' – she was extraordinarily like her niece at that moment, the inspector thought – 'but, you see, I know Jerry Lamont.'

'But you knew Sorrell very much longer, and didn't know the things that mattered in his life.'

'Yes, but that was Bertie. Length of time has nothing to do with it. I heard about everything that happened to Jerry, girls included.'

'Well, thank you for telling me all you did,' Grant said as he stood up. 'If nothing you have said helps Lamont very much, at least it doesn't incriminate him any further. Did you ever have any reason to think that Sorrell wasn't going to America at all?'

'Do you mean that he was going somewhere else?'

'No; I mean that, if he contemplated suicide, his going to America might have been an elaborate blind.'

'I certainly don't think that. I'm sure he intended to go to America.'

Grant thanked her again, and went back to the Yard. From Simpson he learned that Mrs Ratcliffe and her sister were still at Eastbourne, and there was no word of their return.

'Does Mr Ratcliffe go up and down to Eastbourne, then?'

No; Mr Ratcliffe had been down only once since they were there, and then he didn't stay the night.

'Did you find out what the quarrel was about?'

No; the maid apparently had not known. From the secret amusement that radiated from Simpson's freckled face Grant deduced that the interview with the Ratcliffe maid had been more amusing than informative, and he dismissed him dolefully. He would have to go down to Eastbourne and see Mrs Ratcliffe – accidentally; but tomorrow he would have to attend the Lamont case at the police court. It would be a purely formal occasion, but he would have to be there. There was no time to go down to Eastbourne tonight, and get back, with any hope of obtaining the casual kind of meeting with Mrs Ratcliffe that he contemplated. But, if the case was over quickly tomorrow, he would go straight down there. He wished duty did not call him to the court. That was routine, and the visit to Mrs Ratcliffe was not – it was a hunt, a sporting chance, a gamble. He wanted so badly to see what Margaret Ratcliffe's face would look like when he showed her the monogrammed brooch.

CHAPTER 16

MISS DINMONT ASSISTS

Gowbridge Police Court is at no time a cheerful building. It has the mouldering atmosphere of a mausoleum combined with the disinfected and artificial cheerfulness of a hospital, the barrenness of a schoolroom, the stuffiness of a tube, and the ugliness of a meeting-house. Grant knew it well, and he never entered it without an unconscious groan, not for the sorrows that hung about it like invisible webs, but for his own sorrow in having to pass a morning in such surroundings. It was on occasions such as a morning in Gowbridge Police Court that he was wont to refer to his profession as a dog's life. and today he was in a bad mood. He found himself looking with a jaundiced eye on the rank and file of the force as represented by those on duty in the court, on the hearty and self-sufficient magistrate, on the loafers on the public benches. Conscious of his nauseated mental condition, he hunted round as usual for the reason with a view to banishing it, and after a little cogitation, ran it to earth. He was unhappy about giving his evidence! At the bottom of his heart he wanted to say, 'Wait a bit! There's something here that I don't understand. Just wait till I find out a little more.' But being a police inspector with perfectly good evidence and the countenance of his superiors, he could not do that. He could not qualify what he had to say with any remarks of that sort. He glanced across the court to where the lawyer who had Lamont's case was sitting. Lamont would want some bigger guns than that when he came up for his trial at the Old Bailey or he wouldn't have a dog's chance. But big guns cost money, and lawyers are professional men, not philanthropists.

Two cases were summarily dealt with, and then Lamont was brought into court. He looked ill, but was perfectly collected. He even acknowledged the inspector's presence with a slight smile. His arrival created a stir in the public part of the court. There had been no press warning that the case would be dealt with there today, and all those present were either curious idlers or friends of principals in other cases. Grant had looked for Mrs Everett, but she was not there. Lamont's sole friend in court seemed to be the paid one who had charge of his interests. Nevertheless, Grant looked again now for a sign of personal interest on any face. He had found before now that useful information can be obtained from the expressions of presumed strangers in the body of a court. But a careful scrutiny revealed nothing; nothing but curiosity was apparent on any countenance in the audience. But as he left the box, after giving his evidence, he saw a new-comer at the back of the court, and the new-comer was Miss Dinmont. Now Miss Dinmont's holiday did not finish for a week yet, and she had said at that fateful manse tea that since she had holidays only once a year she spent them all at home; and as he sat down, Inspector Grant was marvelling at the girl who would not soften towards a man she believed to be guilty of a terrible thing, but who would cut short her holiday and travel five hundred miles to hear the evidence for herself. Lamont had his back to her, and it was unlikely, unless he deliberately looked round the room as he went out, that he would be aware of her presence. She caught the inspector's eye upon her, and bowed to him, unperturbed. In her neat, dark tailor-made and small hat she looked the complete, self-possessed, charming woman of the world. She might have been a writer looking for copy for all the emotion she showed. Even when Lamont was remanded and led out of court, her good-looking face was not stirred. They were very alike, aunt and niece, Grant thought; that was probably why they did not like each other. He went up to her as she was leaving and greeted her.

'Are you doing anything, Miss Dinmont? Come and have lunch with me, will you?'

'I thought inspectors lived on tablets of condensed beef extract, or something like that, during the day. Do they really have time to sit down to a meal?'

'Not only that, but they have a very good one. Come and see!' And she smiled and came.

He took her to Laurent's, and over the meal she was quite frank about her change of plans. 'I couldn't stay in Carninnish after what happened,' she said. 'And I had an itch to hear the court proceedings, so I just came. I have never been in a court of law in my life before. It isn't an impressive spectacle.'

'Not a police court, perhaps,' he admitted; 'but wait till you see a big trial.'

'I hope I never shall — but it seems that I'm going to. You have a beautiful case, haven't you?'

'That is the word my chief uses about it.'

'And don't you agree?' he asked quickly.

'Oh yes, certainly.' To admit to Mrs Everett that he was not satisfied was one thing, but he was not going to blazon it abroad. And this independent girl was certainly 'abroad'.

Presently she mentioned Lamont directly. 'He looks bad,' she said judicially, using 'bad' in her professional sense. 'Will they look after him in prison?'

'Oh yes,' said Grant; 'they take very good care of them.'

'Is there any chance of their badgering him? Because I warn you he won't stand any badgering as he is now. Either he'll be seriously ill or he'll say that he did it.'

'Then you don't believe he did?'

'I think it's unlikely, but I'm quite aware that the fact that I think so doesn't make it so. I just want him to get a fair deal.'

Grant remarked on her matter-of-fact acceptance of his word at Carninnish as to the man's guilt.

'Well,' she said, 'you knew much more about it than I did. I never saw him till three days previously. I liked him – but that didn't make him guilty or innocent. Besides, I'd rather be a brute than a fool.'

Grant considered this unfeminine pronouncement in silence, and she repeated her question.

'Oh no,' Grant said; 'this isn't America. And in any case, he has made his statement, as you heard, and he is not likely to change his mind or make another.'

'Has he any friends?'

'Only your aunt, Mrs Everett.'

'And who will pay for his defence?'

Grant explained.

'Then he can't have any of the good ones. That doesn't seem to me particularly fair – for the law to keep famous lawyers to do their prosecuting and not famous lawyers to defend poor criminals.'

Grant grinned. 'Oh, he'll have a fair deal, don't you worry. It is the police who are harried round in a murder case.'

'Did you never, in all your experience, know a case where the law made a mistake?'

'Yes, several,' Grant admitted cheerfully. 'But they were all cases of mistaken identity. And that's not in question here.'

'No; but there must be cases where the evidence is nothing but a lot of things that have nothing to do with each other put together until they look like something. Like a patchwork bedcover.'

She was getting too 'hot' to be comfortable in her search after enlightenment, and Grant reassured her and unostentatiously changed the subject – and presently fell silent; a sudden idea had occurred to him. If he went down to Eastbourne alone, Mrs Ratcliffe, however casual his appearance, might be suspicious of his bona-fides. But if he appeared with a woman companion, he would be accepted at once as off duty, and any suspicion his presence might arouse would be lulled until he could get Mrs Ratcliffe completely off her guard. And the whole success of the expedition depended on that – that she should be unprepared for any demonstration on his part.

'Look here,' he said, 'are you doing anything this afternoon?'

'No; why?'

'Have you done your good deed for the day?'

'No, I think I've been entirely selfish today.'

'Well, get it off your chest by coming down to Eastbourne with me this afternoon as my cousin, and being my cousin till dinner. Will you?'

She considered him gravely. 'I don't think so. Are you on the track of some other unhappy person.'

'Not exactly. I'm on the track of something, I think.'

'I don't think so,' she said slowly. 'If it were just fun, I'd do it like a shot. But when it means something I don't know for someone I've never met – you see?'

'I say, I can't tell you about it, but if I give you my word that you'll never regret it, will you believe me and come?'

'But why should I believe you?' she said sweetly.

The inspector was rather staggered. He had commended her lack of faith in Lamont, but her logical application of it to himself disconcerted him.

'I don't know why,' he admitted. 'I suppose police officers are just as capable of fibbing as anyone.'

'And considerably more unscrupulous than most,' she added dryly.

'Well, it's just a matter for your own decision, then. You won't regret coming. I'll swear to that, if you like – and police officers are not given to perjury, however unscrupulous they may be.'

She laughed. 'That got you, didn't it?' she said delightedly. And after a pause, 'Yes, I'll come and be your cousin with pleasure. None of my cousins are half as good-looking.' But the mockery in her tone was too apparent for Grant to find much pleasure in the compliment.

They went down through the green countryside to the sea, however, in perfect amity, and when Grant looked up suddenly and saw the downs he was surprised. There they stood in possession of the landscape, like someone who has tiptoed into a room unheard, and startles the occupant by appearing in the middle of the floor. He had never known a journey to the south coast pass so quickly. They were alone in the compartment, and he proceeded to give her her bearings.

'I am staying down at Eastbourne – no, I can't be, I'm not dressed for the part – we've both come down for the afternoon, then. I am going to get into conversation with two women who know me already in my professional capacity. When the talk turns on hat brooches I want you to produce this from your bag, and say that you have just bought it for your sister. Your name, by the way, is Eleanor Raymond, and your sister's is Mary. That is all. Just leave the brooch lying round until I arrange my tie. That will be the signal that I have had all I want.'

'All right. What is your first name, by the way?'

'Alan.'

'All right, Alan. I nearly forgot to ask you that. It would have been a joke if I had not known my cousin's name! . . . It's a queer world, isn't it? Look at those primroses in the sun and think of all the people in terrible trouble this minute.'

'No, don't. That way madness lies. Think of the pleasantly deserted beach we're going to see in a few minutes.'

'Do you ever go to the Old Vic?' she asked, and they were still telling each other how wonderful Miss Baylis was when they ran into the station; and Grant said, 'Come on

Eleanor,' and, grabbing her by the arm, picked her from the carriage like a small boy impatient to try a spade on the sands.

The beach, as Grant had prophesied, was in that pleasantly deserted condition that makes the south-coast resorts so attractive out of the season. It was sunny and very warm, and a few groups lay about on the shingle, basking in the sun in an aristocratic isolation unknown to summer visitors.

'We'll go along the front and come back along the beach' Grant said. 'They are bound to be out on a day like this.'

'Heaven send they aren't on the downs,' she said. 'I don't mind walking, but it would take till tomorrow to quarter these.'

'I think the downs are ruled out. The lady I am interested in isn't much of a walker, I should say.'

'What is her name?'

'No, I won't tell you that until I introduce you. You are supposed not to have heard of her, and it will be better if you really haven't.'

They walked in silence along the trim front towards Holywell. Everything was trim, with that well-ordered trimness that is so typically Eastbourne. Even the sea was trim – and slightly exclusive. And Beachy Head had the air of having been set down there as a good finish off to the front, and of being perfectly conscious of the fact. They had not been walking for more than ten minutes when Grant said, 'We'll go down to the beach now. I'm almost certain we passed the couple I want some time ago. They are down on the shingle.'

They left the pavement and began a slow foot-slipping stroll back to the piers again. Presently they approached two women who were reclining in deck-chairs facing the sea. One, the slighter one, was curled up with her back to Miss Dinmont and the inspector, and was apparently reading. The other was snowed round with magazines, writing-pad, sunshade, and all the other recognised paraphernalia of an afternoon on the beach, but she was doing nothing and appeared to be half asleep. As they came abreast of the chairs the inspector let his glance fall casually on them and then stopped.

'Why, Mrs Ratcliffe!' he said. 'Are you down here recuperating? What glorious weather!'

Mrs Ratcliffe, after one startled glance, welcomed him. 'You remember my sister, Miss Lethbridge?'

Grant shook hands and said, 'I don't think you know my cousin—'

But the gods were good to Grant that day. Before he could commit himself, Miss Lethbridge said in her pleasant drawl:

'Good heavens, if it isn't Dandie Dinmont! How are you, my dear woman?'

'Do you know each other, then?' asked Grant, feeling like a man who has opened his eyes to find that one more step would have taken him over a precipice.

'Rather!' said Miss Lethbridge. 'I had my appendicitis in a room at St Michael's, and Dandie Dinmont held my head and my hand alternately. And she held them very well, I will say that for her. Shake hands with Miss Dinmont, Meg. My sister, Mrs Ratcliffe. Who'd have thought you had cousins in the force!'

'I suppose you are recuperating too, Inspector?' Mrs Ratcliffe said.

'You could call it that, I suppose,' the inspector said. 'My cousin is on holiday from Mike's, and I have finished my case, so we are making a day of it.'

'Well, it isn't tea-time yet,' said Miss Lethbridge. 'Sit down and talk to us for a little. I haven't seen Dandie for ages.'

'You'll be glad to have that awful case off your hands, Inspector,' her sister said as they subsided on the shingle. She spoke as though the murder had been just as much of an event in Grant's life as it had been in hers, but the inspector let it pass, and presently the talk veered away from the murder and went via health, restaurants, hotels, and food to dress, or the lack of it.

'I love your hat brooch,' said Miss Dinmont idly to her friend. 'I can think of nothing but hat brooches this afternoon, because we've just been buying one for a mutual cousin who is getting married. You know – like getting a new coat and seeing people's coats as you never saw them before. I have it here somewhere.' She reached for her bag without altering her reclining position, and rummaged in it until she produced the blue velvet box. 'What do you think of it?' She opened it and extended it to them.

'Oh, lovely!' said Miss Lethbridge, but Mrs Ratcliffe said nothing for a little.

'M. R.,' she said at last. 'Why, the initials are the same as mine. What is your cousin's name?'

'Mary Raymond.'

'Sounds like a goody-goody heroine out of a book,' remarked Miss Lethbridge. 'Is she goody?'

'No, not particularly, though she's marrying an awful stodge. You like it, then?'

'Rather!' said Miss Lethbridge.

'Beautiful!' said her sister. 'May I have a look at it?' She took the case in her hands, examined the brooch back and front, and handed it back. 'Beautiful!' she said again. 'And most uncommon. Can you get them ready-made, so to speak?'

Grant's infinitesimal shake of the head answered Miss Dinmont's cry for help. 'No, we had it made,' she said.

'Well, she's a lucky devil, Mary Raymond, and if she doesn't like it, she has very poor taste.'

'Oh, if she doesn't like it,' said Grant, 'she can just fib and say she does, and we'll never be a bit the wiser. All women are expert fibbers.'

''Ark at 'im!' said Miss Lethbridge. 'Poor disillusioned creature!'

'Well, isn't it true? Your social life is one long series of fibs. You are very sorry – You are not at home – You would have come, but – You wish someone would stay longer. If you aren't fibbing to your friends, you are fibbing to your maids.'

'I may fib to my friends,' said Mrs Ratcliffe, 'but I most certainly do not fib to my maids!'

'Don't you?' said Grant, turning idly to look at her. No one, to see him there, with his hat tilted over his eyes and his body lounging, would have said that Inspector Grant was on duty. 'You were going to the United States the day after the murder, weren't you?' She nodded calmly. 'Well, why did you tell your maid that you were going to Yorkshire?'

Mrs Ratcliffe made a movement to sit erect and then sank back again. 'I don't know what you're talking about. I most certainly never told my maid I was going to Yorkshire. I said New York.'

That was so patently possible that Grant hastened to get in first with, 'Well, she thinks you said Yorkshire,' before Mrs Ratcliffe inevitably said, 'How do you know?'

'There isn't anything a police inspector doesn't know,' he said.

'There isn't anything he won't do, you mean,' she said angrily. 'Have you been walking out with Annie? I shouldn't be surprised if you suspected me of having done the murder myself.'

'I shouldn't wonder,' said Grant. 'Inspectors suspect all the world.'

'Well, I suppose I can only give thanks that your suspicions led to nothing worse than walking out with my maid.'

Grant caught Miss Dinmont's eyes on him under the short brim of her hat, and there was a new expression in them. The conversation had given away the fact that Mrs Ratcliffe had some connection with the queue murder, and Miss Dinmont was being given furiously to think. Grant smiled reassuringly at her. 'They don't think I'm nice to know,' he said. 'But at least you can stick up for me. Justice is the thing I live for.' Surely she must see, if she thought about it, that his inquiries in this direction could not be very incriminating to Lamont. The chances must be the other way about.

'Let's go and have tea,' Miss Lethbridge said. 'Come along to our hotel. Or shall we go somewhere else, Meg? I'm sick of anchovy sandwiches and currant cake.'

Grant suggested a tea-shop which had a reputation for cakes, and began to bundle Mrs Ratcliffe's scattered belongings together. As he did so, he let the writing-pad drop so that it fell open on the sand, the first sheet exhibiting a half-written letter. Staring up at him in the bright sunlight were the round large letters of Mrs Ratcliffe's script. 'Sorry!' he said, and restored the block to the pile of papers and magazines.

Tea as a gastronomic function might have been a success, but as a social occasion Grant felt that it failed miserably. Two out of his three companions regarded him with a distrust of which he could not fail to be conscious, and the third – Miss Lethbridge – was so cheerfully determined to pretend that she was not aware of her sister's ill humour that she tacitly confessed her own awareness of tension. When they had taken leave of each other, and Grant and his companion were on their way to the station in the fading light, he said, 'You've been a brick, Miss Dinmont. I'll never forget it,' but she did not answer. She was so quiet on the way home that his already discontented thoughts were further distracted. Why couldn't the girl trust him? Did she think him an ogre to make such unscrupulous use of her as she suspected? And all the time his looker-on half was smiling sardonically and saying, 'You, a police inspector, asking for trust! Why, Machiavelli was fastidious compared with a C.I.D. man.'

When Grant was at war with himself his mouth had a

slight twist in it, and tonight the twist was very marked. He had found not one definite answer to the problems that troubled him. He did not know whether Mrs Ratcliffe had recognised the brooch or not. He did not know whether she had said New York to her maid or not. And though he had seen her writing, that helped to no conclusion; a large percentage of women wrote large and very round hands. Her pause at sight of the brooch might have been merely the pause while she read the twined initial. Her veiled questions as to its origin might have been entirely innocent. On the other hand, they most emphatically might not. If she had anything to do with the murder, it must be recognised that she was clever and not likely to give herself away. She had already fooled him once when he dismissed her so lightly from his mind on the first day of the investigations. There was nothing to prevent her from going on fooling him unless he found a damning fact that could not be explained away.

'What do you think of Mrs Ratcliffe?' he asked Miss Dinmont. They were alone in the compartment except for a country yokel and his girl.

'Why?' she asked. 'Is this merely making conversation, or is it more investigation?'

'I say, Miss Dinmont, are you sore with me?'

'I don't think that is the correct expression for what I feel,' she said. 'It isn't often I feel a fool, but I do tonight,' and he was dismayed at the bitterness in her voice.

'But there's not the slightest need,' he said, genuinely distressed. 'You did the job like a professional, and there was nothing in it to make you feel like that. I'm up against something I don't understand, and I wanted you to help me. That's all. That's why I asked you about Mrs Ratcliffe just now. I want a woman's opinion to help me – an unbiased woman's opinion.'

'Well, if you want my candid opinion, I think the woman is a fool.'

'Oh? You don't think she's clever, deep down?'

'I don't think she has a deep down.'

'You think she's just shallow? But surely—' He considered.

'Well, you asked me what I thought, and I've told you. I think she's a shallow fool.'

'And her sister?' Grant asked, though that had nothing to do with the investigations.

'Oh, she is different. She has any amount of brain and personality, though you mightn't think so.'

'Would you say that Mrs Ratcliffe would commit a murder?'

'No, certainly not!'

'Why not?'

'Because she hasn't got the guts,' said Miss Dinmont elegantly. 'She might do the thing in a fit of temper, but all the world would know it the next minute, and ever afterwards as long as she lived.'

'Do you think she might know about one and keep the knowledge to herself?'

'You mean the knowledge of who was guilty?'

'Yes.'

Miss Dinmont sat looking searchingly at the inspector's impassive face. The lights of station lamps moved slowly over and past it as the train slid to a halt. 'Eridge! Eridge!' called the porter, clumping down the deserted platform. The unexpectant voice had died into the distance, and the train had gathered itself into motion again before she spoke.

'I wish I could read what you are thinking,' she said desperately. 'Am I being your fool for the second time in one day?'

'Miss Dinmont, believe me, so far I have never known you do a foolish thing, and I'm willing to take a large bet I never shall.'

'That might do for Mrs Ratcliffe,' she said. 'But I'll tell you. I think she might keep quiet about a murder, but there would have to be a reason that mattered to her*self* overwhelmingly. That's all.'

He was not sure whether the last two words meant that that was all that she could tell him, or whether it was an indication that pumping was to cease; but she had given him food for thought, and he was quiet until they ran into Victoria. 'Where are you living?' he asked. 'Not at the hospital?'

'No; I'm staying at my club in Cavendish Square.'

He accompanied her there against her wish, and said good-night on the doorstep, since she would not be persuaded to dine with him.

'You have some days of holiday yet,' he said, with kindly intention. 'How are you going to fill them in?'

'In the first place, I'm going to see my aunt. I have come to the conclusion that the evils one knows are less dreadful than the evils one doesn't know.'

But the inspector caught the glint of the hall light on her teeth, and went away feeling less a martyr to injustice than he had for some hours past.

CHAPTER 17

SOLUTION

Grant was disconsolate. His radiance was dimmed as the Yard had never known it dimmed. He even snapped at the faithful Williams, and only the surprised hurt on that bland pink face recalled him to himself for a little. Mrs Field blamed it unconditionally on the Scots: their food, their ways, their climate, and their country; and said dramatically to her husband, after the manner of a childish arithmetic, 'If four days in a country like that makes him like this, what would a month do?' That was on the occasion when she was exhibiting to her better-half the torn and muddy tweeds that Grant had brought back with him from his foray in the hills; but she made no secret of her beliefs and her prejudices, and Grant suffered her as mildly as his worried soul would permit. Back in the everyday routine and clearing-up arrears of work he would stop and ask himself, What had he left undone? What possible avenue of exploration had he left untravelled? He tried deliberately to stop himself from further questing, to accept the general theory that the police case was too good to be other than true, to subscribe to Barker's opinion that he had 'nerves' and needed a holiday. But it was no use. The feeling that there was something wrong somewhere always flowed back the minute he stopped bullying himself. If anything, the conviction grew as the slow, unproductive, tedious days passed, and he would go back in his mind to that first day, little more than a fortnight ago, when he had viewed an unknown body, and go over the case again from there. Had he missed a point somewhere? There was the knife

that had proved so barren a clue – an individual thing to
be so unproductive. Yet no one had claimed to have seen or
owned one like it. All it had done was to provide the scar on
the murderer's hand – a piece of evidence conclusive only
when allied with much more.

There was this, there was that, there was the other, but
all of them stood the strain of pulling apart, and remained
in their separate entities what they had been in the pattern
of the whole; and Grant was left, as before, with the belief, so
strong and so unreasonable that it amounted to superstition,
that the monogrammed brooch in Sorrell's pocket was the
key to the whole mystery; that it was shouting its tale at
them, only they could not hear. It lay in his desk with
the knife now, and the consciousness of it was with him
continually. When he had nothing to do for the moment
he would take both it and the knife from the drawer and
sit there 'mooning over them', as the sympathetic Williams
reported to his subordinate. They were becoming a fetish
with him. There was some connection between the two –
between the offering that Sorrell had made to a woman and
the knife that had killed him. He felt that as strongly and
distinctly as he felt the sunlight that warmed his hands as
he played with the objects on the table. And yet both his
own reason and that of others laughed at the idea. What
had the brooch to do with the affair! Gerald Lamont had
killed Sorrell with a small Italian knife – his grandmother
had been Italian, and if he hadn't inherited the knife he had
probably inherited the will to use one – after a quarrel in a
queue. On his own showing he resented Sorrell's departure
from Britain, leaving him jobless and more or less penniless.
Sorrell had had the money to pay for his passage, but had
not offered it. And on his own showing he had not known
that Sorrell had given him any money until two days after
the murder. Where did a pearl monogrammed brooch come
into that? The little silver-and-enamel knife was a *pièce de
résistance* in the case – a prince of exhibits. It would be

photographed, paragraphed, and discussed in every house in England, and the little crack on its boss handle would hang a man. And all the time that pearl brooch, which would not appear in the case at all, glowed a silent and complete refutal of all their puny theories.

It was utterly ridiculous. Grant hated the sight of the thing, and yet he went back again and again to it as a man does to a mocking mistress. He tried 'shutting his eyes' – his favourite resort in a difficulty – and either distracted himself with amusement, or buried himself in work for long periods at a time; but always when he opened his eyes again it was the brooch he saw. That had never happened before – that he had opened his eyes again and seen no new angle in a case. It was borne in on him that either he was obsessed or he had reached the last angle in the case – the vital one – and that it told him nothing; it was there for him to read, and he did not know how to.

Suppose, he would think, just suppose that the murder was an emissary's work after all, and not the result of the quarrel in the queue, what type of person would an emissary be? Not one of those nearest the murdered man, certainly. But no one else had had access to the queue except the policeman, the door-keeper, and Lamont. Or had there been another who had made his escape unnoticed? Raoul Legarde had gone, and Lamont had gone, without attracting notice – the one because the queue was self-absorbed, the other because it was absorbed in the murder. Was it possible that there had been still another? He reminded himself how indifferent to their surroundings the various witnesses had proved themselves to have been. Not one of them had been able to give an adequate account of the people who had stood next them, with the exception of Raoul Legarde, who was more critical because he was a stranger to England, and an English crowd was still an entertainment to him. To the others it had been no entertainment, and they had not bothered

about their neighbours; they had had all the self-absorption
of Londoners and habitual queue-goers. It was still possible
that someone else had got away without being remembered.
And if that were so, what chance was there now of his being
captured? What possible clue had they?

The brooch, said his other self, the brooch!

On Friday, Lamont was again brought up at Gowbridge
Police Court, and his counsel protested, as Grant had
foreseen, about the statement that had been taken from
Lamont. Grant had expected him to protest as a matter
of form, but it was evident that he was protesting from
conviction. He had become aware of the use the Crown
might make of Lamont's admission that he had resented
Sorrell's departure. The magistrate said that he could see no
evidence of coercion on the part of the police. The prisoner
had been evidently not only willing but anxious to make a
statement. But Lamont's counsel pointed out that his client
had been in no mental or physical condition to make such
an important statement. He was barely recovered from a
bad concussion. He was not in a fit state to—

And so the wordy, futile argument went on, and the two
people whom it most concerned – Grant and Lamont – sat
bored and weary, waiting till the spate of words should cease
and they could depart, the one to his cell and the other to
his work and his ever-present problem. Miss Dinmont was
in the now crowded court again, and this time there was
no doubt of her graciousness to Grant. Her interview with
her aunt seemed to have had the strange effect of softening
her in every way, and Grant, remembering Mrs Everett,
marvelled. It was only on the way back to the Yard that it
occurred to him that her aunt's belief in Lamont had bred in
her a hope that had nothing to do with reason or logic, and
that it was the hope that had given her that queer unusual
charm that was almost radiance. And Grant swore. She
might hope that after all Lamont was not guilty, but what
would that avail her if he were convicted?

That pearl brooch! What was it saying? Who had had access to the queue? He flung himself into his room and glared out of the window. He would give up the Service. He wasn't fit for it. He kept seeing difficulties where others saw none. It was sure proof of incompetence. How Barker must be laughing at him! Well, let him. Barker had about as much imagination as a paving-stone. But then he, Grant, had too much of it for the police force. He would resign. There would be at least two people who would be grateful to him – the two men who hankered most after his job. As for this case, he would think no more of it.

And even as he made the resolution he turned from the window to take the brooch from its drawer yet once again, but was interrupted by the entrance of Barker.

'Well,' said his chief, 'I hear they're making a fuss about the statement.'

'Yes.'

'What good do they think that's going to do them?'

'Don't know. Principle, I suppose. And they see a few admissions that we could make use of, I think.'

'Oh, well, let them wriggle,' Barker said. 'They can't wriggle out of the evidence. Statement or no statement, we've got them on toast. Still worrying over the business?'

'No; I've given it up. After this I'm going to believe what I see and know, and not what I feel.'

'Splendid!' said Barker. 'You keep a rein on your imagination, Grant, and you'll be a great man some day. Once in five years is often enough to have a flair. If you limit it to that, it's likely to be an asset.' And he grinned good-naturedly at his subordinate.

A constable appeared in the doorway, and said to Grant, 'A lady to see you, sir.'

'Who is it?'

'She wouldn't give her name, but she said it was very important.'

'All right. Show her in.'

Barker made a movement as if to go, but subsided again, and there was silence while the two men waited for the new arrival. Barker was lounging slightly in front of Grant's desk, and Grant was behind it, his left hand caressing the handle of the drawer that sheltered the brooch. Then the door opened, and the constable ushered in the visitor with an official repetition of his announcement, 'A lady to see you, sir.'

It was the fat woman from the queue.

'Good afternoon, Mrs Wallis.' Grant recalled her name with an effort; he had not seen her since the inquest. 'What can I do for you?'

'Good afternoon, Inspector,' she said, in her rampant Cockney. 'I came because I think this business has gone far enough. I killed Bert Sorrell, and I'm not going to let anyone suffer for it if I can 'elp it.'

'You—' said Grant, and stopped, staring at her fat shining face, beady eyes, tight black satin coat, and black satin toque.

Barker glanced at his subordinate and, seeing him utterly at a loss – really, Grant must have a holiday – he took command of the situation. 'Sit down, Mrs Wallis,' he said kindly. 'You've been thinking too much about this affair, haven't you?' He brought forward a chair and settled her into it rather as though she had come to consult him about heartburn. 'It isn't good to brood over nasty things like murders. What makes you think you killed Sorrell?'

'I don't think,' she said rather tartly. 'I didn't make any doubt about it, did I? A very good job it was.'

'Well, well,' said Barker indulgently, 'let us say how do we know you did it?'

'How do you know?' she repeated. 'What do you mean? You didn't know till now, but now I've told you and you know.'

'But, you know, just because you say you've done it

is no reason that we should believe you have,' Barker said.

'Not believe me!' she said, her voice rising. 'Do people usually come and confess to murdering people when they didn't?'

'Oh, quite often,' said Barker.

She sat in surprised silence, her bright, expressionless dark eyes darting swiftly from one face to the other. Barker raised a comical eyebrow at the still silent Grant, but Grant hardly noticed him. He came from behind the desk as if loosed suddenly from a spell that had held him motionless, and came up to the woman.

'Mrs Wallis,' he said, 'will you take off your gloves a moment?'

'Come now, that's a bit more sensible,' she said, as she drew off her black cotton gloves. 'I know what you're looking for, but it's nearly gone now.'

She held out her left hand, gloveless, to him. On the side of her first finger, healed but still visible in the rough skin of her hard-worked hand, was the mark of a jagged scar. Grant expelled a long breath, and Barker came over and bent to examine the woman's hand.

'But, Mrs Wallis,' he said, 'why should you want to kill Sorrell?'

'Never you mind,' she said. 'I killed 'im, and that's enough.'

'I'm afraid it isn't,' Barker said. 'The fact that you have a small scar on your finger is no proof at all that you had anything to do with Sorrell's death.'

'But I tell you I killed 'im!' she said. 'Why won't you believe me? I killed 'im with the little knife my 'usband brought home from Spain.'

'So you say, but we have no proof that what you say is true.'

She stared hostilely at them both. 'You'd think you weren't police at all to listen to you,' she remarked. 'If it weren't for that young man you've got, I'd walk home right now. I never knew such fools. What more do you want when I've confessed?'

'Oh, quite a lot more,' Barker said, as Grant was still silent. 'For instance, how could you have killed Sorrell when you were in front of him in the queue?'

'I wasn't in front of 'im. I was standing behind 'im all the time till the queue began to move up tight. Then I stuck the knife in 'im, and after a little I shoved in front, keepin' close to 'im all the time so he shouldn't fall.'

This time Barker dropped his complaisant manner and looked at her keenly. 'And what was Sorrell to you that you should stick a knife in him?' he asked.

'Bert Sorrell wasn't anything to me, but he 'ad to be killed and I killed 'im, see? That's all.'

'Did you know Sorrell?'

'Yes.'

'How long have you known him?'

Something in that question made her hesitate. 'Some time,' she said.

'Had he wronged you somehow?'

But her tight mouth shut still more tightly. Barker looked at her rather helplessly, and then Grant could see him turning on the other tack.

'Well, I'm very sorry, Mrs Wallis,' he said, as if the interview were ended, 'but we can't put any belief in your story. It has all the appearance of a cock-and-bull yarn. You've been thinking too much about the affair. People do that, you know, quite often, and then they begin to imagine that they did the thing themselves. The best thing you can do is to go home and think no more about it.'

As Barker had expected, that got her. A faint alarm appeared on her red face. Then her shrewd black eyes went to Grant and examined him. 'I don't know who you may be,' she said to Barker, 'but Inspector Grant believes me all right.'

'This is Superintendent Barker,' Grant said, 'and my chief. You'll have to tell the superintendent a lot more than that, Mrs Wallis, before he can believe you.'

She recognised the rebuff, and before she had recovered Barker said again, 'Why did you kill Sorrell? Unless you give us an adequate reason, I'm afraid we can't believe you. There's nothing at all to connect you with the murder except that little scar. I expect it's that little scar that has set you thinking about all this, isn't it, now?'

'Not it!' she said. 'D'you think I'm crazy? Well, I'm not. I did it all right, and I've told you how I did it exactly. Isn't that enough?'

'Oh no, you could quite easily have made up the tale of how you did it. We've got to have *proof.*'

'Well, I've got the sheath of the knife at home,' she said in sudden triumph. 'There's your proof for you.'

'I'm afraid that's no good either,' Barker said, with a very good imitation of regret. 'Anyone could have the sheath of the knife. You'll have to give us a reason for killing Sorrell before we'll even begin to believe you.'

'Well,' she said sullenly after a long silence, 'if you must 'ave it, I killed 'im because 'e was going to shoot my Rosie.'

'Who is Rosie?'

'My daughter.'

'Why should he shoot your daughter?'

'Because she wouldn't have anything to do with the likes of 'im.'

'Does your daughter live with you?'

'No.'

'Then perhaps you'll let me have her address.'

'No; you can't have 'er address. She's gone abroad.'

'But if she has gone abroad, how could Sorrell be able to harm her?'

'She hadn't gone abroad when I killed Bert Sorrell.'

'Then—' began Barker, but Grant interrupted him.

'Mrs Wallis,' he said slowly, 'is Ray Marcable your daughter?'

The woman was on her feet with a swiftness amazing in a person of her bulk. Her tight mouth was suddenly slack, and inarticulate sounds came from her throat.

'Sit down,' said Grant gently, and pushed her back into her chair – 'sit down and tell us all about it. Take your time.'

''Ow did you know?' she asked, when she had recovered herself. ''Ow *could* you know?'

Grant ignored the question. 'What made you think that Sorrell intended harm to your daughter?'

'Because I met 'im one day in the street. I 'adn't seen 'im for years and I said something about Rosie going to America. And 'e said, "So am I." And I didn't like that, because I knew 'e was a nuisance to Rosie. And then 'e smiled kind of queer at me and said, "At least, it isn't certain. Either we're both going or neither of us is going." An' I said, "What do you mean? Rosie's going for sure. She's got a contract and she can't break it." And he said, "She has a previous contract with me. Do you think she'll keep to that too?" And I said not to be foolish. Boy-and-girl affairs were best forgotten, I said. And 'e just smiled again, that horrid queer way, and said "Well, wherever she's goin', we're goin' together." And 'e went away.'

'When was that?' Grant asked.

'It was three weeks today – the Friday before I killed 'im.'

The day after Sorrell had received the little parcel at Mrs Everett's. 'All right. Go on.'

'Well, I went 'ome and thought about it. I kept seeing 'is face. It had a bad grey kind of look in spite of its bein' so pleasant and all that. And I began to be sure that he meant to do Rosie in.'

'Had your daughter been engaged to him?'

'Well, 'e said so. It was a boy-and-girl affair. They'd

known each other ever since they were kids. Of course,
Rosie wouldn't dream of marrying 'im now.'

'All right. Go on.'

'Well, I thought the only place 'e would be able to see
'er would be the theatre. You see, I went round specially
to tell Rosie about it – I didn't see 'er very often – but she
didn't seem to worry. She just said, "Oh, Bert always talked
through his hat anyway, and anyhow I don't see him any
more." She 'ad such a lot of other things to think of, she
wasn't worried. But I was, I tell you. I went that night
and stood on the opposite side of the street, watching the
people coming to the queues. But 'e didn't come. And I
went to the matinée on Saturday and again in the evening,
but 'e didn't come. And again on Monday night, and on
Tuesday afternoon. And then on Tuesday night I saw 'im
come alone, and I went and stood behind 'im in the queue
at the pit door. After a while I saw a bulge in 'is right-'and
coat pocket, and I felt it and it was hard. I was sure then
that it was a revolver and that he was going to do Rosie in.
So I just waited till the queue moved tight, like I said, and
stuck the knife in 'im. He didn't make a sound. You'd think
he didn't know anything had happened. And then I shoved
in front, like I told you.'

'Was Sorrell alone?'

'Yes.'

'Who was standing alongside him?'

'For a while there was a dark young gentleman, very
good-looking. And then another man came to talk to Bert,
and pushed the young gentleman back next me.'

'And who was behind you?'

'The lady and gentleman who gave evidence at the
inquest.'

'How is Rosie Markham your daughter?'

'Well, you see, my 'usband was a sailor – that's 'ow I got
the knife from Spain – brought me lots of things, 'e did.
But when Rosie was little, 'e got drowned; and 'is sister,

who was very well married to Markham, offered to take 'er and bring 'er up as their own, 'cause they had no kids. So I let 'er go. And they brought 'er up proper, I'll say that for them. A real lady, my Rosie is. I went out charring for years, but since Rosie got money she bought what they call an annuity for me, and I live on that mostly now.'

'How did your daughter know Sorrell?'

'The aunt that brought Bert up used to live next door to the Markhams, and Bert and Rosie went to the same school. They were very friendly then, of course. Then the aunt died when Bert was at the War.'

'But it was after the War that they got engaged, surely?'

'They weren't what you would call engaged. They just had a notion for each other. Rosie was on tour in *The Green Sunshade* then, and they used to see each other when she was in town or near it.'

'But Sorrell considered himself engaged?'

'Perhaps. Lots of men would like to be engaged to Rosie. As if Rosie would think of the likes of him!'

'But they kept up some kind of acquaintance?'

'Oh yes, she let 'im come to see 'er at 'er flat sometimes, but she wouldn't go out with him, or anything like that. And she didn't 'ave 'im very often. I don't think she 'ad the heart to send him away for good, you see. She was letting 'im down gently, I think. But I'm not sure about all that, you know. I didn't go to see Rosie often myself. Not that she wasn't nice to me, but it wasn't fair on 'er. She didn't want a common old woman like me round, and 'er hobnobbin with lords and things.'

'Why did you not tell the police at once that Sorrell was threatening your daughter?'

'I thought about it, and then I thought, in the first place, I 'adn't any proof. Judging by the way you treated me today, I should think I was right. And in the second place, even supposing the police shut 'im up, they couldn't shut 'im up for good. He would just do 'er in when he came out. And I couldn't be always round watching 'im. So I thought it best to do it when I could. I 'ad that little knife, and I thought that would be a good way. I don't know anything about pistols and things.'

'Tell me, Mrs Wallis, did your daughter ever see that dagger?'

'No.'

'Are you quite sure? Think a little.'

'Yes; she did. I'm telling you a lie. When she was quite big, before she left school, they had a play of Shakespeare that had a dagger in it. I don't remember the name of it.'

'*Macbeth*?' suggested Grant.

'Yes; that was it. And she was the heroine. She was always wonderful at acting, you know. Even when she was a little thing she was a fairy in a school pantomime. And I always went to see 'er. And when they were playing that thing *Macbeth*, I gave 'er a loan of the little dagger 'er father 'ad brought from Spain. Just for luck, you know. She gave it back to me when the play was over. But she kept the luck, all right. All 'er life she's been lucky. It was just luck that made Ladds see 'er when she was on tour, so that 'e told Barron about 'er, and Barron gave 'er an interview. That's 'ow she got 'er name – Ray Marcable. All the time she was dancing and singing and what not for him 'e kept saying, "Re-markable!" and so Rosie took that for 'er name. It 'as the same initials as 'er own – at least, as 'er adopted name, see?'

There was a silence. Both Barker, who had been wordless for some time, and Grant seemed to be temporarily at a loss. Only the fat woman with the red face seemed to be completely at her ease.

'There's one thing you must remember,' she said. 'Rosie's name must be kept out of this. Not a word about Rosie. You can say that I killed 'im because of 'im threatening my daughter, who is abroad.'

'I'm sorry, Mrs Wallis, I can't hold out any hope of that. Miss Marcable's name is sure to come out.'

'But it mustn't!' she said. 'It mustn't! It'll spoil it all if she's dragged into it. Think of the scandal and the talk. Surely you gentlemen are clever enough to think of a way of avoiding that?'

'I'm afraid not, Mrs Wallis. We would if we could, but it won't be possible if your story is true.'

'Oh, well,' she said, with surprising equanimity, considering her former vehemence, 'I don't suppose it will make such a very great difference to Rosie. Rosie is the greatest actress in Britain at the present time, and 'er position is too good for anything like that to spoil it. Only you must hang me before she comes back from America.'

'It is a little too soon to talk of hanging,' Barker said, with a faint smile. 'Have you got the key of your house with you?'

'Yes; why?'

'If you hand it over to me, I'll send a man down to verify your story of the sheath of the knife. Where can he find it?'

'It's at the very bottom of the top left-hand drawer of the chest-of-drawers, in a box that had a scent-bottle in.'

Barker called in a man, and gave him the key and the instructions. 'And see you leave everything as you get it,' Mrs Wallis said tartly to the emissary.

When the man had gone, Grant pushed a piece of paper across his desk to her and extended a pen. 'Will you write your name and address there?' he said.

She took the pen in her left hand, and rather laboriously wrote what he had asked.

'You remember when I went to see you before the inquest?'

'Yes.'

'You weren't left-handed then.'

'I can use either hand for most things. There's a name

for it, but I forget what it is. But when I'm doing anything very special, I use my left. Rosie, she's left-handed too. And so was my father.'

'Why didn't you come before and tell us this story?' Barker asked.

'I didn't think you would get anyone unless you got me. But when I saw in the paper that the police had a good case, and all that, I thought something would have to be done. And then today I went to the court to have a look at 'im.' So she had been in that crowded court today without Grant having seen her! ''E didn't look bad even if he was foreign-looking. And 'e looked very ill. So I just went 'ome and cleared up and come along.'

'I see,' said Grant, and raised his eyebrows at his chief. The superintendent summoned a man, and said, 'Mrs Wallis will wait in the next room for the moment, and you will keep her company. If there is anything you want, just ask Simpson for it, Mrs Wallis,' and the door closed behind her tight black satin figure.

CHAPTER 18

CONCLUSION

'Well,' said Barker, after a moment's silence, 'I'll never talk to you about your flair again, Grant. Do you think she's mad?'

'If logic carried to excess is madness, then she is,' Grant said.

'But she seems to have no feelings on the subject at all – either for herself or for Sorrell.'

'No. Perhaps she is crazy.'

'There's no chance of its not being true? It's a far less believable story in my eyes than the Lamont one.'

'Oh yes, it's true,' Grant said. 'There's not a doubt of it. It seems strange to you only because you haven't lived with the case as I have. The whole thing falls into place now – Sorrell's suicide, the gift of the money to Lamont, the booking of the passage, the brooch. I was a fool not to have seen that the initials might as well have been "R. M." But I was obsessed by the Ratcliffe woman at the time. Not that reading the initials the other way would have helped me too much, if Mrs Wallis hadn't turned up with her confession. Still, I ought to have connected it with Ray Marcable. On the very first day of the investigations, I went down to the Woffington to have a talk with the doorkeeper, and I saw Ray Marcable then, and she gave me tea. Over tea I described the dagger to her – the description was going to the Press that evening. She looked so startled that I was almost certain that she had seen something like that before. But there wasn't any way of making her tell if she didn't want to, so I left it, and from beginning to end of the case there has been nothing to connect her with it until now. Sorrell must have intended to go to America as soon as he knew that she was going. Poor devil! She might be Ray Marcable to the rest of the world, and a very big star, but he never got over thinking of her as Rosie Markham. That was his tragedy. She, of course, isn't a bit like that. It's a long time since Ray Marcable thought of herself as Rosie Markham. I expect she made it definite that there was nothing doing when she returned the brooch he had had made for her. A brooch like that wouldn't have meant anything to Ray Marcable. He had really meant to go to America till the Thursday evening, when he got the parcel Mrs Everett talked about. That was the brooch, and that evidently tore it. She may have announced her intention of marrying Lacing, for all I know. You saw that he had gone out on the same boat with her? Sorrell must have made up his mind then that he would shoot her and commit suicide. The Woffington pit isn't the best place for shots at the stage with a revolver, but I expect he counted on the fuss there would be at the end. It isn't so very long since I saw half the pit in the orchestra at the end of a last night at the Arena. Or perhaps he meant to do it as she was leaving the theatre after the show. I don't know. He could have done it in the afternoon quite easily – he and Lamont went to the stalls – but he didn't. I don't think he wanted his friends to know if there was the remotest chance that they mightn't. You see, he tried to fit things so that they would take it for granted that he was on his way to America. That explains the lack of clues. Neither Mrs Everett nor Lamont would connect the suicide of an unknown man who had killed Ray Marcable with the man they thought was on the *Queen of Arabia*. He probably forgot that meeting in the street with Mrs Wallis, or didn't think that his secret thoughts had been so obvious to her. When you come to think of it, it was rather cute of her to spot what he intended. Of course, she had the clue – she knew about Ray. But she was the only one who would be able to connect him with Ray Marcable. Ray Marcable never went anywhere with him, of course. He tried to do the best he could for his friend by handing over his wad, with instructions, as Lamont said, that it wasn't to be opened till the Thursday. Do you think Sorrell thought there was a chance that his friend would never know what had become of him, or do you think he didn't care so long as the deed was well over before they found out?'

'Search me!' said Barker. 'I don't think *he* was too sane either.'

'No,' said Grant, considering, 'I don't think Sorrell was crazy. It's just what Lamont said about him – he thought for a long time about something, and then did exactly what he had intended. The only thing he didn't reckon with was Mrs Wallis – and you'll admit she isn't the kind of quantity you'd expect to find butting around in an ordinary crowd. He couldn't have been a bad sort, Sorrell. Even to the last he kept up the jape about going to America. His packing was perfect – but Lamont was packing at the same time, and probably in and out of the room all the time. He hadn't a single letter or photograph of Ray Marcable. He must have made a clean sweep when he made up his mind what he was going to do. Only, he forgot the brooch. It fell out of a pocket, as I told you.'

'Do you think Ray Marcable suspected the truth?'

'No; I don't think so.'

'Why not?'

'Because Ray Marcable is one of the most self-absorbed people in this era. In any case, she remembered the dagger from my description of it, but she had no reason to connect the man who was murdered with Sorrell, and therefore wouldn't connect her mother with the affair at all. The Yard didn't know Sorrell's identity until Monday, and that was the day she left for the States. I shall be very much surprised if she knows, even yet, that the dead man was Sorrell. I shouldn't think she reads much in the Press but the gossip column, and America isn't interested in the queue murder.'

'Then there's a shock in store for her,' said Barker sorrowfully.

'There is,' said Grant grimly. 'And at least there is a pleasant one in store for Lamont, and I'm glad of it. I have made a complete fool of myself over this case, but I'm happier just now than I have been since I hauled him into the boat from the loch.'

'You're a marvel, Grant. With a case like that I should have been as pleased as Punch and all over myself. It isn't canny. If you're ever fired from the force, you can set up as something in the second-sight line at five bob a time.'

'So that you can descend on me for blackmail, I suppose? "Give us a quid or you'll have the cops in!" No; there isn't anything uncanny about it. After all, in any human relationship you've got to decide for yourself, apart from evidence, what a man is like. And though I wouldn't confess it even to myself, I think I knew Lamont was telling the truth that night when he gave me his statement in the train.'

'Well, it's a queer business,' said Barker – 'the queerest business I've known for ages.' He hoisted himself off the desk against which he had been propped. 'Let me know when Mullins comes back, will you? If he has the sheath, then we'll decide to accept the story. Lamont's being brought up again tomorrow, isn't he? We can bring her into court then.' And he left Grant alone.

And Grant mechanically did what he had been going to do when Barker's entrance had interrupted him. He unlocked the drawer of his desk and took out the dagger and the brooch. Only a little space between the intention and the act, and what a difference! He had been going to withdraw them as the emblems of his despair – mysteries that maddened him; and now he knew all about it. And it was so simple now that he knew. Now that he knew! But if Mrs Wallis had not come—He turned away from the thought. But for the accident that made the woman fairminded even in her madness he would have stifled his misgivings and gone through with the case as befitted a valued inspector of the C.I.D., and in accordance with the evidence. He had been saved from that.

It had been so clear a case where evidence was concerned – the quarrel, the left-handedness, the scar. They had searched for the man who had quarrelled with Sorrell, and he was left-handed and had a scar on his thumb. Wasn't that good enough? And now it was nonsense – like Miss Dinmont's bedcover. The murderer was a woman, ambidextrous, with a scar on her finger. He had been saved by the skin of his teeth and a woman's fair dealing.

His thoughts went back over the trail that had led them so far wrong: the hunt for Sorrell's identity; Nottingham, the youth in Faith Brothers', Mr Yeudall, the waitress at the hotel, all of them remembering the thing they were most interested in, and humanly connecting it with all that happened. Raoul Legarde with his beauty, his quick intelligence, and his complete description of Lamont. Danny Miller. The last night of *Didn't You Know?* Struwwelpeter and the raid on Sorrell's offices. Lacey, the jockey, and that damp day at Lingfield. Mrs Everett. The burst to the north. Carninnish – the silent Drysdale and the tea at the manse. Miss Dinmont with her logic and her self-containedness. The beginning of his doubt and its blossoming with Lamont's statement. The brooch. And now—

They lay on his desk, the two shining things. The dagger winked knowingly in the evening light, and the pearls gleamed with a still small smile very like the smile that Ray Marcable had made famous. He did not think that Gallio & Stein had made a very good job of the monogram; even yet, looked at casually, he would read it M. R. Both Mrs Ratcliffe and Mrs Everett had read it that way, he remembered.

His thought went back to Mrs Wallis. Was she technically sane? He would have said not, but sanity, from a medical point of view, depended on such queer qualifications. It was impossible to anticipate what a specialist would think of her. And anyhow it wasn't his business. His business was done. The Press would be scathing, of course, about the police haste to make an arrest, but his withers would be unwrung. The Yard would understand, and his professional standing would not suffer. And presently he would have that holiday. He would go down to Stockbridge and fish. Or should he go back to Carninnish? Drysdale had given him a very warm invitation, and the Finley would be teeming with salmon just now. But somehow the thought of that swift brown water and that dark country was ungrateful at the moment. It spoke of turmoil and grief and frustration; and he wanted none of that. He wanted a cowlike placidity, and ease, and pleasant skies. He would go down to Hampshire. It would be green there now, and when he grew tired of the placid Test waters there would be a horse and the turf on Danebury.

Mullins knocked, and came in and laid the sheath of the knife on Grant's desk. 'Got it where she said, sir. That's the key of the house.'

'Thanks, Mullins,' said Grant. He dropped the knife into its sheath, and rose to take it to Barker. Yes; he would go to Hampshire. But sometime, of course, he would go back to Carninnish.

The doctors pronounced Mrs Wallis quite sane and fit to plead, and her trial is due at the Old Bailey this month. Grant is convinced that she will get off, and I am inclined to trust Grant's flair so far. Unwritten laws, he says, are not supposed to be valid in this country, but a British jury is in reality just as sentimental as a French one; and when they hear the story as put forward by Mrs Wallis's counsel – one of the most famous criminal defenders of the day – they'll weep bucketfuls and refuse to convict her.

'Well,' I said to him, 'it has been a queer case, but the queerest thing about it is that there isn't a villain in it.'

'Isn't there!' Grant said, with that twist to his mouth.

Well, is there?

THE END

Miss Pym Disposes

Josephine Tey

Ley's Physical Training College was famous for its excellent discipline and Miss Lucy Pym was pleased and flattered to be invited to give a psychology lecture there. But she had to admit that the health and vibrant beauty of the students made her feel just a little inadequate.

Then there was a nasty accident – and suddenly Miss Pym was forced to apply her agile intellect to the unpleasant fact that among all those impressively healthy bodies someone had a very sick mind . . .

'Tey's style and her knack for creating bizarre characters are among the best in her field'
New Yorker

arrow books